PSYCHO

NECESSARY EVILS

PSYCHO

ONLEY JAMES

PSYCHO

NECESSARY EVILS BOOK TWO

Copyright © 2021 Onley James
WWW.ONLEYJAMES.COM

This book is a work of fiction and does not represent any individual living or dead. Names, characters, places, and incidents either are products of the author's imagination or are used fictitiously.

Cover and Interior Design by We Got You Covered Book Design
WWW.WEGOTYOUCOVEREDBOOKDESIGN.COM

ISBN: 978-1-68524-043-1

PROLOGUE
DR. THOMAS MULVANEY

This boy would be his youngest find yet. His first subject, who Thomas had named Atticus, had been eight upon his adoption. He was a gifted child, a born mimic, with the ability to turn his personality on and off like a light switch. It was fascinating.

The boy behind the glass was much younger. Barely four. He huddled in the corner, headphones in his ears, a thick paperback book on his knees. He was painfully thin and pale and had dark brown hair that fell over big eyes. Thomas ached for him. He looked so small in the large room, lit only by the small lamp beside him.

Thomas was wary of bringing in another boy so soon but felt it necessary for the study to have subjects of various ages, to see how each one did with the tools he would give them.

Initially, he'd thought to adopt just one, but any good experiment meant having a large subject pool. Since Thomas was doing this without the watchful eye of a review board, he couldn't have the amount of subjects he'd like. At

least, not without resorting to keeping the boys behind lock and key. And he wouldn't do that. He wanted these boys to think of him as a father, a confidant, not a prison warden. He wasn't a supervillain. He understood the potential hidden away behind that glass, and it only worked with patience and care.

The door behind Thomas opened, and a man with snow white hair and a beard appeared. "Dr. George Stryker," he said in lieu of a greeting. "Sorry to keep you waiting."

"Dr. Thomas Mulvaney," Thomas said, extending a hand.

The elderly doctor shook it. "I know who you are. We have mutual acquaintances. That's why I called."

His project was top secret, but there were a small number of people in the fold, those with the contacts Thomas needed. People who wanted to see his experiment succeed so they could recreate it, and others who watched, hoping he'd fail. But Thomas didn't care about those people. They were a means to an end. He knew he was right about these boys. His research subjects.

His sons.

"What's his name?" Thomas asked, nodding towards the boy beyond the glass.

"According to his birth certificate, Isaiah. But he doesn't respond to it. He doesn't respond to much, if I'm being honest. But given how he was found, that's not surprising."

Thomas's heart rate accelerated. This part was always the hardest—hearing about their pasts, especially when he had to leave them behind. "Tell me."

"He was found during a wellness check on the mother.

She suffered from severe schizophrenia. Both auditory and visual hallucinations. But, for a time, she was stable on her medications, which is why she was permitted to keep her child, but with scheduled supervision for the first year of his life to ensure medication compliance. Sometime after the year was up, she clearly went off her medications."

"And nobody noticed?"

"He wasn't old enough for school, so there was nobody to notice. Her neighbors had concerns about her behavior, but they didn't even know she had a child."

Thomas's gaze strayed to the other physician. "She was abusing the boy?"

Stryker sighed. "According to the woman's diaries, she thought the boy was a changeling."

"A changeling? Like out of Irish fairy tales?" Thomas asked, unable to keep the surprise from his voice. "She thought somebody replaced her real son with a fae child?"

Stryker nodded grimly. "She was deeply disturbed. When she saw his remarkable intelligence at a young age, she convinced herself it had to be supernatural."

Thomas looked back at the small boy, shaking his head. "That's…"

The older man wasn't finished. "She locked him in a room sometime after he turned two, and that's where he stayed. They found a stained crib mattress, a stack of books, one light, and a bucket on the floor. He was filthy. It took the nurses hours to get him clean, mostly because he wouldn't stop fighting them."

"He's aggressive?" Thomas asked.

Dr. Stryker shook his head. "It's more complex than that. He's been deprived of human interaction for at least a year and a half, maybe longer, during his most formative years. He was only found because the mother killed herself. A neighbor heard the gunshot and called the police to check on her. While doing a sweep of the house, they found him."

"Jesus," Thomas muttered.

"He's not overtly aggressive. He will not become violent unless somebody attempts to touch him. He's been deprived of light and touch and sound. He reacts violently to all three. The only exception seems to be music. We're not sure why, but he keeps headphones in almost round the clock."

Interesting. Thomas would have to bring him into the real world slowly and with great care. "Diagnosis?"

The man picked up the folder from the metal holder beside the window, opening it. "Attachment disorder. Panic disorder. Post traumatic stress disorder. But I called you because, even though we cannot make a definitive diagnosis, he certainly displays many psychopathic tendencies. He has no sense of fear. He reacts violently to any unwanted attention. He lies easily. Is extremely possessive of anything given to him."

Thomas mulled that one over. This one would be difficult, but he was up to the task. He wanted a vast array of psychiatric maladies as well as the psychopathy. He needed to understand how the research affected each of them.

Stryker sighed. "While I can't say for certain, I suspect he was born a psychopath. I think his behavior helped shape his mother's delusions. He's exceptionally gifted, especially given his lack of education. I can see how the mother believed his abilities to be unnatural. The boy can read. Far beyond his years. Hell, far beyond mine. We've had him for a week and he's blown through every book in our library including the Bible, the Koran, and Stephen Hawking's *A Brief History of Time*. He's also since taught himself to write with the help of a handwriting workbook one of the nurses brought him."

Thomas scoffed. "You're joking."

"I'm not. He reads faster than anyone we've ever seen and has a great understanding of concepts far beyond his years. We tested his IQ. 155. Just a few points shy of Hawking himself." Thomas couldn't hide his startled response. "So you can see our problem."

Thomas nodded. "If he's a psychopath with that level of intelligence, he would be a plague on society and smart enough to hide in plain sight. Any bed-wetting, arson, harming of weaker children?"

"Not so far. In truth, he lives in his head. He listens to music and reads. He's bored, no doubt. There's nothing in this facility that could keep a child like him entertained. Being locked in that room, in silence, with nothing but the few books his mother gave him must have been torture for a boy with that level of genius."

"He'll lack for nothing with me," Thomas assured him. "I'd like to meet him now."

"I'd advise you not to touch him. Also, do not turn on the overhead light. He becomes quite…feral."

Thomas nodded, making to leave the observation room.

"Will you keep me apprised of his progress?" Dr. Stryker

asked, expression tight.

"Of course."

Thomas opened and closed the door to the room quickly to keep the harsh fluorescent lights of the hallway away from the child. Once inside, the child didn't acknowledge him in any way. He moved forward, dropping to sit cross-legged near the boy, but not close enough to touch him.

"What are you reading?" Thomas prompted, unsure whether the boy could hear him over the music playing in his headphones.

He responded by lifting it enough for Thomas to read the cover. *Light in August.*

"Faulkner, huh? That's a pretty advanced book for your age."

The child flicked an irritated gaze towards Thomas, like he was intruding. Perhaps he was.

"What if I told you I have a library in my home with thousands of books?"

This time, the boy tugged a headphone free, eyeing Thomas suspiciously. "Have you read them all?"

Thomas chuckled. "No, and I suspect you might beat me to it. You speak very well."

The boy shrugged. "I could speak before I could walk. It frightened my mother. She was…unwell."

He spoke with the vocabulary and affect of a grown man. Thomas wasn't entirely convinced the boy wasn't, in fact, a fairy tale creature or perhaps an extraterrestrial. "I heard. I'm sorry for what you had to endure for the first few years of your life."

The boy shrugged again. "She couldn't help who she was."

It was such a simple statement of fact. No bitterness or malice.

"They tell me you don't like to be touched," Thomas said.

The boy's expression looked almost prim as he said, "Not against my will, no."

Thomas couldn't help but smile. "That is valid. Nobody should touch you without your consent."

Once more, the boy observed him shrewdly, as if trying to guess at his motivations, but said nothing.

"Would you like to come live with me and read your way through my library?"

"Why?"

"Why what?"

"Why would I want to live with you? Other than your library?"

Thomas shook his head. "Well, to be honest, I have a lot of money but no family. Just one son who is a bit older than you. I want to fill my house with boys just like you."

"Like me?" he queried, frowning.

"Yes. Children who are gifted. Children who have a certain psychological makeup."

The boy nodded as if that made perfect sense. "Do you have any more books like the one by Mr. Hawking? I find his theories—" He paused as if looking for the correct word. "Thought provoking."

Thought provoking… This child might be too smart for even Thomas. But he had resources. Far more resources than anybody else, thanks to an accident of birth that left

him with more money than he could ever spend.

"If you come live with me, we can stop at the bookstore on the way home and you can choose as many books as you like." At the boy's apprehension, Thomas corrected himself. "Or you can tell me what books you'd like and I'll have them delivered."

The boy narrowed his eyes at him, as if he thought it might be a trick. "Any books?"

Thomas might regret this but he said, "Any."

The boy nodded once. "Then yes."

Now, to the other task at hand. "They tell me your name is Isaiah."

His lip curled. "I hate that name. My mother was very religious but also quite superstitious."

Thomas leaned in closer. "Well, my family has a somewhat silly tradition of giving siblings names that all start with the same letter. My brother was Teddy, and my sister was Thea. I'm Thomas. You have a brother at home, who I've called Atticus. Would you like to choose another name? One that starts with A?"

The boy closed his book, eyes glued to the cover. "August. Can I be August?"

Thomas grinned. "Absolutely. Would you like to come home with me, August?"

August gave a huge sigh. "Yes, I think I would."

ONE

AUGUST

Vivaldi filled August Mulvaney's ears as he stared down at his phone screen and the self-evaluation form he was tasked with filling out by the end of the day. This new bizarre corporate hoop-jumping was ridiculous to him. They weren't a law firm, they were an ivy league university. Asking a tenured professor to describe themselves in three words or less was absurd. Most couldn't describe what day of the week it was without an APA formatted dissertation and review board approval.

Three words to describe him? Which him did they want? The brilliant quirky weirdo or the deviant homicidal psychopath? Both were true enough, though one was most definitely more palatable than the other. Yet neither of them could go on a self-evaluation.

He sighed, gazing out over the quad. The sky overhead was as ominous as his mood. Dark gray storm clouds hung low, just waiting to unleash on the students who refused to yield their space until the last possible moment. It was

uncharacteristically chilly for this time of year. He took a sip of his coffee, keeping himself tucked up against the building as he watched the rain move closer. It was slated to rain all day according to the forecast, but August put as much stock in forecasts as he did horoscopes.

Bianca Li, an assistant professor of astrophysics, tucked herself in beside him, tugging her sweater across her body and wrapping her arms around herself. Her black hair whipped across her face, and her black framed glasses sat perilously close to the end of her nose. She was easily older than August by at least ten years but could still pass for a grad student.

He pulled his earbuds from his ears. "How would you describe me in three words?" Before she could answer, he took a finger and pushed her glasses up the bridge of her nose.

"Weirdo without boundaries?" she asked, batting his hand away.

"Weirdo was the first thought that came to mind for me as well. I don't think that would fly with the board."

Bianca shrugged. "You've got tenure. What are they going to do about it?" She snapped her fingers. "I got it. Absent-minded professor."

August rolled his eyes. "I'm not absent-minded. I have... selective hearing."

"Children have selective hearing. You live in your own world," she pointed out.

August waved her statement off. "You're exaggerating."

"You almost walked into the fountain...twice."

She wasn't wrong. The thing was, August was absent-minded by choice. When a person is burdened with an

affliction that causes them to remember—verbatim—every word ever spoken to them, their brains become a chaotic mess, a tangle of conversations from yesterday and decades ago. A single word could trigger a cascade of memories that could trap him in his thoughts for days.

So, August remained selectively absent-minded. His observations were a thing he'd trained himself to turn on and off at will rather than lose his mind absorbing pieces of conversation with every step he took. By shutting out the things he considered static, he was able to focus on the things that mattered, like spintronics or light scattering and optical wave mixing techniques, semiconductor quantum dots, and, sometimes, even laser physics.

On campus, he rarely interacted with anybody but his immediate coworkers and, of course, his students. He made a point to view his surroundings without absorbing them, never letting his gaze focus on any one thing for too long unless it was life or death. Yet, the moment he caught sight of the man walking across the quad, he couldn't look away.

The man walked with his hands in his pants pockets, shoulders hunched against the wind. From where August stood, he could see he was attractive, though somewhat haggard, dressed in jeans and a zip front olive green cardigan. His clothes said faculty, but his messy blond hair and the two days worth of growth on his perfectly square jaw screamed student. Maybe he was a teacher's assistant.

As August predicted, the sky opened up. Students hurriedly gathered books and papers, stuffing them in backpacks before making a run for it. The man didn't run

but he did pick up his pace, heading straight for August and Bianca, who stood near the building entrance. When he passed, he glanced up, locking eyes with August, holding his gaze for a solid five seconds before turning away again and disappearing inside the building. His eyes were a deep green, almost the color of his sweater.

August turned to watch him through the windows of the corridor, feeling strangely empty once he was out of sight. He shook his head, taking another sip of his coffee. This weather made him broody and weirdly sentimental for a monster.

"He's pretty, isn't he? Too bad he's crazy."

"Who is he?" August finally asked.

She gave a dreamy sigh. "Lucas Blackwell, Adjunct Professor of Criminal Psychology."

August took another sip of his coffee. "Lucas Blackwell," he repeated, liking the way the moniker felt on his tongue. "That doesn't sound like a real name. They hired a crazy person to take O'Malley's job? Doesn't that seem counter productive?"

"The whole psych department is batshit crazy. He'll fit right in."

"You seem to know a lot about him," August observed.

Bianca snorted. "You really don't know who he is?"

August's brow furrowed. "Should I?"

Bianca looked him up and down. "You should write hopelessly oblivious professor on that form. The faculty has been positively ravenous for all the scandalous details for weeks, ever since Everly hired him. But, before that, he was all over the news."

"Why's that? He a Kennedy or something?"

She shook her head. "Former darling of the FBI's behavioral profiling unit. Whiz kid. Recruited straight from college because he spoke three languages and had near perfect test scores on his entrance exam."

Lucas Blackwell couldn't have been more than thirty at most. "Former? Was he injured?"

"You could say that. Suffered some kind of massive nervous breakdown and was put on permanent desk duty. They offered him a teaching gig at Quantico, but he bailed for our school."

"How do you know all this?" August asked, somewhat in awe of her ability to study the asteroseismology of white dwarfs and stay up to date on the latest campus gossip.

"How do you *not* know this? I know you're usually taxing that big brain of yours with entanglement theories or whatever, but you love all that spooky shit, and Lucas Blackwell… He's spooky."

"How so?" August's love of 'spooky shit' was well known around campus. Theoretical physicists weren't really known for their love of parapsychology. But they just considered it another one of his quirks. He supposed it was.

Bianca leaned in a bit as the rain began to splash their shoes. "You know how most behavioral profiling is done at a desk?"

He nodded. "It's basically making a living out of educated guessing. I doubt that requires much leg work."

She snickered. "Well, Lucas was real hands on. *Too* hands on. Liked to handle evidence and visit crime scenes. Said it helped his process."

"I'm failing to see the spooky," August said, wanting Bianca to get to the point before the wind blew the rain any farther under the overhang.

"It's pretty fucking out there. Rumor has it, he thinks he's... What's the word when you can get, like, psychic visions by touching things?"

August's brows ran for his hairline. "Clairvoyant?"

"Yes! He claims he's clairvoyant."

"So, our university hired a mentally unstable criminologist who claims to have supernatural abilities?"

"Yep."

August chuckled. "He'll fit right in."

Bianca laughed. "You know, this is the most I've ever heard you ask about another human being and I've known you for six years."

He turned, tossing his coffee cup in the trash. "True, but your life is mundane. No offense."

She rushed to keep up with him as he made his way back towards his office to grab his things.

"You can't just say no offense after saying something offensive," Bianca said, though she didn't seem offended in the least.

Nobody could afford to worry about feelings in a field like theirs. Half the professors on this side of campus had brains far too complex to hold even the simplest of conversations. They were all varying degrees of neurodiverse. The sad truth was, the smarter a person was the less they bothered with societal expectations. They spoke in blunt terms without any worry about sentiment.

Scientists couldn't afford ego. When you dealt in theory, there was always somebody standing in line ready to tell you you're insane or trying to debunk your research. That was the nature of their work. August was only as... domesticated as he was because his father had insisted on it. Being a quirky genius was fine. Being an unfeeling, uncaring psychopath was not—not in public, anyway.

"There's a faculty meeting at four. Will you be there?"

"Is it mandatory?" August asked.

Bianca nodded. "Yes."

August shrugged. "Probably not. I'm having lunch with my brother before he leaves for the airport."

"August..."

"I'm a tenured professor. What are they going to do? Fire me?" he repeated, shooting her a grin.

August went left to the hallway where his office lay, and Bianca went right to take the long way to the other side of the campus. When he was alone once more, he replaced his headphones. Vivaldi had finished, and Chopin now filled his ears. He let himself disassociate, mulling over his research assistant's topic for her thesis.

He didn't see the other man until they collided. Hard. August's phone flew from his fingers. The other man's hands shot out, grasping for anything to keep him upright. August grabbed the man's forearm just as he gripped August's shoulders.

That was when August got a good look at him. Lucas Blackwell. The moment they touched, the other man wrenched away with a gasp, falling to the ground and

scrambling away from August like he was a serial killer.

Which, technically, August supposed he was. But Lucas Blackwell didn't know that.

Though it was beside the point, August couldn't help but notice the terrified man was even more beautiful up close, like a sculpture come to life. High cheekbones, square jaw, full lips. Lips that were pulled back in horror.

August extended his hand to help him up, but Lucas flinched away. "Don't. Don't…touch me."

Apparently, it wasn't just the physics department that lacked any sense of decorum. He pulled his now useless headphones from his ears. "I'm sorry. I was so into my music that I wasn't watching where I was going."

Lucas said nothing, flushing when he noticed the other faculty members staring at him. He stood, giving one last panicked look over his shoulder before all but sprinting down the hallway.

August picked up his phone, sighing at the now cracked screen. He'd been called off-putting before but usually only by his brothers after a particularly gruesome kill. And there were many. August liked the wet work. Liked getting his hands dirty. Killing gave him a thrill like nothing else did.

He was almost to his car when it hit him. Bianca said Lucas Blackwell was clairvoyant. That he could see the past—or the future, August supposed—simply by touching an object. August was a logical man. While he found the paranormal fascinating, he recognized it for what it was, pseudoscience. There was no way Lucas Blackwell was actually clairvoyant.

He couldn't be.

Yet, he'd looked at August like he was a monster. Which he was. But there was no way Lucas could know that. It was impossible. *But what if he did?* What would that mean for him? His family lived by a code. They didn't kill the innocent. But they'd only ever run into this situation once before, months ago when his brother had decided to fall in…not love, but maybe obsession, with a little wounded bird named Noah.

Noah knew their secret, had figured it out before he'd even met Adam face to face. But Noah was like them. He understood some people just didn't deserve to live. Noah had killed alongside them. He had an investment in keeping them all off the police's radar.

But Lucas was a former Fed. He probably believed strongly in trials and justice and the long arm of the law. He probably wasn't a fan of vigilante justice. Which didn't bode well for his life expectancy if he truly had somehow figured out exactly who August was when the mask was off.

Shit.

As much as August loved killing, the idea of chopping up the pretty blond professor into bite-size pieces left him feeling hollow. August had never met a problem he couldn't solve, but Lucas Blackwell was going to be a problem. A big one. And August had no idea what the hell he was going to do about it.

TWO

LUCAS

Lucas couldn't get to his office fast enough. As soon as he crossed the threshold, he shut the door and locked it, as if the devil himself chased him. Maybe he did. The things Lucas had seen when he'd touched him, the man he'd thought attractive just moments before... He blinked the sweat from his eyes, willing his heart to stop thundering in his chest before he lost consciousness.

It was his first day. His first fucking day. There had to be some sort of explanation for the blood and the screaming. Maybe he'd been in the military and seen combat? Maybe he worked in law enforcement? No. That didn't make any sense. Those screams... Those men were being tortured.

He brought his knees up, bracing his elbows on them to cradle his head in his hands. Lucas knew better than anyone that serial predators hid in plain sight. Sometimes, right under your nose. He dug the heels of his palms into his eyes until little sparks of light danced behind them. This was his first. Fucking. Day. He couldn't go accusing a coworker of

18

being a murderer. Not after last time. He couldn't handle anybody else looking at him like a…crazy person. He'd just left that environment.

"Have you thought, perhaps, you're projecting your impulses onto your co-worker?"

"You must admit it's far-fetched, Lucas."

"You have to understand our concerns given your behavior."

"He's a federal agent. We think, perhaps, you just need a break."

"You're not well."

"You can't just attack people."

Their words swirled around in his head on repeat. There was nothing worse than having people who once respected him suddenly look at him as if he were crazy. He'd spent his life as an outcast. As a child, he was too small, too quiet. An easy target. Afraid of everything. Every object had the potential to send him into a downward spiral of pain and suffering. But, at the bureau, he'd had a home.

Unlike many law enforcement agencies, the FBI had lots of people like him. People who were more brain than brawn. People who were accountants and statisticians. He'd had a home there, even as the book nerd. But that was all gone, ripped away from him because he'd had the audacity to put aside his self-preservation to let his higher ups know they had a wolf among them.

They'd repaid him by branding him a lunatic and throwing him in an institution for weeks. He shook his head. Maybe they were right. Maybe he was crazy. Things he'd once been so sure of now seemed impossible. The meds they put him on just made it worse, made him doubt who

he was and what he saw. Made it harder to shield himself from unwanted visions.

When his heartbeat settled into a normal rhythm, he stood, walking to his desk, attempting to mentally pull himself back together. There was no way his peers weren't out there gossiping about his collision and hasty escape. The man—the one he collided with—had to be faculty. He'd had a lanyard around his neck like Lucas. But he hadn't been able to view what it said.

He needed to stop being so reactionary and do what he'd been trained to do… Investigate. He pulled up the directory for the school. It only took two pages of scrolling the faculty before he had a name. August Mulvaney, Ph.D. Professor of Quantum Physics.

That man was a physicist? He was in good shape. There was no hiding that. When they'd collided, Lucas felt like he'd hit a brick wall. Torturing people was probably taxing on the body. He concentrated on the man—August's—face, hoping maybe he could pick up any more flashes without having to touch him. Sometimes, it worked with photographs, but this wasn't a photo. It was a computer monitor.

Lucas placed his hand over the picture on the screen. Nothing. He sighed. August Mulvaney looked like that actor. The one from all those kid movies. Daniel something? But taller and with broader shoulders.

Harry Potter!

That was it. Harry Potter…if he moonlighted as a stripper. Lucas didn't consider himself a person who made assumptions, but he imagined physics professors as older nerdy guys with pocket protectors and glasses. Men who wore blazers with patches on the elbows.

August had thick brown hair that swept away from his face in a wave and the beginnings of a beard over a strong jaw. His nose was just the tiniest bit crooked, like he'd broken it, and his top lip was slightly smaller than his bottom, which in no way detracted from his attractiveness.

Lucas dragged his gaze away from the man to his profile. Christ. A brief scan of his curriculum vitae showed the man not only held a Ph.D. in quantum physics but also in biomedical engineering and two masters degrees, one in applied mathematics and the other in…Russian literature?

Who the fuck was this guy? That many degrees didn't seem remotely possible. He couldn't be much older than Lucas. He clicked on the awards tab, brows raising when he had to scroll to see them all. There were pages full of honors with names like the *Presidential Early Career Award for Scientists and Engineers*, *Alfred P. Sloan Research Fellowship* and *Rackham Graduate School One Term Dissertation Fellowship*. Lucas wasn't dumb, but he didn't know what any of that shit meant.

Lucas closed out the tab and pulled up Google, typing in August Mulvaney, expecting to find a link to the same CV listed on the school's website and maybe a LinkedIn profile. Instead, he found article after article about not only August but the entire Mulvaney family.

August Mulvaney was the second oldest son of billionaire Thomas Mulvaney. One of seven adopted children. August's list of accomplishments were well documented. He could

read and write at a college level by five. He had an IQ that rivaled the likes of Einstein and Hawking. Was the second youngest member to ever be inducted into MENSA at age six. Finished high school level classes before he reached double digits, attended college when most kids were hitting puberty. Achieved his first Ph.D. at eighteen. That had to be enough to make anybody a little crazy. Right?

Lucas opened his drawer and popped two of his clonazepam before leaning back in his chair. He ran the flashes over and over in his mind. Blood. Knives. Screaming. Body parts. Nothing made sense other than murder. A shiver of fear ran along his spine.

Lucas couldn't go accusing the genius son of a famous billionaire of being a serial killer, especially without proof. And Lucas had learned the hard way that passing off an ability people didn't understand as intuition only got him so far. The Fox Mulder and *X-Files* references used to be funny, just camaraderie among colleagues.

Until one of those colleagues turned out to be a killer. A killer, who was still getting away with murder. Fuck. Lucas had already lost his reputation, his credibility, his job. He couldn't very well tell authorities that he'd touched a fellow professor in a hallway and saw, psychically, that he'd tortured people. He sounded like a fucking nut, even to himself.

Maybe he *was* crazy…like his mother. They'd practically run her out of town with all her talk of visions and auras and psychic bonds. Even Lucas hadn't believed her until it started happening to him. By then, it was too late. His mother was long gone and he was left alone with his grandfather,

who was determined to beat Lucas into toughening up. He learned to hide quickly—not just his abilities but his love of books, his soft heart, and his attraction to boys, not girls.

Lucas shook off his memories. His past didn't matter. If August Mulvaney was a murderer, why did Lucas even care? The last time he'd stuck his neck out for what he believed was right, the FBI had lopped it off. They'd ruined his life. He no longer believed in the infallibility of the police. He no longer believed in much of anything.

There was a soft knock at the door. Lucas ran his hands over his face and shut out of his browser before turning the lock and swinging the door open to find…August Mulvaney.

He looked so…normal. His expression affable, his hands tucked into the pockets of his perfectly tailored pants. Lucas's heart rate began to gallop once again. August was even hotter now that they were face to face. Not that it should matter. The man was likely a murderer. His brain seemed completely okay with that. Lucas ran a hand through his messy hair but then crossed his arms to keep from fidgeting.

"Can we talk?" August asked, voice deep and smooth, almost cheery.

Lucas sniffed. "I'm not really feeling that great. I skipped lunch and I think my blood sugar is low."

"Let me take you to lunch," August offered. When Lucas opened his mouth to refuse, August held up a hand. "We can go somewhere public if you like, say the faculty lounge."

Lucas's tongue shot out, licking over his lower lip. Did he know? Did he know Lucas could…see things? Of course, he did. He'd been the talk of the campus for weeks. But

why would August care what Lucas saw if he had nothing to hide? And, if he had nothing to hide, why would he think Lucas would only want to talk in public? Wasn't that as good as an admission of guilt?

Something withered within him as reality sank in. Admission to who? Him? Lucas already knew he was right. Clearly, August did, too.

"Why? Why would I want to go to lunch with you?" Lucas asked, unsure how else to frame it.

August took a single step, just one expensive loafer crossing the threshold. But it was enough for Lucas to smell his expensive cologne, something spicy that made Lucas want to lean in, to press his face against August's throat where the scent would be strongest.

"I think you know."

Lucas swallowed hard. "Do I?"

August's smile was wolfish. "You know, I don't believe in psychics or mediums. But, given the way you reacted when you touched me, I'm willing to suspend my disbelief."

"I don't know what you mean," Lucas lied.

August examined his face. "You're really very pretty."

Lucas blinked at the unexpected compliment. "What?"

"When I saw you on the quad, I thought you were attractive, but up close…you're almost pretty. Delicate even. I always pictured cops as being these big, tough, former military types, but you're…kind of sweet looking."

"You do realize you're speaking out loud, right?" Lucas asked, unnerved by both his lack of manners and the raw hunger in the other man's eyes.

"I'm aware."

"Do you often speak to strangers like this?" Lucas asked, hating how raw his voice was.

"No. But most people haven't been inside my head. I figured we'd moved past politeness."

"I can't tell if you're trying to threaten me or flirt with me," Lucas admitted, willing his pulse to stop hammering in his throat.

"You could call this flirting. I don't really make threats. Threats imply that the threatened has a chance to escape punishment. That's never the case with me. The guilty are always punished."

"So, you admit it," Lucas whispered. "You admit that you're a killer?"

"Was that ever in question? Do you not believe your own visions?" August asked, head tilted like he was trying to figure Lucas out, like Lucas was somehow the odd one.

Lucas stuffed his shaky hands in his pockets, his gaze dipping to his shoes. "I believe them. Most others don't."

"I work in quantum and theoretical physics. Many people think my work borders on science fiction. I don't know about clairvoyants, but I do know how you reacted when you touched me. You weren't faking that."

Lucas's head was spinning. This man, this killer, was standing there telling Lucas he believed him, believed his gifts. August Mulvaney was a murderer and he knew Lucas knew it. "And you...what? Just wanted me to know that you know? Why are you here?"

August shrugged. "I had hoped to offer you an explanation.

Something to appease your panic. I imagine, given your past, the idea of working beside a killer would seem daunting."

"Who are you?" Lucas asked.

August held out his hand as if they were at a faculty mixer. "August Mulvaney." Lucas just looked at it until August dropped it once more. "Alright. Well, if you don't want to have lunch with me, I have no reason to cancel lunch with my brother. But if you change your mind, my cell phone number is on the back. We could always do dinner."

Lucas looked down at the card offered, hesitating before he took it. What was happening? The man in front of him was clearly a psychopath. Lucas had interviewed enough of them to know they didn't understand societal norms enough to fake them.

His blood felt hot in his veins as anger took root. "You can't flirt or threaten your way out of this. I know what you are."

August chuckled. "And what am I?"

"A killer," Lucas said again. They were just talking in circles and it was making him dizzy.

The look August gave him was so devoid of emotion it made his stomach feel hollow. "Oh, I'm so much more than that. But if you want to know the rest, you'll have to go to dinner with me."

"I could just go to the police," Lucas snapped, clenching his teeth until his jaw ached.

"You won't do that," August said, that wolfish smile returning.

Lucas shifted from one foot to the other. "And why's that?"

August leaned in close enough for his breath to fan

over Lucas's ear, his voice a low rumble as he murmured, "Because we both know nobody would believe you."

With that, he turned and walked away, leaving Lucas to stare after him with his card practically burning his fingers.

Shit.

THREE
AUGUST

"Are you really not going to see Dad before you go?" Adam asked.

The question wasn't directed at August but at their other brother, Aiden, who sat across from him. It was a breezy day, so they were gathered at a table at the far end of the patio, one far from the prying ears of neighboring tables. Lunch with the Mulvaney boys was always a lively affair, even when only four of them were present, like today, and the topic of conversation was rarely palatable for public consumption.

Aiden was rarely in town. In fact, this was his younger brother's first trip home in years. He stayed in touch with them via text or email, but nothing more, not even a phone call. Nobody knew why. Well, one other person knew why, but he wasn't talking either. So, they'd staged an intervention before his flight.

Aiden gave Adam, the youngest, an irritated look. "He's your dad, not mine."

August just didn't understand the venom directed at their

father. He wanted to know more, to poke at Aiden with something sharp and pointy until he spilled his secrets. Instead, he took a sip of his fizzy water. "Funny how you don't say that about us, your brothers. Only Dad."

Atticus, the eldest, threaded a hand through his ginger hair before pushing his glasses up the bridge of his nose. "Yes, excellent point. Why have you disowned Dad, but not us?"

Aiden rolled his eyes. "This is why I don't come back here. You guys are so dramatic. I didn't disown anybody. He was never my father. I was almost seventeen when he 'adopted' me," he said, using air quotes around the word *adopted* as if that was somehow untrue. "I just never viewed him as a father, and he never saw me as his son."

"Bullshit," Adam said, reaching for his sugar laden soda, downing half of it in one go.

August couldn't help but note the girls who gazed at his brother, a former model. He was gay and taken, but that never stopped them. If anything, when he was out with Noah, it only made things worse. Somehow, it never bothered Adam. Maybe it was because he was the baby and used to all the attention.

August took in the black nail polish on Adam's short, blunt nails. It was chipped in several places, but it seemed as if even that was a deliberate fashion choice. His black hair parted in the middle, flopping into his husky blue eyes. He wore ripped jeans and a faded designer t-shirt that probably cost a thousand dollars, even though it looked as if he'd pulled it straight from the garbage. Adam made laziness chic.

August turned his attention back to Aiden. "No, there's

something more to it. We'll figure it out eventually, so why not just tell us?"

Aiden pushed his plate away, glowering at the two of them. "Because there's nothing to tell. You're literally making something out of nothing. How did six psychopaths become such gossips? There's no tea here."

Aiden didn't look well. His reddish brown hair now fell to his shoulders with his face half-covered by an unkempt beard. As always, there was a hardness to him, like the world never stopped letting him down, even though their father, Thomas, never denied him anything. Even if Aiden refused to acknowledge it.

"Your words say one thing, but your body language screams that you're lying," Adam said, looking Aiden up and down. "You can't lie to us."

The muscle in Aiden's jaw began to tic. "Is this why you asked me to lunch? To grill me about why I don't get along with your dad?"

Atticus snapped his fingers. "See, that. That right there. *Our* dad. What the fuck, man? Even after all these years, you still have a chip on your shoulder about something. Can't the two of you just work it out?"

Aiden took a sip of his scotch. "We have worked it out. I live on the other side of the country, he gives me assignments and pays me for my time. You're the only ones who seem so pressed about it."

"Because Dad hasn't been the same since you left. It's like he's just…sad. You could have at least gone to see him while you were here. Said hello or something," Atticus chided, his tone chock full of eldest child superiority.

Aiden forced his chair back with a loud scrape of iron over concrete, drawing the attention of the other patrons. "This has been fun, guys. Let's not do it again."

"Sit. Down," Atticus said, tapping a finger onto the table with each word.

Aiden flicked him off. "You're not the boss of me."

Atticus opened and closed his mouth like a fish out of water, while Adam snickered. It was clear Aiden had no intention of staying.

August did the only thing he could to keep them all there. "I think somebody knows about me."

His bickering brothers all turned to look at him at once.

"Knows?" Adam echoed. "Like, *knows* knows?"

"Somebody other than Adam's pet?" Atticus asked, looking flummoxed.

This time, it was Adam who gave him the finger. "Noah is not my pet."

"Focus," Aiden muttered. "Who knows about you?"

August sighed. "A new professor."

"How would that even be possible? Is he related to another victim? Did he hear something? See something?" Atticus asked, not bothering to let August answer.

"Nothing like that," August assured him.

Aiden fell back into his chair. "Why do you think this co-worker knows about you?"

August sighed. "Because he said, 'I know what you are.'"

"Maybe he just meant you're an ass," Adam said.

"Or off putting," Atticus offered.

Aiden nodded. "Or just weird."

August rolled his eyes. "He said he knew I killed people. Used the word *killer*. I don't think it was a metaphor for something."

"How would he know that?" Atticus asked, his pale face pinking like a hairless cat.

August took another sip of his water, liking the feel of the bubbles on his tongue. "He's clairvoyant."

His brothers volleyed looks back and forth between them before glancing at him as if waiting for August to deliver the punchline, but none came.

Finally, Aiden said, "You're joking."

August shook his head. "I'm not."

"You can't possibly believe this. You're a scientist, for God's sake," Atticus said.

"I mean, the dude said he was a killer. I don't think he was talking about his personality," Adam said. "Regardless of how he knows, we still need to take it seriously. What are you going to do?"

"I don't know," August said.

"You don't know?" Adam echoed. "You have a look on your face that says you do know."

August shook his head, struggling to find the right words. Words that could somehow convey the feeling that had struck him when Lucas had looked at him. "I kind of want to…play with him?"

Was that even the right way to phrase it? August wanted to open him up, see what made him a person. He wanted to poke him and prod at him, like a dog with a toy. August wanted to see if he could make Lucas squeak.

"P-Play with him?" Atticus sputtered.

"Like paper dolls or like a cat wants to play with a mouse before he maims it?" Aiden asked, not sounding particularly bothered by whatever August's answer might be.

"I don't want to hurt him... Not much, anyway. Just a little. I want to see what I can do...what he'll let me get away with before he pushes back."

Atticus's eyes bulged. "What are you talking about? You need to tell Dad. We need to neutralize the threat."

"Neutralize the threat," Aiden said, cracking a smile for the first time since they'd sat down. "You're such a tool, man."

"Excuse me for trying to keep us all out of prison," Atticus said, pouting.

Adam waved Atticus off, giving August his full attention. "What do you mean?"

August thought about it. "I don't know. Nobody will believe him. He has no proof other than his intuition. He's lost all credibility. I don't even consider him a threat, really."

"So, why bring him up?" Aiden asked, frowning.

August sighed, holding his glass to his lips, feeling the carbonation spring up and burst on his skin but not taking a drink. "He's really...pretty."

A grin spread across Adam's face. "Oh, shit. I think August is crushing on his co-worker."

Was he? He hadn't really ever thought of men as anything but a means to an end. He rarely had sex, and when he did it was all rather perfunctory. He was unable to form attachments, and it had never seemed fair to any

unsuspecting person to attempt a relationship when he spent many of his nights neck deep in entrails. "I just… like the way he smells. I look at him and I find myself wondering what his skin tastes like."

"Oof. Easy, Dahmer," Adam said. "Maybe don't start with that."

"Don't start with anything. He thinks you kill people," Atticus said, practically apoplectic at that point.

"He does kill people?" Adam reminded. "Noah doesn't care that I kill people. Military spouses don't care that their soldiers may kill people in combat. Maybe his little psychic connection won't mind either."

Aiden shook his head, a half smirk on his face. "Who is he?"

August flicked his gaze upward. "He's the new criminal psychology professor."

"Why not just date a cop?" Atticus snapped, hands flying upward, clearly beside himself.

"Um, a psychologist and a cop aren't the same thing," Adam said. "Stop trying to shut him down."

August shrugged. "He used to be an FBI agent."

Atticus gestured wildly. "See?" To August, he said, "You're supposed to be the smart one."

August flattened his mouth, giving Atticus a withering look before he said, "I am the smart one. I have papers to prove it and everything."

"Then maybe start acting like it and stop thinking with your dick?" Atticus shot back.

August bristled. "My dick has no bearing on my thought

process. There's just something about him…"

Adam leaned in, bracing his forearms on the table, eyes shining. "Like what?"

August thought of Lucas, with his dirty blond hair and green eyes. "He's…soft. Vulnerable. Fragile even. I want to…test his limitations."

"Right, a fragile FBI agent," Atticus huffed.

"He is. He's a profiler. He sat at a desk. Something happened to him and it, like, fractured him."

"You want to test his limitations?" Aiden prompted, brow raised.

August made a noise of frustration. "Have you ever just looked at someone or something and thought, I want to keep it? Like, I want to protect him from the outside world but, at the same time, his helplessness and fear are so… intoxicating? I want him to be soft just for me."

"Oh, Jesus," Atticus muttered.

August knew he wasn't explaining himself right. But he didn't know how to say he wanted to be the one who put Lucas together and took him apart. The one who could make him beg but also made him feel safe. The idea of playing with Lucas, teasing him, torturing him, maybe making him cry just a little…had August harder than he'd ever been, and he was grateful for the table blocking his lap.

"I get it," Adam said. "It's how I feel about Noah. Not the helplessness and fear, that's a little fucked up—not that I'm judging—but the second I looked at him, I knew he was mine. Maybe it's an evolutionary thing?"

Atticus rolled his eyes. "Leave the science to the people

who know what they're talking about. Obsession isn't evolutionary."

August cut his gaze to Atticus. "Well, I do know science, and I know exactly what I'm talking about. I want him. He already knows who I am. What I am. What's the worst that can happen?"

"He uses you to gather evidence and then exposes us all? There's a trial, a spectacle, Dad's experiment goes up in flames and he dies disgraced," Atticus said. "Just spitballing here."

Aiden sighed. "He's already made up his mind. Look at him." He gestured to August. "Have you ever seen him look this cow-eyed and dopey when talking about anything but string theory or murder?"

August had no choice but to endure the three of them examining him like a slide under a microscope.

"Dad's going to freak out," Atticus muttered.

Adam shrugged. "Maybe not. He'll likely just use it as another experiment, like me and Noah. You know how he likes to drop us in new environments and situations and see how we react."

Aiden scoffed. "Daddy's adorable little lab rats. How cute."

"Bitter much?" Adam asked.

Aiden shrugged. "I just know what happens to rats once the experiment is over. While he won't kill us, he will do whatever it takes to keep his project under wraps. Anybody you invite into this fucked up family runs the risk of being merced the moment they step out of line. They should know that going in."

August contemplated the idea of Lucas as part of the

Mulvaney family. Adam's boyfriend, Noah, had melted into the fold without issue. But he'd endured a rough childhood and understood that, sometimes, people just needed killing. Could Lucas ever come to understand that? Did August even want him to? Did August want to take Lucas and bind their lives forever? They'd only just crossed paths that morning.

But the idea of keeping Lucas...having him all to himself, made August's insides quake. The power of having somebody like Lucas trust somebody like him, it heated something inside him until he could focus on nothing else. Would he open up to August? Make himself vulnerable to a man like him? Would he trust August enough to give himself to him in every possible way?

"I have to get to the airport," Aiden said, looking at his watch.

"I'll drive you," Adam offered.

Aiden shook his head. "I'll grab an Uber."

"It's a ride to the airport, not a marriage proposal. Stop being fucking weird."

Aiden sighed. "Yeah, fine." To August, he said, "Let me know if the psychic thing blows up in your face and I have to go on the lam, yeah?"

August waved a hand dismissively. With that, Adam and Aiden left, heading straight from the patio to Adam's black BMW 7 Series. Well, likely Thomas's BMW. Adam used their father's garage as his own personal car lot.

When the server came, he gave her one of his cards, ignoring Atticus as he continued to glare at him from across the table.

Finally, Atticus said, "You know you can't do this. It puts us all at risk."

August shook his head. "He's already onto me. We're already at risk. At least, from the inside, I have a chance at changing his mind."

"You? You find torturing people amusing. You actively tune out ninety percent of the world. You spend hours in your own head trying to solve riddles most people could never hope to understand. He probably likes sports or video games or—I don't know—stamp collecting. Even if you weren't a stone cold killer, you'd have nothing in common."

August grinned. "I don't know, he likes to catch killers. I am one. That's something, right?"

Atticus stood, giving him one last disgusted look. "Christ. You're going to get us all killed."

"Have a little faith, brother," August said, his mind already wandering to all the things he wanted to do with his—What did Adam call Lucas? Right, August's new little psychic connection. He needed to pay him another visit.

Tonight.

FOUR

LUCAS

Like most nights, Lucas woke screaming, his heart hammering in his chest, body shaking, sweat soaking his sheets and boxer briefs. The nightmares never stopped, even after months, even after drugs and therapy and all the techniques he used to shield his mind from the visions that plagued him. Sometimes, he wondered if this was all that was left. Blood and pain and fear.

Did he want to live like this? Was he even living at this point? It felt more like existing. Getting up, going to work, coming home, eating. It was just…muscle memory, just reliving the same day over and over again.

He rubbed his eyes, then rolled off the bed, padding into his bathroom. He didn't turn the light on, navigating his movements by the small night light near the sink. He wrenched the water in the shower to the coldest setting and stepped beneath the icy spray, the shock tearing a gasp from him. He just stood there, eyes closed, hoping to wash away the remnants of his visions.

Women screaming, begging, crying. Blood. The whirring of a motor of some kind, almost like a dentist's drill. He slammed his fist into the wall, trying to will it all away, but nothing worked.

Finally, he turned off the water, toweling dry and walking naked to the bedroom. He pulled on a pair of black boxer briefs before heading back to the bed. He'd intended to strip the sheets but, instead, just dropped to the edge of the mattress and stared at the wall.

His shoulder throbbed. It was always worse after the nightmares. Maybe the doctors were right. Maybe it was all in his head. It had been three months since the attack, since a fellow patient at the hospital had plunged a shard of glass into his shoulder. Lucas had never seen it coming.

The little hairs at the back of his neck suddenly stood at attention, a terrible realization hitting him as some deep, dark recess of his brain began to scream *danger*. He wasn't alone. He turned his gaze, scanning the darkness, brain short-circuiting at the figure sitting in the chair in the corner, shrouded in shadow.

Lucas snatched the knife he kept on the bedside table, grateful it was still there. He didn't stand, though, just whispered, "Who's there?"

He hated the fear in his voice, especially when, the truth was, he'd known this day would come eventually. It was only a matter of time before Kohn came to finish what that patient had started, or maybe he'd hired somebody, just like last time.

The stranger's body shifted until only his face was in shadow. "Do you always wake up screaming?"

Tension drained from his body. Not Kohn. August. August Mulvaney. The *other* serial killer to enter his life. Equally as deadly, probably more so, but he hadn't arranged to have Lucas killed, so he was still better than the alternative.

"How did you get in?" Lucas asked, gripping the knife handle.

August rose, prowling closer until he loomed over Lucas, partially illuminated by the slice of moonlight that cut through the bedroom. Lucas sat hunched over on himself, but he lifted the knife just enough to show August he was armed.

"Stay where you are." There was no heat in his words. He was just so fucking tired. He wanted it all to be over already.

August's voice was low, almost crooning. "You're holding it all wrong."

"What?"

August dropped to his knees before him, his face finally revealed. Lucas had to fight the urge to reach out and run his hands along the scruff on his chin. He'd never wanted to touch a person so badly in his life. Touch had always meant bad things for Lucas.

He shook the thought away. Normal people didn't find murderers attractive. How had Lucas ever passed the FBI's psych evaluation? They should have just locked him up on sight.

He sucked in a breath as August's fingers began to trail over his forearm, the pads of his fingers tickling the hair there in a way that gave Lucas goosebumps. There were no

flashes this time, just the barely-there caress of his touch that had his cock hardening. He watched, transfixed, as August's fingers advanced slowly until he reached the hand holding the knife.

"Are you here to kill me?" Lucas asked, finding the thought didn't scare him like it should.

August gave him a cryptic smile but didn't answer. He gently unwrapped Lucas's grip from the hilt of the weapon. He hoped he'd just plunge the blade into his heart and be done with it.

Instead, August turned the knife, point out, then closed Lucas's fingers around the hilt once more. "Holding a knife like that will get you killed. The blade's no good pointed at the floor." He gripped Lucas's wrist, placing the tip of the knife over his own heart. "Like this, you can stab here." He moved the blade to rest beside his throat. "You can slice me open here. I'd bleed out in seconds. With the blade like this, every glancing blow will cut your opponent. Even if it doesn't kill them, they'll be in pieces before you finally end their suffering."

There was no malice in his tone, only a trace of amusement.

"Is this funny to you?" Lucas asked, trying to make sense of any of it. "I'm not going to tell anybody, if that's what you're worried about. Like you said, who would believe me anyway? If you're going to kill me, just do it."

August gave him a pitying look, brushing the back of his hand along Lucas's cheek. "Are you alright?"

Lucas choked on a sob. Was he alright? No. Of course, he wasn't alright. He was losing his mind. He saw things, heard things. He'd lost his career, his credibility, the full use of his right arm. He woke up screaming each night and needed a dozen pills just to be a functioning human being. He didn't want to do this anymore.

"Please," Lucas begged, closing his wet eyes. "Just do it already."

He waited for the pain to come, but it never did. Instead, warm soft lips pressed against his in a kiss that lingered. Lucas didn't pull away. It didn't even occur to him. But then it was over.

When his lids fluttered open, August said, "I work for an organization that eliminates dangerous people. People who slip through the cracks in our justice system."

Lucas frowned. "You're a genius, billionaire, crime-fighting vigilante? You're…Batman?"

August grinned. "Exactly. You don't have to be afraid of me. I'm a good guy."

"A good guy who tortures people and kills them?" Lucas deadpanned.

"Yes," he said, as if it were the most normal thing in the world.

There was something so unsettling about August. He was trying so hard to be a person, but it just didn't work. His smile, his intense gaze. He was a psychopath. That much was obvious. He'd suspected it in his office, but this confirmed it.

Still, Lucas didn't want him to leave. He imagined it was like somehow befriending a wolf. He might eat him, but the thrill of being near such a creature was too exciting to

pass up.

Lucas shook his head. "That's... You sound crazy."

August's gaze met his. "Crazy is such a hurtful word. You'd think somebody with a degree in psychology would know that," he chided. "Touch me. See for yourself. You can look around my brain for as long as you like."

"Are you trying to get me to put down the knife?" Lucas asked, realizing how stupid that sounded, even to him. August could have disarmed him at any time. Lucas was basically a sitting duck. A big, half-naked sitting duck.

August pushed Lucas's knees apart, leaning in until the blade pierced his skin, red blooming across the snowy white fabric of his dress shirt. "You can keep the knife if it makes you feel better. I don't want you to be afraid of me."

Lucas's brows knit together. "Why?"

"Why?" August echoed, making no attempt to hide his amusement, seemingly unworried about the fact that he was now bleeding, leaning in even more, like he'd let the knife sink into the hilt just to be closer to Lucas.

Lucas had to be dreaming, or maybe he shouldn't have taken his meds with that shot of whiskey, but he'd just wanted a single night of peace. But that was long gone. "Yeah. Why don't you want me to be afraid of you? Why do you even care what I think?"

"Because I want you," August said simply.

"For what?" Lucas blurted.

August's gaze raked over him, all trace of amusement leaving, replaced with a raw hunger that made Lucas shiver. "For many things. But none of that can happen until I know you believe me."

Lucas pulled the knife free of August's chest, setting it on the bed beside him. "You're bleeding."

"I'm fine." He lifted Lucas's hands and pressed them to his face, eyes closing, like August was in need of comforting. "Do it."

Lucas shook his head at the other man's stubbornness. He took a deep breath and dropped his shields, opening his mind to August, bracing himself for whatever came next. But there was no blood. No screaming. This time, the visions were…orderly, like August was guiding him somehow. There were files and computer screens, flashes of mugshots, a conference room of men, faces pinned to a white board. There was no one image that proved August's words, but he could feel the truth of them.

Lucas opened his eyes, still cupping August's face. "You're…a superhero."

August laughed, the sound rich and smooth, pouring over Lucas like cool water. "You're the one with superpowers. But we don't kill innocent people. It's against the rules. I won't hurt you."

Lucas believed him. He just didn't know what to do with that information. It explained everything and nothing. They were total strangers. Yet, they were sitting in Lucas's apartment in the dead of night, August on his knees and Lucas half naked, sharing an experience more intimate than sex to Lucas.

"Why did you break into my house?"

August's gaze lowered, his expression sullen. "You never

called or texted. I needed to see you."

"You needed to see me?" Lucas parroted.

August looked up, nodding earnestly. "Very much."

Lucas blinked. "You needed to see me, so your first thought was to bypass my complicated as fuck security system to break into my house to watch me while I slept? You could have texted me, you know."

August shrugged. "You didn't give me your number."

"I didn't give you the code to my alarm system either, but that didn't slow you down too much," Lucas pointed out.

"Would you have let me come over if I had? Texted you?" August asked, sounding genuinely curious.

Lucas thought about it. Would he have allowed August to enter his home knowing what he knew? "I don't know," he answered honestly. "But you can't just break into my house every time you want to see me."

"Alright," August said, voice cheery, as if he'd won a major point in whatever weird contract they appeared to be negotiating. "Can I kiss you again?"

Lucas felt a bemused smile starting to form. "No."

August pouted. "Fine. Can I stay with you tonight?"

"What? No?"

"Why not?" August pressed, clearly offended.

Lucas floundered. "What do you mean, why not? Because you're a stranger, Batman or not."

"What if I promise not to touch you?"

That was the problem. Lucas wanted August to touch him. That part of him that had once believed in logic and reason had died, leaving behind the worst, most reckless parts of

Lucas. The parts that wanted August to stay, wanted him to touch him. How long had it been since Lucas had let anybody close to him in that way? "Why do you want to stay?"

"To keep you safe. Protect you."

"You can't protect me from my own brain."

"I can try," August said. "You could at least let me try."

Lucas examined August. He looked so sincere, like he was trying so hard. "This is crazy. I feel like I'm hallucinating."

"Please, let me stay," August said, giving him his biggest, saddest eyes.

Lucas snorted. "Now, you're just manipulating me."

"Of course, I am. Is it working?"

Lucas took a huge breath and let it out. Yeah. Yeah, it fucking was. They should have left him locked up in that psych ward. "Fine. But take your shirt off." A smirk spread across August's face as he began to unbutton his shirt. "You're bleeding," Lucas reminded him.

August glanced down as if he'd forgotten. When he peeled his shirt off, Lucas realized he'd definitely made a mistake. August wasn't built like a stripper, as Lucas had originally imagined, but he was toned, his chest and belly coated with dark curls. He should have let him keep the bloody shirt.

August helped Lucas change the sheets. Lucas slipped between them, then erected a pillow barrier between them.

August watched, clearly amused. "Can I take my pants off?"

Lucas gave a surprised laugh. "No."

"Please?"

"Ugh, fine." He gave in, just wanting another couple of

hours of sleep before he had to get up for work. August dropped his pants, then slid between the sheets. Lucas closed his eyes. August's head popped up over the pillow wall. "Can I take you to breakfast in the morning?"

"No."

August flounced back onto the bed. "I can't kiss you or touch you or take you to breakfast? You're taking all the fun out of this sleepover."

Lucas chuckled. "Then go break into another man's home."

August reappeared. "There's no other man. Just you."

Lucas wasn't August's man, but he didn't say as much. It wouldn't matter if he did. August was nothing if not stubborn, and he seemed to have come to some internal conclusion that Lucas was his. The idea of being the sole focus of a homicidal psychopath should have sent Lucas into another panic attack. Instead, he rolled over and quickly drifted off to sleep.

FIVE
AUGUST

"You broke into his house and watched him sleep?"

August rolled his eyes at Adam's amused statement. "When you put it like that, it makes me sound like a stalker."

August had stopped by Adam's loft on his way to the college to try to figure out how to make Lucas love him… or, at least, like him more than other people. They sat at the kitchen table with Adam's boyfriend, Noah, and their other brother, Archer.

Noah always looked like he'd just come from a church social with his big brown eyes and freckled cheeks, in direct opposition with his brother's inky black hair and pale blue eyes. Yet, they seemed a perfect match.

"You *are* a stalker, dude. You can't just break into a guy's apartment and sneak up on him while he's sleeping," Noah chastised.

August frowned. "Why? Didn't Adam do the same thing to you?"

Noah stopped short, looking at Adam. "You totally did.

Your whole family is creepy."

"My whole family murders people. You knew that going in. Seems like it says more about you than it does me," Adam said, grinning at Noah before pulling him in to kiss the top of his head.

"That. The whole kissing and cuddling thing. I want that," August said.

Archer made a disgusted noise. "Christ. I'm not drunk enough for this."

August hadn't expected to find Archer at Adam's place. It was surprising to find Archer anywhere before noon. A professional poker player and amateur reprobate, Archer had somehow turned his vices into a lucrative career.

As usual, he looked like he'd rolled off a pirate ship, dark hair askew, a few days worth of scruff on his chiseled face. All he was missing was a bottle of rum, which Archer had no doubt already downed before leaving his apartment.

Noah waved Archer off. "Don't mind him. If you want to get this guy, you—and I can't stress this enough—cannot listen to any advice offered up by these two idiots. Or anybody else with the last name Mulvaney, honestly."

"Hey," Adam said, feigning hurt.

"No, he's got a valid point. I can show you how to get anybody into bed, but I don't have a clue what to do with them once the sex is over," Archer said, kicking his booted foot up on the kitchen chair beside him. "You probably shouldn't get your relationship advice from a bunch of psychopaths."

August shifted his gaze to the only non-psychopath in the room. "How do I make him like me?"

Noah leaned in, tongue sweeping across his lower lip before he asked, "Well, how did you leave things with him this morning?"

August's mind drifted back to that moment. He'd woken to find Lucas had breached his own pillow barrier and infiltrated August's side of the bed. He'd stared down in amusement at Lucas's face smashed against August's bicep, both hands wrapped around his forearm like he was his own personal pillow. He liked being Lucas's pillow. "I just snuck out before he woke up."

"You fucked him and then ghosted?" Noah asked, sounding horrified.

August's brows knitted together. "What? No. We didn't have sex. I just asked him if I could sleep with him."

Noah rubbed both hands over his face. "You're all androids. It's like you've never watched a single romantic comedy in your lives." He pointed at August. "You can read an entire book in, like, thirty minutes and you've never cracked open a single one on relationships?"

August shrugged. "Why would I? I've never wanted a relationship. Until now. I went there last night to tell him that."

"And how did he react?" Noah prompted.

August grinned. "He pulled a knife on me."

Archer snickered. "Smart man. I like him already."

"Is that why there's blood all over your shirt?" Noah asked. "He stabbed you?"

August frowned. "Not exactly. I did it."

Noah's mouth fell open. "You stabbed yourself? You need

to start at the beginning."

August did his best to recall all the details of the night before. When he was done, he found himself staring at three dumbfounded faces. "Well, help me."

"Dude, you broke into a stranger's house, told him you were Batman, kissed him, impaled yourself on a blade, and then asked to spend the night. I don't know that God could help you," Noah said.

"I don't ever want to hear that I'm bad at romance," Adam told Noah, expression smug.

Noah grinned and patted his cheek before turning back to August. "Okay, so, this isn't that bad." At the others' incredulous looks, he said, "Okay, it's a little bad." When they continued to blink at him, he blurted, "Okay, it's really bad, but we can fix it."

"How? How do I fix this?" August asked, genuinely wanting to make things right. He wanted Lucas to be excited to see him, not terrified of him.

"Well, to start, you have to be more Bruce Wayne and less Batman," Noah said.

August frowned. "I don't know what that means."

Noah blew out an exasperated breath. "It means less creepy vigilante and more suave billionaire."

"August? Suave? Good luck," Archer quipped.

Noah glared at Archer. "Unhelpful, dude," To August, he said, "Okay, so maybe not suave but, like, sincere. Do nice things for him. Find out what he likes. Bring him coffee. Ask him on a real date."

What nice thing could August do for Lucas? He didn't

even know him, knew nothing about him, except that he smelled like rain and spice and looked soft and vulnerable when he slept and that August had watched him drool on his arm that morning and found it…comforting. "I want to keep him."

"Bruh. Those are thinking thoughts not speaking thoughts," Noah coached. "You can't just go around telling strangers you've imprinted on them like some werewolf in a *Twilight* movie. They won't get it."

August shrugged. "He already knows I'm a psychopath."

Noah bobbed his head. "I mean, that's good. Congrats on that first hurdle. But it's a long way between knowing you're a psychopath and wanting to spend his life with one. He's a former FBI agent and you're a murderer. As far as relationship issues go, I'd say this is like the Montagues versus the Capulets on steroids. It's kind of a big hurdle and you could both end up dead."

Something twisted inside August. "You don't think he'd want somebody like me."

"We didn't say that," Noah soothed.

"I'm saying it. No fucking way. Not a chance in hell," Archer muttered. "Do you have any booze in this place?"

"Noah has his emotional support vodka in the freezer," Adam said, pointing a thumb in the direction of the kitchen.

Noah's lip curled, glaring at Archer. "It's not even nine in the morning."

"I haven't been to bed yet, so it doesn't count," Archer said, taking the bottle and pouring himself a healthy dose into an orange juice glass.

"I think you have a chance," Adam said, patting August's hand stiffly.

"That!" Noah said. "That right there. You guys have got to work on looking more like people and less like…cyborgs pretending to be people. Adam needs to work on his fake empathy face and you have to learn to smile without looking like a fucking supervillain."

August blinked at him. "I smile like a supervillain?"

"You smile at the wrong things, at the wrong time. You're never happier than when you're about to kill somebody or when you're thinking of killing somebody. You have to work on that. Smile less." August wiped all expression from his face. "Yeah, okay, that's not going to work either."

August flopped back in his chair. "This would be a lot easier if I could just club him over the head and drag him back to my cave."

"You know what," Noah said, "fuck everything I just said. If Lucas is going to like you, he's going to have to take you as you are. Just show him who you are without a knife in your hand. Show him the things you like outside of murder."

What did August like better than murder? Music. Silent movies. That wasn't really enough to build a relationship on.

Archer gave August a wolfish grin. "In other words, you're doomed."

Noah threw a fork at him. "Shut up. You've never had a relationship with anything that didn't have an alcohol percentage on the label."

"Touché," Archer said, raising his glass in a mock salute.

How did he show Lucas what he liked outside of murder? What did he like? Would Lucas still want him when he realized August was put together all wrong? In every way. "What about sex?"

Archer spit his drink onto the table with a laugh, shaking his now wet hand.

Noah glared at the man before giving August a patient look. "What about it?"

"How do I get him to like the things I like...sexually?"

"I'm shocked you've even had sex," Adam said, sounding genuinely surprised and a little relieved.

August frowned. "Why's that?"

"You're creepy, bro. What person is going to have sex with you without wondering if you're going to turn them into a lamp shade when it's over?" Noah slapped Adam's arm hard enough to make him flinch. "What? He asked."

August shrugged. "I usually use sex workers. It makes things less complicated. They don't ask questions and they're discreet."

Noah began to squirm but looked determined. "Okay, so you're not a virgin. Win. Why wouldn't Lucas like what you like sexually? Are you into some weird fetishes? Necrophilia or, like, licking feet?"

"A foot fetish comes after necrophilia for you?" Adam asked, chuckling.

Noah glared at Adam. "Shut up." He looked back to August. "Seriously, what is it you worry he won't be into?"

"I like..." He struggled to put a name to it that didn't make him sound even creepier than they already found

him. "A power exchange."

"BDSM?" Noah asked, shoulders sinking in relief. "Oh, thank God, it's something normal. Like, I can't guarantee he wants to be spanked or tied up or whatever, but you could always just have the conversation whenever you get there."

August clearly wasn't explaining himself correctly. A problem he'd never had before. "What if I want him to do those things to me?"

Noah's eyes widened as understanding dawned. "Oh."

"I did not see that one coming," Adam said.

"I totally did," Archer muttered, pouring himself another serving of vodka.

"You still need to talk about it—with him. But maybe you should worry about getting him to like you before you worry too much about getting him to spank you."

Archer scoffed. "I'm not drunk enough for this conversation."

"Me either," Adam said, reaching for the vodka bottle.

Noah smacked his hand away. "You haven't even had breakfast this morning."

That. Whatever that was. That was what August wanted. With Lucas. A total stranger. It made no sense, and he couldn't describe it to another living soul with any elegance, but he wanted a person of his own. He wanted Lucas to be his person. But Noah was right. August was weird and off-putting and he said and did everything wrong. How did he make Lucas see that August couldn't love him but he could protect him? Keep him safe.

He left Adam's house with a promise to keep Noah

apprised of the situation as it unfolded. The moment he slid into the driver's seat, he pulled up Google and typed in books on relationships, choosing the first one called *The Five Love Languages*. August was great at languages. He spoke seven. How hard could it be to learn five more?

He sat in his car scrolling page after page, learning about acts of service, quality time, words of affirmation, receiving gifts, and physical touch. He wanted to touch Lucas and wanted Lucas to touch him, too. But he needed to start small.

Coffee. August could do coffee. He loved coffee. Did Lucas love coffee? He drove back to Lucas's apartment, breaking into his house once more. Lucas was gone, a half eaten piece of toast sitting on the counter and a full thermos left beside it as if he'd left in a hurry, too distracted to remember to grab it.

August continued to prowl around, opening the kitchen cabinets, pausing when he saw the numerous medicine bottles on the bottom shelf. There were mood stabilizers and antidepressants, anti-anxiety meds, and painkillers. Something bad had happened to Lucas, and August was determined to find out what it was.

In a spare bedroom, he hit pay dirt; a thick file folder sat on a desk. Inside sat a stack of missing person posters, several neatly written notes, and a photo of a man in an FBI jacket with a lanyard around his neck that stated he was Special Agent Laurence Kohn. Across that photo somebody had written one word in blood red marker.

GUILTY

Guilty of what? What had happened to Lucas that made him wake up every night screaming? What could have caused a man who had lived with a burden like being clairvoyant to suddenly snap after years with the FBI? Who the fuck was Special Agent Laurence Kohn, and what was he guilty of?

August pulled his phone out and began to snap pictures of the missing person photos. They were all women, all indigenous. The youngest appeared to be barely thirteen, the oldest forty-five. Had Lucas stumbled upon a serial predator? Was that predator a fellow agent? That would be enough to drive anybody over the edge. Had Lucas realized it with just a touch like he had August? No wonder Lucas had been terrified of him.

He put the folder back where he found it and made to leave. He was going to bring Lucas's thermos but thought better of it, returning the apartment to exactly as Lucas left it before locking up and heading back downstairs. At the base of the stairs, there were businesses on either side. To the left was the near empty coffee shop he'd seen when he'd arrived. Coffee.

Inside was a girl with pink hair and a nose ring, scrolling through her phone. She perked up when she saw she had a customer. When August got to the counter, he smiled, doing his best to make sure he wasn't smiling like a supervillain. It must have worked because she didn't look spooked like strangers usually did.

"What can I get you?" she asked.

That was a good question. He had no idea how Lucas

took his coffee or even if it had been coffee in the thermos. With the meds he was on, caffeine wasn't good for him.

Still, there was always decaf. "Weird question, but do you know the man who lives upstairs? Six foot, blond hair, pretty eyes?"

The girl grinned. "Lucas?"

August nodded, relieved. "Yes. I don't suppose you know his coffee order?"

The girl examined him closely. "Yeah. He gets the same thing every day."

Damn. Maybe he'd already had his coffee. "Did he come in this morning?"

The girl's brow wrinkled. "Actually, no. Kind of weird."

"Would you get him whatever his usual is?" he asked. "But make it decaf." When she frowned, he added, "I'm worried about his stress levels."

She gave him a simpering look, like she thought he was sweet. That boded well, he supposed. "He your boyfriend or something?"

August sighed. "Not yet. I'm trying to find out his love language."

The girl nodded. "Right on. Acts of service. Good start."

"Thanks."

She gave him a conspiratorial look. "You should write something cute and flirty on the cup."

August's brain short-circuited. "Like what? I'm really bad at dating."

A devious grin crossed her face. "Do you trust me?"

"Of course not. I don't even know you. But you're bound

to write something better than I would. I'd probably tell him I like the way his atoms are put together or something."

The girl pouted. "Aw, that's so nerdy and cute. But let's try something a little flirtier."

With coffee and a chocolate chip muffin in hand, August gave a wave. "Thank you."

"I'm Cricket, by the way," she called as he pushed the door open.

"August."

She smiled again. "Nice to meet you, August."

"You too."

Lucas wasn't in his office, so August made his way across campus to the Social Sciences wing. Lucas was sitting at his desk in front of a large projection screen, and students were just starting to filter in and find their seats in the stadium-like seating.

Lucas looked sexy as hell in an olive green sweater the same color as his eyes, his blond hair just messy enough to look deliberate. The students noticed his good looks, too. Girls giggled and pointed, whispering to each other. It made him want to cut off their ponytails.

Lucas looked up in surprise when August reached his desk. "Hi."

"Hi. I brought you breakfast," August said, setting his goodies on the desk.

Lucas gave him a somewhat bemused smile. "I said no

breakfast."

August shook his head. "No, you said I couldn't take you to breakfast. You never said I couldn't bring breakfast to you."

Lucas paused, but then nodded. "Oh. I suppose you're right."

"I got your order from Cricket downstairs. But it's decaf."

Lucas frowned. "Decaf? Why?"

"I saw you take Effexor. Both caffeine and Effexor can increase your blood pressure, and you're already under a great deal of stress."

August hoped Lucas would see this as what it was: his attempt to take care of him.

"How do you know what meds I take?" Lucas asked, taking a tentative sip of his coffee.

"Oh. I broke into your apartment this morning and looked around."

Lucas gave a heavy sigh, opening the pastry bag and pulling out the muffin. "Of course, you did. I should just give you a key."

"That would make it much less time consuming," August agreed. "Can I take you to lunch later?"

Lucas laughed, shaking his head. "No."

"Can I bring lunch to you later?" August tried again.

Lucas rolled his eyes but smiled like he couldn't help himself. "Maybe."

August grinned. "I'll see you at one."

"I didn't say yes," Lucas called after him.

"But you also didn't say no," August pointed out, turning and leaving before Lucas rectified that.

He had three classes before their 'maybe' date. He didn't know if he could wait that long to see Lucas again, but he'd try. In the meantime, he needed to have Calliope deep dive into Laurence Kohn. Had he hurt Lucas? August would happily rip this Kohn guy's tongue out if it made Lucas happy.

Was murder an act of service?

SIX

LUCAS

August was gone before Lucas really had a chance to look at the to go cup and realize there was writing on it.

I HOPE YOUR DAY IS AS NICE AS YOUR ASS.

Lucas found himself smiling, ignoring the voice in his head screaming he clearly had a death wish. Maybe he did. It was no secret that August was dangerous. A killer. A man who had tortured countless men. He could decorate a stadium with all the red flags August had waved.

He'd broken into Lucas's apartment—twice—watched him sleep, gone through his things, looked at his endless medication regimen. Lucas should have felt violated, indignant, angry. Instead, he was relieved. He wouldn't have to explain himself to August. He already knew Lucas's deep, dark secret and hadn't run screaming in the other direction.

Because he's a murderer.

Nobody's perfect, right?

Lucas snickered at his own nihilistic thoughts. He had spent most of his life believing there were only two sides. Good and evil. Black and white. And all that thinking had done was leave him with a false sense of security and a piece of glass buried in his shoulder.

Now, he wasn't sure what he believed. Kohn was out there. Kidnapping. Raping. Torturing women society had forgotten. When Lucas had done the right thing, gone through the proper channels, he'd almost been killed for his trouble. Women had lost their lives.

So, what was Lucas supposed to do now? When a person had exhausted every conceivable legal way to keep society safe, what was left except people like August? Wasn't it better to kill one man to save a hundred more potential victims?

Maybe he was just rationalizing. Maybe he'd fallen so far into rock bottom he was willing to dismiss the crimes of a vicious psychopath just to feel normal in his own skin. He missed the person he used to be. Confident. Funny. Cocky even. A year ago, Lucas had thought he had the world figured out until one touch had confirmed he was a fool. Now, he had no idea what to think.

August was a depraved killer, who seemed to enjoy torturing people. But he also had a strict moral code. And yeah, he was weirdly honest and inadvertently funny and sexy as hell, especially when he had looked at Lucas with that raw intensity, like nobody else in the world existed but him.

But no matter how he looked at it, August was the villain, Batman or no. Still, the devil he knew had to be better than the devil he didn't. Especially if that devil was on Lucas's

side. As much as Lucas hated to admit it, he'd already made up his mind about August. He'd let August do whatever he wanted, even to his own detriment.

There was no longer any part of Lucas that felt safe in this world. Kohn would come for him eventually. He'd made no secret of all the horrors he planned to inflict on Lucas for attempting to ruin his plans. He might as well enjoy his time on the planet while he could.

What did August think of Lucas? He'd gotten on his knees and told Lucas he'd wanted him, had pushed a knife into his chest just to be near him. Did he want to know the truth? He looked down at the cup August had brought him. One he'd held in his hand. One Lucas could probably get a read off if he dropped his shields.

Lucas looked out over the sea of faces. They all whispered about him, some more obviously than others, but none of them would dare say anything to his face, not when he controlled their grade in a much-needed class. Still, he'd be crazy to drop his guard there in the classroom just to get a peek into August's head.

Fuck it. If August could go through Lucas's medicine cabinet, he could go through August's head. He gripped the cup in both hands, letting his eyes fall shut. He saw Cricket—the perky blonde cashier—heard her ask if Lucas was his boyfriend, and tried to ignore the warmth that bloomed in his chest. Heard August say his idea of a compliment was saying he liked the way Lucas's atoms were put together. He would have found that far more charming than what had ended up on the cup. Even though Cricket

was right. Lucas did have a nice ass. It was after the goodbyes that things took a turn for the…steamy.

The images were far less detailed, flashes really, but still enough to send fire shooting through his blood. Lucas holding August's wrists above his head. August kneeling, hands bound, head bowed, with Lucas looming over him. August on all fours with Lucas behind him. Lucas on his back with August riding him. He sucked in a gasp as he forced his eyes open.

There were a couple of startled giggles from the front row, but most people just looked at him like they were afraid he was moments away from snapping, when, in truth, he was rock hard behind his desk. Lucas could not teach a group of budding criminologists with an obvious erection. He'd be tossed out on day one.

And yet, he couldn't stop thinking about August wanting to submit…to Lucas. Fuck. He needed to maintain some objectivity, but having complete control over August— using him however he liked, knowing August craved that dominance—made him hot and shivery.

Lucas viewed sex with a certain amount of trepidation. It usually required laser focus for him because, if he slipped up, he might make the experience far more intimate than his partner wanted. Nothing ruined sex like accidentally letting his guard down and realizing the person he was with was thinking of somebody else, or had abhorrent sexual fantasies, or was actually a monstrous predator.

Lucas was hardly a blushing virgin but, with his clairvoyance, his sexual encounters often ended with hurt

feelings or as a one night stand. He could count on one hand the amount of times he'd been intimate with another human being and it hadn't ended poorly. Or awkwardly. And, in one case, catastrophically.

But what was there he could learn about August that he didn't already know? While he had no interest in seeing what he'd seen the first time he'd touched August, last night, August's touch had brought nothing but an unexpected pleasure that had shot heat through his core. The truth was, August and Lucas already knew the worst things about each other, and knowing that was almost hotter than the thought of August on his knees for him. Almost.

Fuck, he'd looked so hot on his knees for Lucas. Maybe Lucas had already crossed the line into insanity because the thought of controlling and dominating August—an unconscionable killer, a psychopath who lacked an ability to feel remorse—had him rock hard. He wanted that. Wanted August. On his knees. On all fours. Hell, anyway he could get him.

Shit.

He needed to stop this line of thought immediately. He had a job to do. He finished his muffin in two bites, put his shields back up, and downed his coffee in one go, clicking the remote to the overhead projector. "Okay, let's get started. Who read the chapter on aggression and violent behavior?"

Once morning classes ended, Lucas went back to his office, unsure whether August would make good on his lunch offer but knowing he had other things he needed to focus on. Like Kohn. He sat at his desk and pulled up the missing persons database, scrolling through an endless sea of faces. It was like looking for a needle in a stack of needles, searching for one face in a sea of thousands, and there was a good chance the needle wasn't there at all.

Lucas wasn't sure how long he sat there before knuckles rapped against his door, which swung open before he could issue an invitation. August. Lucas's heart began to thud hard behind his ribs at the sight of him. Had any man ever made Lucas's pulse flutter before?

He held up two bags. The smell of the food hit Lucas hard, making his stomach growl.

"I hope you like Chinese," August said in lieu of a greeting.

"I do," Lucas confirmed. "You know, most people wait for a person to invite them in before they just barge in."

August gave him a sheepish look. "I didn't want to give you the chance to think about it for too long."

August's honesty was annoyingly endearing. He gestured towards the worn leather sofa against the wall, and Lucas nodded in agreement. Once they were seated on opposite sides of the small couch, August set the bags between them and handed Lucas chopsticks. "There's also a fork in the bag just in case you don't know how to use them."

It was said almost like a challenge, a wide grin spreading across his face before faltering and dying completely. Lucas split the cheap wooden utensils, rubbing them together as he contemplated August's sudden lack of expression.

"Are you okay?" Lucas asked.

August's eyes darted to his. "Yes. Why?"

Lucas grabbed the container of beef and broccoli. "Because you went from grinning like the Joker to looking like I kicked your puppy in the span of about fifteen seconds. It was a little disconcerting."

August shrugged, gaze shifting to somewhere over Lucas's shoulder. "My brother's boyfriend said my smile freaks people out. I don't want to freak you out."

August's admission made Lucas's heartbeat fall off rhythm. "I like your smile."

"You don't think I smile at the wrong things?"

"No. I one hundred percent think you smile at the wrong things. But I find it strangely charming."

"Oh," August said, as if he was chewing over that answer.

After that, they ate in relative silence, swapping containers and making occasional small talk. When they were finished, August asked, "Did you get my message?" Lucas frowned. Message? He reached for his phone. August reached out and touched his hand. "No, not that one. The one on your cup."

Lucas snickered, doing his best to ignore the heat of August's fingers still gripping his fingers. "About my ass? Yes. I also know it was Cricket who liked my ass, not you."

August shook his head, voice earnest. "Cricket isn't the only one who likes your ass. I like it very much. I like it so much I'd like to take it out to dinner, but you keep saying

no. But that's not what I meant. I… Did you pick up any thoughts when you touched the cup?"

Understanding dawned. "Are you saying you deliberately left impressions on my cup hoping I'd snoop around in your head?"

August grinned. "Yes. It seemed a shame to waste an opportunity. It was just an experiment. I figured if you can pick up thoughts and feelings from objects, then, it stands to reason, I can leave those impressions there for you to find."

Lucas could feel color creeping up his neck to his face. "You left those thoughts…deliberately?"

August nodded. "I wanted you to see I was trying."

"Trying?" Lucas echoed.

"Yeah, to romance you."

Lucas's eyes widened. The things he saw…had nothing to do with romantic gestures. Well, maybe in the loosest sense of the words. Supplication could be seen as romantic, but Lucas didn't think that was what he meant. He leaned in close. "What exactly is it you tried to show me?"

"The coffee shop conversation."

Lucas studied August's face. "What about after the coffee shop conversation?"

"After?" August enquired.

"Yeah, what I saw had nothing to do with coffee."

August tilted his head, his tongue darting out to wet his lip. "What did you see?"

Lucas almost lied but then decided he didn't want any lies between them. "You. On your knees. For me."

August swallowed hard. "Like last night?"

Lucas shook his head. "Definitely not."

"Oh." August didn't sound embarrassed when he asked, "Did you like it? Me on my knees…for you?"

"Yes," Lucas said, his cock once more hardening behind his zipper. "Too much."

August moved closer until their knees slotted together. "Can I kiss you?" he whispered.

Lucas shook his head, though he didn't know why.

"Why not?"

"Because this is a bad idea. I just got out of a mental health facility. I'm being stalked by a maniac. I've lost everything. I can't think of a worse time to try to have a relationship."

"Oh," August said, seemingly running that through his big brain. "Then will you kiss me?" he asked, his voice low.

"You're not going away, are you?" Lucas pressed.

August met his gaze. "I can't."

"Why?"

"Because some part of me chose you and now, I can't let you go. Don't ask me to explain the way my brain works."

Lucas should have been horrified. A psychopath had just told him he'd claimed him as his own. Instead, Lucas reached up and cupped August's face. "This doesn't mean we're in a relationship," he said.

"What doesn't—"

Lucas crashed their mouths together, lightning exploding in his veins as August yielded instantly, melting against him. His submission made Lucas bolder, his tongue darting inside to explore. August's hands flailed, then caught in Lucas's shirt. He did catch flashes of August's thoughts, but

there was nothing distasteful about them. Just more of what he'd seen earlier. Flashes of naked flesh and panting breaths and August saying his name like a plea.

"Fuck."

He ripped his mouth from August's and gripped his knees, yanking hard enough to get him beneath him, blanketing his weight on top before delving back in to kiss him once more. August spread his legs, letting Lucas settle between his thighs, both groaning when their bodies collided, both of them hard.

This wasn't at all what Lucas had intended. Hell, he hadn't intended anything but he couldn't stop, didn't want to stop. He'd thought August might be a fling. A dangerous impulse thing he could look back on and marvel at, but he'd never imagined somebody like August would want anything long term. Lucas wasn't even sure he'd be alive in six months.

Still, he didn't stop. He couldn't. He liked August beneath him, the way he was rolling his hips against Lucas's, the tiny hitched breaths he expelled every time Lucas did something he liked.

Lucas had never just made out with somebody before. Not ever. Not even in high school. And he was suddenly realizing what he'd been missing. He tore his lips away to explore August's jaw, his earlobe, the corded tendon of his neck.

"We should stop," he said, even as his hands untucked August's shirt, pushing it up so he could thread his fingers through the springy curls that covered his chest and belly.

"Okay," August panted, catching Lucas's mouth in another dirty kiss.

Lucas ground himself against August's rocking hips, almost positive he could come just from the heat and friction and the feel of August's lips beneath his. But they couldn't. This was Lucas's first day of work. August was a stranger…and a co-worker…and a psychopath, who wanted to mate with Lucas for life.

Lucas launched himself off August, forcing himself all the way back against the far end of the couch. "Seriously. We're at school. We both have classes starting in fifteen minutes."

August crawled closer, his hand going for Lucas's zipper. "I can get you off in less than fifteen minutes."

The confidence in August's words threw Lucas's train of thought far off its track. "What?"

August's eyes raked over him, gaze hot enough to melt steel. "I can make you come in fifteen minutes or less."

Lucas's cock throbbed at his offer. He glanced at the door, then at August. He wanted to let him. Nobody would ever know. But he shook his head. "Not here. My place. Later. After work. Where we have some privacy. I have another class and then I'm working on a…research project."

It wasn't a lie.

"Kohn?"

Lucas's erection instantly flagged at the name. "How do you know that?"

August shrugged. "I told you, I went through your apartment. Who is he? Other than a special agent that is?"

Lucas sighed. "He's a field agent with the FBI. Big shot, started at Quantico the same time I did."

"And you think he killed all those women in your file?"

Lucas shook his head. "Not all of them, no. But some of them. Not that anybody will believe me."

"I believe you."

Lucas gave him a smile. "Thanks, but that won't help me put him in prison."

August ran a hand through his dark hair. "Maybe prison isn't what he needs."

Lucas's eyebrows ran for his hairline. "You mean kill him?"

August nodded. "Sure. If he murdered those women, he meets the code."

Lucas's mind reeled. Life would be so much easier if he could just let August do what he did. "That's the thing. I don't think he did it alone. I think he has a partner. And I think they keep these women for a long time and then, when they're done, they get rid of them somehow. I just don't know how or where or even who. I just know they're out there hurting people and I can't do a thing about it."

"Let me help. I have resources."

"You have better resources than the FBI?" Lucas said, incredulous.

"Yes, I have a Calliope."

"A what?"

"Not a what. A who. Calliope. Let me help you."

Lucas thought about it. August wasn't going anywhere. Lucas could pretend the thought bothered him, that it scared him or worried him. That was what he should feel when in a situation like that. But he wanted him there, wanted his touch and his obsession. And his help. Lucas wanted his help.

"Okay, but not here. My place. Tonight. Dinner."

August blinked in surprise. "Like a date?"

His voice was so adorably hopeful there was no way Lucas was going to say no, even if he was being manipulated. "Yes. Like a date."

SEVEN
AUGUST

August taught his remaining classes on auto-pilot. Luckily, he was only teaching level one physics classes that afternoon. He could talk about time evolution and the Schrödinger equation in his sleep. But he wasn't sleeping. He spent the whole lecture remembering the feel of Lucas's tongue sliding into his mouth, the hard length of him pressed against August's hip, how Lucas had to physically tear himself away from August.

He ended his last class early by twenty minutes, shoving his earbuds in his ears before heading out into the drizzling rain. He pulled the collar of his jacket up but didn't bother with his umbrella as he cut through the quad on his way to the parking lot, thoughts still firmly on Lucas.

August had never had anybody truly lust after him before. Sex was purely transactional. He'd needed it that way. If there was an exchange of goods and services, August didn't have to worry about being creepy or weird. He was paying them to overlook all of his off-putting idiosyncrasies, of

which he had many.

He didn't have that luxury with Lucas. He had to somehow want August as he was. Their kiss had seemed to suggest he was open to at least a physical relationship with him, if not an emotional one. August lacked the necessary requirements for a love match, but he needed Lucas to understand that his brain had already decided their fate. There was no way to say that without sounding like a psycho.

Except, he was a psycho.

He was a psycho and Lucas was crazy. Maybe that made them perfect for each other? Still, he didn't want to fuck this up before it even got started. And if anybody was going to fuck it up before it started, it would be August.

He was almost to the parking lot when a hand tapped him on the arm. Bianca.

He pulled his headphones from his ears. "What's up?"

She pushed a lock of dark hair behind her ear, her tone conspiratorial. "Did I see you leaving Special Agent Crazy-Pants' office at lunch looking a little mussed?"

August raised a brow, a strange rush of adrenaline filling him at Bianca's casual insult of Lucas. "I don't know. Did you?"

"I'm serious," Bianca said, smiling and nudging him.

August didn't smile back but did his best to not let the real him bleed through. "So am I."

Bianca rolled her eyes and laughed. "Seriously? Spill. What's he like? Is he really as out there as people say? Are you trying to hook up with him? Is that your type? Hot and crazy?"

Yes.

"Hook up?" August said, closing his now shaking hands into fists. She remained oblivious to the heat rising under his skin.

"Yes, you automaton," she teased. "Are you trying to hook up with him?"

"Why do you care, exactly?" August asked, making no attempt to hide his growing annoyance, even though his father would have cautioned him against it.

Bianca shrugged. "We kind of just assumed you were asexual, but you and Captain Crazy actually makes sense."

"*Don't.* Call. Him. That."

Bianca's eyes went wide at the icy warning in his tone. "I-I didn't realize you were so…close. I apologize."

August needed to pull himself together. If his father thought he couldn't handle being in a relationship with Lucas, he wouldn't let him keep him. He took a deep breath, forcing his face into a serene expression. "No. I'm sorry. I didn't get much sleep last night. I was looking over a student's dissertation and, clearly, I didn't realize how tired I was until now. I'll see you around, okay?"

He didn't wait for Bianca to say goodbye, just turned and walked the few steps to his Mercedes G-class, clicking the alarm off and throwing open the door. Only once he was locked inside the cab alone did he finally let himself go, gripping the steering wheel and shaking it hard, a raw scream falling from his lips.

The fucking audacity. She had no right to talk about Lucas that way. He wasn't crazy. He was perfect. He was sweet and sexy and strong. They were the ones who were gossips, constantly looking down their noses at others, feeling they were entitled to make snide comments because of some sense of superiority.

He threw the SUV into reverse and stomped on the gas, tires screeching as he jerked the wheel. As he turned onto the street, he engaged the Bluetooth button. "Call Adam."

"Calling Adam," an electronic voice repeated.

Adam didn't answer the first time. Or the second. The third time was the charm.

"Somebody better be fucking dead," Adam growled into the phone, breathing heavily.

"Somebody almost was."

That seemed to bring Adam up short. "What happened?"

"Somebody said something mean about Lucas and I just… I wanted to break her in half." He couldn't stop his voice from shaking.

Adam's voice took on a certain hesitancy when he said, "What did she say about him?"

"She called him Special Agent Crazy-Pants and Captain Crazy."

"Those aren't even good insults," Adam said.

"I wanted to punch her in the face. I've never felt angry like this before."

"I get it, but you gotta rein it in, bro, or Dad will try to take him away from you. So, pull it together, okay? Good talk."

"Wait! I need Noah," August said.

Adam sighed heavily. "He's a little…tied up right now."

August let out a breath through his nose, his rage still sending shivers along his skin. "It will only take a minute. This can't wait."

Adam groaned. "Do you have any idea how long it takes to tie these restraints? He'll call you later."

August frowned. "Oh. You meant literally tied up?"

There was a long-suffering sigh. "Yes. Literally. I have him literally tied to our bed right now. Call back later."

Noah's muffled voice came from somewhere nearby. "Oh, my God, Adam. You cannot just tell people you have me tied to the bed."

"Why not? You are. Besides, it's not people. It's August." To August, he said, "He'll call you later."

August's mouth flattened into a hard line. "But I need him now. I have a date."

"A date?" Adam said, perking up.

"Put him on speakerphone," Noah demanded.

"You can't be serious?" Adam asked, clearly not talking to August. Noah gave a muffled response before Adam said, "Ugh, fine. Five minutes. That's all you get. You hear me? Five."

"Deal," August agreed.

He didn't need long, anyway. He just needed to know what he was supposed to do on a date. They'd had lunch together, and that had led to kissing and petting and rubbing off on each other in a way August found…most agreeable. But was that a date? Like, didn't dates involve fancy restaurants or movies or walking on the beach? August didn't know what the hell he was doing.

"Wh—" Noah's breath hitched. "What's up, dude?"

His voice was strained, but August knew firsthand that being tied up could be stressful. "I'm supposed to go on a date with Lucas. Like tonight."

"That's good," Noah assured him, voice filled with false cheer.

"I've never been on a date before," August said, his voice now as tense as Noah's.

Once more, there was a sudden sharp intake of breath. "Okay. Well, where are you going?"

"His place."

"Oh, yeah. Fuck, keep doing that," Noah whispered.

August frowned. "Doing what? I'm not doing anything."

"Not you," Noah said.

August rolled his eyes. "We're supposed to have dinner and talk about his killer ex-coworker."

He heard Adam snicker but paid no attention.

"Most people just make small talk on a first date, but, honestly, this seems right on brand for you," Noah mused.

"Are you sure it's a date?" Adam asked, sounding doubtful.

August frowned. "It is. I asked. He said yes."

Noah still sounded unsure. "Okay, well…good."

"Help me," August begged. "What does somebody do or say or wear on a first date?"

There was a long silence punctuated with breathy sighs and muffled whispers, then Noah was back. "Um, full disclosure. I've never been on a date. Adam just sort of showed up at my trailer and never left."

"God, that would make this so much easier," August

admitted, wishing he could just brand Lucas as his and let the world know he was protected.

Adam's voice popped up. "Don't get too dressed up. You'll look like a dweeb. Jeans, a nice shirt."

"Bring flowers. Oh, or wine," Noah added.

"*Do not* talk about how much you like eviscerating people to pop music…or your weird obsession with Celine Dion. Or your knife collection. Or the swords. Or the array of medieval torture devices you have. Honestly, just steer clear of weaponry altogether."

August nodded along as if they could see him. "Wine. Flowers. No evisceration. No Britney or Gaga. I think I can do that."

Adam was suddenly right up on the phone. "Your five minutes are up."

"Good luck," Noah called, then moaned long and low.

August stabbed at the disconnect button. Noah and his brother fucking was not a soundtrack he wanted on a loop in his head for all eternity. He turned on the stereo and let Bach sooth his ragged edges, a wave of…something washing over him. Not panic or anxiety—August didn't experience those things. But he did respond to rewards, and when Lucas kissed him and touched him, that had felt like the best possible reward. And he wanted more.

August arrived at Lucas's apartment at exactly seven, a bag in one hand and a bouquet of flowers in the other. He'd forgone

the wine due to Lucas's extensive med list, but the woman at the gourmet shop had assured him his replacement gift would be more than acceptable for a dinner.

After the shop, he'd stopped at the florist to pick up flowers, but that hadn't exactly gone to plan either. When he'd explained they were for a date, she'd immediately taken to making a bouquet based on looks. Pink roses, red carnations, eucalyptus leaves, and daylilies. August had turned away. She'd clearly never learned there was a language to flowers and she was getting the message all wrong.

August had read a book on it once in first grade. Each flower meant something specific. He didn't know if Lucas knew that, but he didn't want him to get the wrong idea or think he hadn't made an effort. But it was too late now. He was there with his expensive cheese and more expensive— yet grossly misleading—flowers.

He knocked, looking down at his jeans and zip front sweater. Was he casual enough? Too casual? He hated feeling like he was out of his element. He needed Lucas to like him. For both of their sakes.

When the door opened, August was not prepared for a wet haired, barefoot Lucas. He wore black jeans slung low on his hips and a hastily buttoned chambray shirt.

"I half expected you to just let yourself in," he said, a rueful smile on his face. He was truly beautiful.

August held up his offerings. "My hands were full."

Lucas grinned, like August had made a joke. "Of course. Makes perfect sense."

"Here," August thrust the gifts at him.

Lucas took the flowers and the bag, bringing the bouquet to his nose, sniffing them deeply. "Pretty."

August preened. "They are. Even if the message is filled with contradictions."

"Did you leave another message on my gifts?" Lucas asked, tilting his head.

"Not intentionally."

Lucas looked at the bag, peeking inside. "Is this…cheese?"

"Yeah, the woman at the shop said it was just as good as wine. I didn't think you drank given your medications."

Lucas studied him for a long moment. "Thank you. That's…weirdly thoughtful of you."

"I feel like you're making fun of me," August said. "But I'm not sure."

Lucas leaned forward and smacked a quick kiss on August's lips. "Just a little."

August found that he didn't mind Lucas teasing him if it made him smile. He liked his smile. His whole face transformed. He didn't look like a man whose life had been shredded. Lucas had a nice mouth, perfect teeth, and soft lips. August liked being the reason Lucas smiled, even if it was at his expense.

When he took August's offerings and walked into his small, tidy kitchen, August followed. When he realized August was behind him, he threw a puzzled look over his shoulder. August couldn't help but move closer, trapping Lucas against the counter, nuzzling his face into his neck.

"Hi," Lucas said, sounding both amused and slightly breathless.

August continued to cling to him. "Hi."

"Whatcha doin'?" Lucas asked.

"I just needed to touch you." It abruptly occurred to August that maybe Lucas didn't like being touched without warning. "Is…this okay?"

Lucas leaned back against him slightly. "Yeah, it's nice. But I thought you were into…submission. I didn't think you'd make the first move. Unless breaking into my apartment was the first move?"

August understood the confusion. He let his lips trail along the sensitive skin at the back of Lucas's neck, liking the shiver that ran along his skin. "There's power in submitting. But that's not why I do it."

"Why do you do it?" He sounded genuinely curious.

August pressed his forehead to Lucas's shoulder. "There's no way to explain it without sounding like a monster."

"I already know you're a monster," Lucas reasoned. "What do you have to lose?"

You. "Submission keeps whoever I'm with…safe. Because I don't trust myself."

"You don't trust yourself how?"

August took a deep breath, certain he was about to end this relationship before it started, but like Lucas said, he already knew August was a monster. He blew out a breath and just told him the truth. "I love hurting people. I know it's not the right thing to say. My father has told me a thousand times. But I'm good at it. I like making bad men suffer. I don't like their screaming or crying—it gives me a migraine—but I like knowing they died in pain. Because of me."

Lucas's back was rising and falling rapidly now. "What does that have to do with sex?"

"If I let myself go there, if I truly decided to let myself go, I think I would hurt somebody…somebody like you, and I'd like it so much I couldn't stop. When I'm there… in that headspace, it consumes me. If I was to hear you cry out, whimper, moan, I might lose myself, take it too far. It's better if I'm…contained."

Lucas turned in August's arms. "Do you truly think you could hurt me? Do you really think your bloodlust is so strong that you'd lose yourself with me?"

August searched Lucas's face for any hint of disgust, surprised when he didn't find it. "Bloodlust? No. Losing myself with you? I already have."

Lucas cupped August's face like he'd done the night before. "I think you underestimate yourself."

August shook his head. "But, if you're wrong, the cost could be your life. I can't feel guilt or remorse, but the thought of not seeing your face or touching you, kissing you, makes me feel…like there's a hole in my chest. Does that make sense?"

"Yes. But then why would you think that you'd ever snap like that with me? Is it because you think I'm weak? Fragile? Timid? Is my victimhood an attractor for you?" There was a sort of contempt there under his words, not for August but himself.

He leaned forward and brushed their lips together in a kiss that lingered. "The rabbit in you attracts the wolf in me. I can't help that. It's instinctive. Sometimes, you smell…

vulnerable. Nobody ever lets themselves be vulnerable around me. Some part of their id recognizes the predator in me. People keep their guard up around me instinctively. But not you. When I look at you, I don't *want* to hurt you. I want to protect you, keep you safe."

Lucas wrapped his arms around August's neck, kissing him like he couldn't stop himself. "You answered your own question. You want to protect me, not hurt me. But, the truth is, I can protect myself. I know everything you've seen of me undermines that statement, but it's true. I had to go through training just like any other agent. I'm just…going through a rough patch."

August crushed Lucas against him, holding him tight, tighter than he'd ever held anybody. "I know you can protect yourself. But I don't want you to. I want to be that person. Your person. My brother and his boyfriend… neither of them are weak. Adam is every bit the psychopath I am, and Noah is…not, but he's no saint either. They work because they trust each other, they have each other's backs, flaws and all. Nobody has ever accepted all my deficiencies, and there are many."

"Is this your usual first date talk?" Lucas finally said.

"I've never been on a date before," August confessed.

Lucas smiled. "I sort of figured. I've never had a guy give me cheese as a gift before."

August shrugged. "I probably should have told the lady this was a date and not just dinner. It seemed like a good idea at the time."

"Maybe you should just trust your own instincts with

something other than murder?"

August scoffed. "That's a terrible idea. I probably would have brought you a ceremonial knife from Peru or something."

"You have a ceremonial knife from Peru?" Lucas asked, perking up.

August shook his head. "My brother said I shouldn't talk to you about that. Or any of my other weapons. Or my kill playlist. Or my love of pop divas."

The smile fell from Lucas's face and he was suddenly kissing him, turning him so the sharp edge of the counter dug into his hips. "You are one of a kind, August Mulvaney," he said against his lips.

"So I've heard," August said, darting his tongue into Lucas's mouth. He tasted like toothpaste.

"I'm still not sure I'm on board with happily ever after and all that."

"I can live with that. At least through dinner."

EIGHT
LUCAS

As they ate, they talked. Well, August talked. He talked about string theory and the relative state formulation, about whether he truly believed there were parallel worlds, and how some of his co-workers thought his theories were too out there. Lucas could have interrupted, could have changed the subject, but he found himself fascinated and more than a little turned on by how passionately August spoke about a subject he clearly loved.

August's hands gesticulated wildly, his forest green eyes bright and cheeks flushed as he somehow made huge abstract concepts palatable and easy for a lay person like Lucas to understand. When August was in his comfort zone—teaching—all his awkwardness seemed to melt away. Lucas didn't really care for any science, except the social ones, but August explained his ideas in a way that made the universe seem magical and full of possibilities.

How did a vicious killer, a man who admittedly enjoyed hurting people, have such childlike wonder when it came

to all the world's possibilities? Lucas envied him. He envied a serial killer. If anything should have signaled he'd hit rock bottom, that was it, but he just didn't care. August was a huge radiant beacon and Lucas was a moth, desperate to get closer, using that light to blind him to the shitshow his life had become.

"Your students must love you," Lucas finally said.

August paused, his gaze darting to his right, like he was thinking about it. "I think they do, yes. I get many requests for my classes and excellent evaluations."

Lucas smiled. August lacked the ability to fake any sort of humbleness or humility. He was confident in his brilliance. "I can see why."

August tilted his head in that way he did whenever Lucas said something any other person in the world would have seen as flirty. "Why's that?"

Lucas looked August up and down. "Because you're sexy when you talk physics," Lucas said. "Which is a phrase I never thought I'd ever utter out loud."

The change in August was...palpable. His affable good-nature morphed into a feral intensity that had Lucas's cock hardening. Yeah, August's particular brand of crazy was definitely Lucas's kink.

August studied him, gaze hot enough to melt steel. But almost as quickly, it disappeared, replaced once more by polite August who cleared his throat, gaze falling to his half-eaten chicken.

"Except, I'm being rude, dominating the conversation," August said, not like he meant it but like he was trained to say it, trained to know the niceties needed to pass as human in the outside world. "I want to know about you."

That Lucas believed. August looked at him like there was still something salvageable in there, and it made him jittery, like he'd had too much caffeine, even though he hadn't had any because August had thought of his medications. How could a psychopath be the most attentive person Lucas had ever met?

"You do?" Lucas asked.

August frowned. "Of course. If I'm going to marry you someday, I should probably know what I'm getting into."

His words sent a shock wave of awareness rolling across Lucas's nerve endings. There wasn't even a trace of humor. August Mulvaney—a killer he'd known less than three days —was sitting at his table casually talking about how he had settled on Lucas someday becoming his husband.

It was a testament to the weirdness of Lucas's life that it just seemed like one more surreal thing in a long, long list of bizarre events. Where was his fear? His sense of self-preservation? This man had just said he was going to marry him like it was a foregone conclusion and it didn't scare him. It just made him…horny. And made him feel safe. And Lucas never felt safe. Or even wanted. Something he would never say out loud to anybody.

Fuck. They should have never let him out of that facility. He'd clearly cracked. "What do you want to know?"

August leaned in, his sudden wide grin fading to an amiable smile, like he wasn't sure which was the appropriate option. "Why did you become a profiler?"

Lucas wanted to tell August he didn't have to fake it with him, that he didn't care if he smiled or not. That he wanted him to be comfortable around him.

Instead, he took a sip of his water before saying, "I have this talent, right? I can touch things and get impressions, visions, know things I shouldn't."

"Psychometry."

Lucas blinked at him, surprised. "Yeah, people always want to say I'm clairvoyant, but that's somebody who gets visions unprompted. I have to touch the person or object."

August studied him. "No wonder you don't like to be touched."

Had he told August that? He was starting to think he was the psychic. "Yeah, it sucks to know that even your own family thinks you're a freak."

"I can relate to that," August said. "Imagine being the weirdest psychopath in a house full of psychopaths."

Lucas laughed softly.

August examined his face. "Surely, somebody in your family cared for you? Took care of you? You had nobody to talk to?"

Lucas's heart squeezed. "I could've talked to my mom. She was like me. But nobody believed her. Hell, I didn't fucking believe her, not until it started happening to me. But by then, she was gone. She'd left me with my grandfather and took off."

"Your grandfather didn't believe in your gifts?"

Lucas snorted. "My grandfather was a movie villain. The haggard farmer with a chip on his shoulder, who believed in

men being men and that all questions could be answered by reading the scriptures. I didn't tell him I could see things. He already thought I was weak. Too quiet, too skinny, too into books. He'd wanted some corn-fed, stocky football-loving grandson, not some sniveling kid who cried too much and was afraid of the dark."

August stood abruptly, startling Lucas. He walked around the table to sit beside him stiffly before threading their fingers together. This time, it was Lucas who tilted his head, giving August a curious look. "What are you doing?"

August shrugged. "Your face has that pinched look around the eyes, like you did the night I broke in."

"You mean last night?" Lucas said, amused.

August frowned. "Was it just last night? Seems like a million years ago. But I don't like you sad."

Who was this man? "I'm not sad, not anymore. It was a long time ago."

August stared at him. "Your eyes say you're lying. You seem sad in your soul."

It was such a spot-on assessment, it took Lucas's breath away. He was sad. Deep down, in a place he never talked about, Lucas never stopped being sad. If he did have a soul, his was bruised and battered, aching for some kind of release.

"A physicist who believes in things like souls and clairvoyance? They're going to run you out of the university," Lucas teased, trying to ease the sudden lump in his throat.

August's intense gaze didn't waver. "I believe in you."

"You can't say things like that," Lucas whispered, swaying forward to brush their lips together.

"Why not?" August answered, pupils dilating.

Lucas snagged the back of August's head and dragged him forward to slant their mouths together, letting his tongue explore before saying, "Because it makes me want to do dirty things to you."

August's hand threaded through Lucas's hair, his kiss consuming. He let August control the kiss, trying to show him he trusted him, even if August didn't trust himself. When August pulled him closer, he slipped from his chair to straddle his lap, moaning when he realized he was already hard. Lucas's hand slipped between them, letting himself palm over the hard line of August's cock.

Lucas had never wanted anybody as bad as he wanted him. It made him bold. He opened August's pants, plunging his hand inside, wrapping his fingers around his erection, thumbing over his uncut cock. "Fuck," he whispered. "Is this okay?"

August trembled, eyes wide as he watched Lucas's hand jerking him. "You should tie me up first."

Lucas continued to slowly stroke him, his lips hovering close enough to feel August's panting breaths. "No. You're not an animal. I'll be happy to play those games with you, but not because you think you're going to lose it and hurt me in some crazed psychotic break."

"You have a death wish," August whispered.

A slow smile crawled across Lucas's face. "Yeah, that's kind of why they locked me up."

August growled, capturing Lucas's mouth in a kiss that curled his toes, a startled cry falling from his lips as August

stood, his hands falling to Lucas's ass, leaving him no choice but to wrap his legs around August's hips. When they reached Lucas's bedroom, August dropped him on the mattress, pulling his sweater up over his head as he gazed down at Lucas like he was going to eat him alive. It sent a little shiver along his skin.

He couldn't hide his surprise at the ink tattooed on August's skin. He hadn't seen that one coming. A snake trailed up his left bicep, the scales of justice were on his side, a skull and crossbones sat on his chest, and he had a pair of dice on his shoulder. Did they all mean something to him? Fuck, he was hot. Especially shirtless, in his unbuttoned jeans, black boxer briefs peeking through the vee of his open zipper.

"Come here," Lucas begged.

August ignored him, instead grabbing Lucas's ankles and tugging him closer so he could get his pants off. Lucas lifted his hips to help. He had no idea what he was doing but he didn't even fucking care. God help him, he would let August do anything he wanted.

When both their pants were off, August fell on top of him, his nose nuzzling the space behind his ear, inhaling deeply. Lucas had never had anybody try to inhale him like he was a drug. But August wasn't done. He dragged his cheek along Lucas's chest, letting his lips brush over one nipple before his tongue teased the taut peak, sucking until Lucas's hands gripped his comforter. "Fuck."

August gave his other nipple the same attention before placing biting kisses over his ribs, his belly, dragging his teeth along his hip bones before nosing along the side of

his cock, which was currently tenting his briefs. The sounds August was making were almost…animalistic. Throaty, grunting noises that went straight to Lucas's dick. It was like August was trying to consume him. It was overwhelming but also so fucking hot. "August…"

Fingers hooked into the waistband of his underwear, tugging them out of the way, and then Lucas's aching cock was enveloped in the tight heat of August's mouth. "Oh, fuck," he groaned, hips bucking against his will.

August's arms snaked under Lucas's thighs, curling over to grip his hips— holding him in place—like he couldn't be trusted to hold still. It was a good call. August's mouth was perfection, and each sucking draw of his lips from base to crown had him gasping, his hands threading through August's dark hair. "Please…"

Lucas didn't even know what he was asking for other than to experience the orgasm welling within him. It was like August had been edging him since they met two days ago and Lucas was finally so close to getting what he craved.

August pulled off, chuckling at Lucas's noise of frustration, before catching his legs beneath the knees, spreading him wide to spear his tongue against his hole. His eyes rolled as August did his best to literally consume Lucas. "Oh, fuck. That feels good."

He didn't mean to let his shields slip, but he couldn't help it, he couldn't concentrate. But instead of the usual barrage of unwanted images, the thoughts and sensations overwhelmed him in the best possible way.

August was imagining burying himself in Lucas but also

pondering Lucas doing the same to him. His thoughts were vivid, possessive, almost as addictive as the feel of the soft slide of his tongue over his entrance.

August was thinking things that had Lucas moaning, his hand floating toward his cock, desperate. His hand was almost where he needed it when August's hand darted out, snaking around Lucas's wrist, keeping him from touching himself.

"August…"

He stopped, his gaze pinning Lucas in place. "You had your chance to control the situation. You refused. You can come when I'm done."

His voice was a low growl, as if daring him to move. This was the real August, the torturer, the tormentor. Not all torture was pain. Sometimes, it was giving just enough to leave someone desperate for more.

Lucas dropped his head back onto the mattress with a shaky breath. August didn't release his wrist, just held it in a vise grip as his other hand slipped into the dark furrow between his cheeks, circling his entrance before impaling him on one spit slick finger. "Fuck… August."

He ignored him, his tongue licking around his rim as his finger pumped in and out, the combo sending Lucas's senses into orbit. He was never one to beg, but he was contemplating it. Part of him worried August would only prolong it to toy with him more. He did the only thing he could think, mindlessly impaling himself on August's finger, moaning every time it glanced across that bundle of nerves that set fire to his blood, making him groan.

When August finally closed his mouth over his cock once more, Lucas couldn't control the movement, working his hips, unable to decide which he liked most—the finger moving within him or the perfect suction that was August's mouth.

August still had his wrist in his grip. Lucas was afraid to say anything, to cry out, to even tell August he was close… and he was so close.

Still, they'd never been together like this before; they hadn't even discussed boundaries. Did August even believe in boundaries that didn't involve ropes or chains? "I'm so close. Please, don't stop. Please."

He didn't stop. If anything, his head bobbed faster, driving Lucas closer to the cliff until he finally tumbled over with a shout, flooding August's mouth with his release, shuddering as he moaned.

As soon as August's finger slipped free, Lucas rolled them, snatching August's arms and pinning them overhead, kissing him deep to taste himself on his tongue. "My turn," he snarled.

The change in August was lightning fast, his muscles relaxing, his eyes going soft, like he'd been submitting his whole life. It was somehow just as much of a turn on as August's animal side, maybe more so. What had August said? He leaned down to bite at August's ear. "Who's the rabbit now?"

August's nostrils flared, his pupils blown. "You are. But it seems I'm at your mercy." There was a slight tinge of humor to his tone, one that let Lucas know he'd play along, that he wanted this, too.

"Hands on the headboard. Don't move."

August threaded his fingers together, resting them near the headboard, eyes never leaving Lucas. If he could have gotten hard again, that look would have done it. August's quiet submission. The way he looked at Lucas like he was something worth having. He was so fucking sexy.

Lucas sat back between August's splayed thighs, looking over his torso and the dark hair dusted over his toned chest and belly, following the trail to his uncut cock, hard and flushed red, jutting from a nest of dark hair.

Lucas had no idea where to start. August was a buffet with too many options. But he'd taken his time with Lucas, and part of him wanted to do the same. See if he could take August apart a piece at a time.

Lucas raked blunt nails from August's collar bones to his hips, watching the red lines emerge along his skin. Goosebumps erupted over his whole body. He leaned down and bit August's one nipple while he gently teased the other, loving the way August hissed, his hips arching against his will. Lucas repeated his experiment as he switched sides. Lucas used his teeth to tug and scrape, then his tongue to soothe.

When he sat back once more, August's hard cock was leaking. Lucas bent down and licked over his slit, pre-cum slightly bitter on his tongue. August growled when Lucas slid his lips up one side of his shaft and down the other before taking him in hand and working him with his fist. August's lids fluttered closed, the muscle in his jaw pulsing as he tried to fuck into Lucas's hand.

"Uh-uh. You had your chance. It's my turn," he teased, as August had moments ago.

August's eyes snapped open, a slow smirk spreading across his face. "I'd respectfully like to remind you that my hands aren't actually tied."

Lucas laughed softly. "I would respectfully like to remind you that it's you who's worried about losing control, not me. You're the one who thinks you need a choke collar, not me." Lucas arched a brow, returning August's smirk. "If you're feeling froggy, leap."

Lucas never saw it coming. One minute, he was peering down at August, the next, he was on his back, August looming over him, straddling his chest.

"Careful," he purred.

Lucas didn't care about being careful. He lifted his head, rubbing his lips across whatever he could reach, August's chest, his ribs. He ran his palms up his thighs before guiding him closer until August's cock hovered above his lips. Lucas took him in his mouth, moaning around August as he gently threaded his fingers through Lucas's hair.

August seemed in no hurry, watching as he worked himself deeper into Lucas's mouth with each slow roll of his hips. "Fuck. You're so fucking beautiful. Can you take more?"

Lucas didn't answer, just swallowed him down, shivering as August groaned, one hand tightening in his hair and the other gripping the headboard. Lucas's cock was trying so hard to rally as he watched August watch him, his ab muscles contracting with each thrust, his lips parted, eyes rolling as he fucked his mouth.

"I'm close," August rumbled, his hips moving faster, his breathing heavier, and then suddenly, he was pulling free, his cum splashing over Lucas's lips and face. August still loomed over him, sucking in breaths. After a minute, he reached down, that same feral gleam in his eye as he slid his fingers through the mess on Lucas's face, pushing it between his lips with his fingers. Lucas sucked his cum from his fingers, laughing when August tried to clean up his face by wiping his palms across it. August laughed too before shifting so he could kiss him long and deep, then inexplicably dropped a kiss on his forehead.

"You okay?" he finally asked when they were side by side.

Lucas thought about it for a minute. "Yeah, actually. Better than okay. And you didn't even kill me or anything."

August's smile faded. "Not yet."

NINE
AUGUST

"Did you say all of your brothers are psychopaths?"

They were back in Lucas's bed after a brief shower. August lay on his back, sheets wrapped around his legs. Lucas laid across the bed, his head resting on August's stomach while he contented himself with trailing his fingers around Lucas's hairline.

"No, I intimated that they are. Which would infuriate my brother, Atticus, who thinks you're just out to prove we're all killers so you can take us out in some epic sting operation."

Lucas rolled towards him. "I've known you two days, hardly enough time to set up surveillance or any kinds of bugs, especially since I'm no longer an FBI agent. I'm a former FBI agent who had a mental breakdown and accused his co-worker of being a serial killer."

That's right. The man who had hurt Lucas so bad he woke up screaming every night. "We're going to have to talk about that."

"First, I think I deserve to know what you meant by being the weirdest psychopath in a family of psychopaths."

August sighed, trailing his knuckles along Lucas's cheek. "I'll tell you everything. But if you betray me, there's going to be a lot of blood on your hands."

Lucas sat up, looking August in the eye. "Are you threatening to kill me?"

August swayed into his space, catching his mouth in a kiss that lingered. "No. I'm threatening to kill them. You're mine, whether you know it yet or not. But if you tell the world who we are...what we do...you'll ruin years of my father's hard work and my brothers will want your head. Don't make me kill my family to protect you."

"I've heard of love at first sight, but this is a little intense."

August kissed him once more. "I don't love you. I can't. You know that. You're choosing to ignore years of training because you haven't felt anything in so long and whatever this is between us is better than feeling numb. I imagine, a year ago, things between us would have been much more... complicated."

"Which one of us is the profiler?" Lucas asked, a sadness seeping into his tone.

"I'm not profiling you. But I see you. Hell, since I saw you walk across the quad, all I see is you. And I know that's a lot. Noah said it's a lot for people who aren't like us."

"Is Noah one of your brothers?"

"No, he's my brother's boyfriend. He and my father are the outliers. The two sane men in a sea of psychopaths. Noah loves my brother even though my brother can't love

him. But Noah had nobody, nothing, and my brother's protection and possessiveness were enough for him, even knowing my brother couldn't love him. Whatever they have is all consuming. I want that, too, with you. But you're not Noah and I'm not Adam."

"No, I'm not. I have no idea what this is. Maybe I am playing with fire just to feel something. Does that change anything? You still kill people and I'm still crazy. I'm not going to tell your secret. Like you said, nobody would believe me anyway. But you need to understand, being with me comes with its own hazards. Kohn will come for me. He's just playing with me."

Something exploded behind August's ribs, a white hot rage that licked through his veins at the thought of anybody attempting to harm Lucas.

He pressed his forehead to August's. "It's not worth losing your mind over. He's coming for me either way."

"Start at the beginning," August said, his voice a low rumble.

Lucas sighed, then returned to using August's belly as a pillow. "I met him four years ago. Special Agent Laurence Kohn."

August brought his knee up until his heel was flat on the mattress, and Lucas's fingers began to trail along the underside of his thigh, like he was trying to soothe August's fury. "Was he a partner or something?"

Lucas shook his head. "He was a field agent. I was a criminal psychologist. We only crossed paths because I happened to be in New Mexico giving a talk on profiling.

An officer with the tribal police reached out to me about a case they had, and asked if he could pick my brain about it."

"Did that happen a lot?"

Lucas shrugged. "I have a reputation within the bureau. There were rumors about me touching evidence, wanting to see crime scenes. Shit grunts like me didn't do. Because of this, people tend to seek me out. This man was no exception."

"How did Kohn factor in?"

"He was the FBI liaison between the tribal police and the FBI, working on a string of missing persons cases on the reservation. I didn't want to step on his toes, but Kohn seemed happy to have the help."

Lucas snorted after that statement, his disgust with himself apparent. He blamed himself as the architect for his own misery. He was so sensitive, so soft. It made August feel...protective. Vengeful. He hadn't even heard the whole story and he was ready to show this man his own liver. Lucas was his. August would protect what was his.

"Don't indigenous women go missing at an alarming rate?" August asked, determined to focus on letting Lucas tell his story.

"Yes. But these women disappeared in rather rapid succession and were all of similar age. It was possible they were trafficked. That also happens with many indigenous women, but the officer in charge of the case, a man named Dan Adakai, was certain there was more to it.

"Unlike most people who hear the rumors about me, Adakai took it seriously. But there was nothing for me to hold or touch. At least nothing associated with the

disappearance. I got some impressions from clothing they owned, but nothing related to who took them. They didn't know where they went missing, so there was no way of knowing where they'd find something I could pull information from. I did my work the old fashioned way, but without a body, it was hard to provide much help."

"Because there was no MO?" August asked.

Lucas nodded. "I apologized and offered to help if any new information came up."

August combed his fingers through Lucas's messy blond tresses. "I'm assuming you found more to go on?"

Lucas's gaze grew unfocused. "Within a week, we had a body."

August frowned. "The timing seems suspect."

"Very. Almost like they were…throwing us a bone, daring us to come after them. I asked my boss for permission to return to New Mexico as a consultant. They reluctantly agreed and only because the tribal police and Kohn requested me."

"Kohn requested you?"

Lucas snorted again. "Yeah."

August could see why Lucas was so furious. The actual killer inviting him in, testing him, playing with him…still playing with him. It would be such a violation of trust for somebody like him.

"What did the body tell you?" August asked, trying to pull Lucas from his shame spiral.

"The victim was fifteen-year-old Malia Etsitty. She was the first to go missing. Her body was fresh, so she'd only

recently been killed. She'd been raped and tortured over a prolonged period of time. Her breasts and genitals had been mutilated anti-mortem, which meant we were dealing with an organized non-social lust killer, who likely moved about the world undetected. He'd posed the body, left it where it could be easily found."

"Showing off," August said.

Lucas nodded. "He was proud of his work and needed us to know he was out there. Despite the clear mutilation, he'd washed her before he'd staged her. In some cases, that might appear like remorse or like somebody who knew the victim, but in this case, it seemed almost like a forensic countermeasure."

August agreed. "What kind of impressions did you get when you touched her?"

Lucas closed his eyes. "Horrible things. I've taught myself to block out the pain and the suffering. I had to in order to survive. I have to do that so I can focus on the anomalies. The things that shouldn't be there."

"Shouldn't be there?" August echoed.

Lucas opened his eyes, looking at August. "Yes. What's different about him than other lust killers, what is out of place? Doesn't fit? Doesn't belong?"

"What did you see?"

"A rectangular room without windows. If I had to hazard a guess, I would have said a box truck or a type of shed or private storage unit, maybe even a small shipping container. Somewhere he wouldn't be disturbed."

"Makes sense."

"It was designed with torture in mind. This killer took his time. This was like his dream home. A place where he could live out any and every sick depraved fantasy he might have."

"Did you find what didn't belong?" August asked.

"Maybe. I couldn't see the killer's face because he wore a mask, which struck me as odd. Why wear a mask if you intend to kill your victim? You aren't worrying about them identifying you."

"Maybe he hadn't intended to kill her? Maybe he just took it too far?"

"I considered that, but lust killers, especially organized non-social types, achieve their sexual gratification in not only torturing but murdering these women. It's a culmination of weeks or months of fantasizing. The kill is the release they need, the mutilation is the foreplay. So, the mask was a red flag."

August nodded. "He was hiding his identity from somebody, but not the victim."

"Exactly," Lucas confirmed.

"Was that the only thing that stood out to you?"

"There was one other thing, but I don't think it's necessarily a clue. Possibly just a preference."

"What was it?"

"A red light."

"A red light?"

"Yes, all of the lighting was clinical but rudimentary, like somebody had rigged up lights in a place that shouldn't have any. But there was this red glow that sort of panned around the room, almost like a lighthouse beam."

"That's…odd."

"Yes."

"How did you figure out it was Kohn?" August asked.

"I didn't." He instantly corrected himself. "I mean, I obviously did but not by using any training. I gave our profile of the killer to the New Mexico bureau and the tribal police and went back to Virginia. A few months later, Kohn showed up at Quantico for a week-long training and sought me out. Which, in retrospect, was bizarre but, at the time, didn't seem all that weird. He was friendly, called me Mulder, teased me about being able to *see* things."

"Flirting with you?" August couldn't hide that the thought irked him.

Lucas gave a humorless laugh. "Yeah, that should have been my first clue that something was up."

August's mouth was a hard line. "Why's that?"

"He didn't ping my gaydar at all. Not even as a closet case."

"He was trying to get close to you. See what you knew."

"Yes. And I never saw it coming."

"Why would you?" August asked. "An FBI agent tasked with solving the murder he executed. It seems pretty outlandish outside of a psychological thriller."

"Outlandish like a family of crime-fighting psychopathic billionaires?" Lucas asked, lips twitching.

"Technically, my father is a billionaire. I make a professor's salary."

"No, *I* make a professor's salary. You make a tenured ivy league professor's salary, which I've been told is quite nice."

August smiled. "I do just fine. And my father is very

generous with his children. Now, finish telling me your story."

Lucas sighed. "I always keep my shields up whenever we're not on a case. Otherwise, I get bombarded with visions every time I so much as pick up a fork. People think it would be great to get a glimpse into people's heads, but it's not true. Kohn was no different. He flirted, texted, asked my opinion about the New Mexico case. When he asked me out, I refused. Dating while psychic has too many pitfalls."

"Dating while psycho comes with similar issues," August said, a teasing smile on his lips.

Lucas couldn't help but laugh. "I imagine it does. Kohn was pestering me every day, so on his final night, I invited him out to dinner. It was awkward and sealed my belief that he was straight, but I thought maybe he was just…testing the waters, unsure of his sexuality."

August threaded their fingers together and brought Lucas's hand to his lips, kissing it, having no idea how to actually soothe Lucas. He was clearly embarrassed, though he had no reason to be.

"When I dropped him off at his hotel, he surprised me by leaning over and kissing me. I was so surprised, I didn't have time to shield myself."

"What did you see?"

"At first, the same thing I saw when I touched Malia. A boxy room, a flickering fluorescent light, that strange red glow. But then I saw other things. Kohn sliding on the mask in his bedroom, dropping a curved knife into a duffle bag."

"What did you do?"

"I froze. At first, he thought I just wasn't into him. Made

a joke of it, apologized. I thought I'd escaped without him figuring it out. Even once I got home, I didn't really think he was a murderer. We worked on the same case, and had the same knowledge. Maybe Kohn liked to put himself in the killer's shoes. But that didn't explain how his knowledge of that room looked exactly like mine. No matter how I explained it, he would never have been able to recreate it with that level of detail. You know?"

August nodded. "When did he figure it out?"

Lucas closed his eyes, his mouth a hard line. "I went to my Supervisory Special Agent. He heard me out, even showed some level of concern, right up until I had to tell him why I believed Kohn needed to be investigated. I tried to explain I'd seen him in a mask with a knife—I left out the part where I'd seen it psychically—but, eventually, I came clean and explained that I truly was clairvoyant, it wasn't just a joke or some process I had. I was immediately placed on desk duty pending a psych eval."

"What did they do about Kohn?"

"Nothing. While he was in Virginia, another body dropped in New Mexico and I looked like a lunatic."

"But you didn't let it go?"

"No. Though, sometimes, I wish I had."

"You don't mean that," August said.

Lucas huffed out a sigh. "Of course, I don't. Not that I've done any good. Those girls are still dead and more have gone missing and I have no way of knowing whether Kohn and his partner are still killing. Have they taken more girls? Are they still being hurt?"

"What happened after your psych eval?"

"They cleared me to return to work, but I was obsessed with proving Kohn was a killer. I took personal time, returned to New Mexico, followed him, looked for any indication on who his partner might be. He called my supervisor, accused me of stalking, and threatened to call the police. The more I tried to prove what I knew to be true, the crazier I looked. Hell, the crazier I became. Then he was waiting for me in my car one night. I thought he was going to kill me but, it turns out, he liked playing with me instead."

"He was taunting you."

"He told me he was going to keep raping and torturing girls, that I couldn't do anything about it. Touched me and forced me to see…all of it. The things he did, the way he hurt them, everything. But worse than that…I felt it. I felt their pain and agony, heard when they begged, cried out, called for their family members. By the time I made it back inside to my office, I was gone. They put me on a seventy-two hour psych hold claiming I was clearly a danger to myself and others. I didn't do myself any favors. I refused to stop rambling about what I'd seen."

"I imagine that would have been horrific for you. But you did get out."

"Kohn tried to kill me in there."

"What?"

"He got another inmate to stab me with a piece of glass. Not that anybody believed me then either. Another inch and he would have gotten my heart. Instead, he severed a nerve in my shoulder, causing a permanent numbness in the tips of my fingers that put me on medical leave. Then they offered me a full-time teaching position in Quantico, saying I was good at what I did but they thought the stress of profiling had finally gotten to me."

"But you left instead."

"Yeah. I don't want to work with people who think I'm insane or unstable. Even if I am."

"Why do you think Kohn is still after you?"

Lucas met his gaze. "Because he moved here a couple of months after I did and women are already missing."

"You're certain it's him?"

Lucas nodded, rubbing his eye with his free hand. "Not that I can prove it. I can't even prove he's responsible for the disappearances, but I know it's him. He's going to keep tormenting me until he gets bored and then he's going to kill me. That's what he said in the car. He said he thought this was almost as fun as torturing women." Lucas sat up abruptly. "We should probably get some sleep. We both have classes in the morning."

August studied his pinched features. "Okay, that's enough for tonight, but this isn't over. Kohn needs to be dealt with."

Lucas dropped down beside him and curled against his side, tugging the blankets over them both.

"No pillow barrier tonight?"

Lucas kissed August's furry chest. "No, not tonight."

TEN
LUCAS

Like the day before, August was gone before Lucas woke, but there was a note on his pillow that said, 'Check your phone.' Lucas stretched until his joints popped, a smile forming as he rolled to grab said phone from the charger.

He found a text from August. Attached was a picture of Lucas, sprawled out, arms and legs askew, mouth gaping. August captioned it: **You're sexy when you're sleeping.**

Lucas's smile widened. **Don't hate me because I'm beautiful.**

August: Lunch later?

Lucas: Can't. I have a meeting with Brenner. Dinner?

The three dots danced. **I have a thing early this evening. But I can come over after? Dessert?**

August was all the dessert Lucas cared about in that moment. **Definitely.**

August: Have a good day.

Lucas stared at the ceiling for a good five minutes with a goofy smile on his face. Brenner was the head of the

114

psychology department, and meetings with him were about as exciting as watching CSPAN—if CSPAN had a thing for collecting antique dolls. There was an old saying that only crazy people went into psych. They were likely talking about Brenner.

After he showered and changed, he hit the coffee shop below, finding Cricket in her usual spot. Her hair was purple today. She looked genuinely excited to see him. "Hi, Lucas."

"Hey, Cricket."

Lucas imagined the quiet shop was boring. The Starbucks that had just opened a block away had stolen the small coffee shop's morning rush, which was great for Lucas and the others in their building but probably not for the owners.

She turned and started making his usual without being prompted. "I saw your boyfriend this morning," she teased, throwing a sly look over her shoulder.

Lucas felt his cheeks pinking. "He's not my boyfriend."

Cricket snorted. "Don't tell him that."

Lucas snickered. August was persistent. And sweet and charming. *And a murderer.* It was worrisome how that detail bothered him less and less with each passing moment. August was a good man. Could somebody say that about a person who admitted to wanting to torture people? Was Lucas just pushing his moral line further towards darkness to justify crushing on an actual serial killer? Would it matter? Three days in and Lucas was too far gone to even care.

"It wouldn't matter if I did. He's pretty stubborn," Lucas admitted, unable to hide how much he liked that about August.

Cricket handed Lucas his coffee cup and his chocolate chip muffin. "I know. He already paid for your breakfast and gave me a twenty dollar tip for giving you decaf, even if you didn't ask for it."

This time, it was Lucas who snorted. "Yeah, he's impossible. So, this is decaf?" he asked, holding up the cup.

"I couldn't take his money and not give you decaf. That would be dishonest," Cricket said. "But the saying was all him."

Lucas frowned, turning the cup to see a masculine scrawl on the cup.

Even if there was no gravity, I'd still fall for you.

Lucas's heartbeat skipped. "He's ridiculous."

"He's smitten," Cricket corrected. "He's also smoking hot. You two would make a super sexy couple. Like Lance Bass and his husband but, like, nerdy hot. Way better than that other guy."

Lucas took a sip of his coffee, wincing at the burn. "Other guy?"

"Yeah, the one who came in asking about you? Said he was your ex-boyfriend. Flashed his badge at me. Asked which apartment was yours."

Lucas's pulse skyrocketed, his fingers curling tight around the top of the paper bag. He'd been so wrapped up in the newness of August that he hadn't given a single thought to Kohn for the first time in over a year. He'd let his guard down and now, he'd just been sucker punched.

"What did you tell him?" He hated the sharpness in his tone, but he was trying to keep his legs under him.

"I told him I'd never heard of you, and if he couldn't figure out where you were on his own, he probably wasn't a very good FBI guy. He gave me the creeps, though. He smiled like a reptile. Sorry if he's actually somebody you wanted to talk to, but there was just…something about him."

"No. You did the right thing." He pulled out his business card, taking the pen from the cup on the counter, circling his cell phone number. "Listen, if he comes back or you see him poking around, can you text me?"

Cricket leaned across the counter, flicking Lucas's card. "Is he really your ex-boyfriend?"

"No. Not even close. If you see him around, just let me know. But stay away from him. He's a really bad guy. Okay?" Lucas held up a twenty dollar bill and placed it in the cup.

"Damn, you and your not-boyfriend are paying my rent this month."

Lucas gave her a smile but it didn't quite meet his eyes. He'd known this would happen. It was only a matter of time. Still, some part of him had hoped Kohn would be too afraid to try it. Hoped they would have at least taken some of Lucas's visions seriously.

Had Kohn taken a break from stalking and killing women to chase down Lucas? Was his partner picking up the slack while he was gone? The thought of women being hurt because Lucas couldn't convince the right people he wasn't crazy made him feel like he'd swallowed battery acid. If he could have just found one solid piece of evidence,

anything that could have backed up his vision…

But Kohn was too good for that and had used his position to create a safety net between the authorities and his victims. Unlike most serial killers, he was cunning as well as sadistic. Lucas knew if Kohn had a partner, that partner was much less likely to be the ringleader. They would have a lower IQ, defer to Kohn. They were basically a subordinate or acolyte. Somebody who almost worshipped Kohn.

But then there was the mask. Was that who Kohn was truly hiding from? Maybe his partner didn't know who he really was? That would afford him a level of safety. Still, Lucas's vision never showed a third party when he was in that room with his victims. Maybe he was filming himself? But even then, why hide? Most serial killers were notoriously proud of their kills. It wasn't like he was sending the videos to the police. No, Lucas was his sole focus.

August was right. Lucas needed help. He was no closer to unraveling this mystery and he no longer had the FBI's resources. Whoever this Calliope was, she had to have better access than Lucas currently had. He'd ask August tonight. The thought of seeing August sent a bolt of lightning through his dick. He tried not to think about August and his insanely talented tongue or the way he'd held Lucas's wrist as he'd sucked him off.

"Morning."

Lucas pulled himself from his dirty thoughts to look around for the voice. It was the woman whose office was across from his. Belinda? Bianca? Something with a B. She was locking up her office, bag thrown over her shoulder,

probably heading to her morning class. She studied him with an eerie intensity that made him want to cover his crotch, like she could see his dirty thoughts about August.

"Morning," he managed.

She gave him a tight smile and a curt nod before taking off down the hall, her low heels clicking as she walked. Lucas listened until the sound faded away entirely before fishing for the key to his office door. When he turned the key in the lock, he realized there was no click. His door was unlocked.

He frowned, pushing open the door. Everything was as he'd left it, not a thing out of place. He hung his bag on the coat rack behind his door, doing one more sweep across his office, before finally dropping into his leather chair, gaze falling to a message scrawled on a yellow sticky note.

I MISS YOU.

Lucas rolled his eyes but couldn't stop smiling. Of course, August had broken into his office. It was entirely something he would do. He left the sticky as it was, opening the bag from the coffee shop and taking a bite of the huge muffin. He was suddenly starving. He was about halfway through his breakfast when he saw it: August's scrawled message on his cup.

Lucas's gaze fell to the note, then back to the cup. The handwriting was not the same. Not even remotely. The sticky note was written all in caps, with a heavy hand. August's writing was as chaotic as he was, words slanting,

119

letters crowded. The ink on the cup wasn't Cricket's either. She wrote in funky block letters, nothing like either of the notes before him.

Lucas couldn't tear his gaze from the note. He stared at the yellow sticky like it was a venomous snake, poised to strike. He wanted to crumple it up and toss it in the trash, forget about Kohn and his crimes. Nobody believed Lucas anyway. Maybe he should just let August do what he did? But that wouldn't stop Kohn's partner or rescue any possible victims they might be holding—hurting—even as he sat there. He couldn't sacrifice them out of some sense of greater good.

As Lucas gazed at the Post-it, he wondered...could he pull anything from it if he dropped his shields? If Kohn's feelings or emotions were strong enough, even if he'd only held it for a moment, it might be enough for him to see something. He glanced at his closed office door. Nobody was likely to disturb him.

After another bite of his muffin and a sip of his lukewarm coffee, Lucas dropped his shields, opening himself, taking a few deep breaths so he was relaxed enough to see even the slightest shred of evidence left on the Post-it. He hated how badly his hands shook as he reached for the stupid piece of paper.

The moment he touched it, a gasp ripped from his lungs. Screaming. Terror. Pain. So much pain. Blood. The buzzing of something electrical. That weird fucking red glow. A girl strapped to a chair, leather binding her wrists and across her forehead. Letters carved into her skin. Three letters. I-C-U.

I see you.

"Lucas? Lucas!"

Lucas's eyes snapped open to see August on his knees before him. They were both on the floor. How had he gotten on the floor? August's hands were cupping his face, and they felt cold against his heated skin. Pain flooded Lucas's senses, making him feel dizzy and feverish. It hurt so bad. Everything hurt. His muscles, his skin, his insides. But more than that, his heart hurt. The girl had been filled with this overwhelming sense of dread and despair. Resigned to the rest of her short life being filled with agony.

"He set me up," Lucas managed between chattering teeth.

"What? Who did? Kohn? He was here?"

Lucas couldn't answer. When August sat beside him, Lucas curled against him, tucking himself under August's arm. His mouth was so dry, his lips cracked and bleeding. His eyes hurt. Why did his eyes hurt? He couldn't feel his hands. It was the straps. The ones across his forearms... They were cutting off his circulation. There was so much pain, his brain tried to reject it, losing consciousness, only to drag him to the surface of that pain once more.

August squeezed him against him. The pain began to fade, his hammering heart slowing as the dingy box of torture was replaced with a frozen lake and silence. Blissful silence. He could feel the frigid air on his face, the stillness of the space. It was vast and isolated, nothing around for miles, except for the occasional whistle of the wind through the empty branches of the trees.

"What did you do?" Lucas mumbled.

"Is it working?"

"Yes," Lucas said, still looking out over desolate wilderness. August was there, standing behind him, arms around him, chin hooked over his shoulder. "This shouldn't be possible."

"Why?" August asked, his breath hot against Lucas's ear. "If you receive impressions from the things you touch, there's no reason why I can't control what you see when you're touching me. It's just science."

Just science. Not according to anybody who knew what Lucas could do. They didn't think it was science. They thought he was crazy. A liar. Only August seemed to truly embrace Lucas's gift. Even though that gift had revealed August's biggest secret. A secret that seemed smaller with each passing day.

If Kohn had taught Lucas anything, it was that some people didn't deserve to breathe the same air as others. That the world would be a safer place with them gone. August and his family provided a service. They kept people safe. Maybe he was rationalizing. Maybe he just wanted August so bad he was willing to do whatever mental gymnastics allowed him to keep the other man, but he didn't care.

Life was short. Kohn was determined to make Lucas's life hell—to torture him until he tired of their game—and then kill him. Maybe August would save him, maybe not. Lucas had no doubt August could save himself, but he wasn't sure he could save them both. Lucas was determined to soak up whatever time with August he could. Time didn't mean much when it was borrowed. They were living their lives on

some kind of accelerated timeline, hurtling through every milestone at light speed.

Lips pressed against the top of his head. "Do you feel better now?"

Lucas closed his eyes, leaning against August's weight. "Yes. I think so."

"Do you want to stay here another minute?"

Lucas studied the icicles hanging from the barren branches. "Yes. Please."

As time ticked by, Lucas's pulse slowed, his body temperature returning to normal, the pain and sadness seeping away. When he finally blinked his eyes open to his dimly lit office, it was disorienting, like tripping and falling down a hole, finding himself in an unexpected place.

August stood, pulling Lucas to his feet and leading him to the sofa, the same sofa they'd made out on just yesterday. Had it only been yesterday?

"Can you tell me what happened?"

"Kohn's fucking with me," Lucas managed, voice raw.

August grimaced. "I gathered, but how?"

Lucas recounted his conversation with Cricket as well as the sticky note incident, relieved when August just accepted him at his word. No matter how accepting August was of Lucas's talents, there was always the underlying fear he'd stop believing.

"I'm canceling my plans for the night."

Lucas shook his head. "No, you're not. You can't spend your whole life as my bodyguard. We have classes, you have your…volunteer work. I can't hide away or Kohn

wins anyway."

August's mouth was a hard line, his breath blowing out through his nose like an angry bull. "I'm going to kill this man, slowly and with as much pain as I can manage. I need you to know that. When it's all over and we get to the bottom of his serial killing duo, I'm going to skin him alive."

Lucas should have been repulsed by the venom in August's words, but they soothed his frayed nerves. "I'll watch. I just want to make sure those girls are safe. The things he was doing…"

"I'm not like him," August said.

Lucas's head jerked up. "What?"

August scanned Lucas's face. "I need you to know that. I need you to know that I'm not like him."

Lucas cupped August's face. "I do know that. The day I met you, I might have panicked, but even when you broke into my home, some part of me knew you weren't the same."

August leaned forward, his lips fitting with Lucas's in a kiss that lingered. Lucas opened his mouth, moaning when August's tongue dipped inside. He tasted like coffee. "I'm still making sure somebody is there to look out for you tonight," August said against his lips.

"Somebody like who?" Lucas asked, dreading the idea of another stranger traipsing through his home.

"I'll figure it out."

Lucas looked at his watch; he didn't have time to argue. "We're both very late for our first class."

August hesitated. "If anything happens, you text me right

away. I don't care if I'm teaching or not." Lucas nodded, but that didn't seem enough. "I need you to promise me."

"I promise," Lucas said. "Can we go do our jobs now?"

August slanted his mouth across Lucas's in a kiss that curled his toes before standing. "Text me. Even if nothing happens. Just…text me."

Lucas smiled. "I will. Now, go to class."

August seemed torn but then finally left, leaving Lucas sprawled on the couch. What would have happened if August hadn't decided to visit him that morning? Kohn had left that note for him like a dirty bomb, knowing Lucas would try to use it to get into his head. Fuck. Why was it that the only two people who believed he could do what he did were two psychopaths?

August said he and Kohn were nothing alike, but that wasn't exactly true. They were mirror images of each other, yin and yang, dark and light, fire and ice…the very best and worst of what could happen to a person who couldn't feel guilt or remorse. A person who reveled in the pain of others.

Lucas dug his palms into his eyes, trying to shake off the morning. He had a full class and, by now, they were likely watching the clock, tempted to dip out before he arrived.

Kohn was future Lucas's problem. Right now, he just had to get through his day.

Alive.

ELEVEN

AUGUST

"You want us to babysit your new boyfriend? The former FBI agent?"

August glowered at his brother, but before he could justify his statement, Noah blurted, "We'd love to."

The look on Adam's face told August the 'we' in the statement was subjective. He had no doubt Noah wanted to get a look at Lucas, to see what exactly it was about him that drew August to him. If he could've just sent Noah, he would have, but that wasn't an option.

Adam would never let Noah go alone, no matter how capable he was of taking care of himself. It was like Adam was sure Noah would make a run for it if they didn't spend every waking moment together. No matter how obvious it was that Noah was just as cow-eyed over Adam.

It didn't escape August's attention that Lucas was also capable of defending himself, but—unlike Noah—Lucas had a very obvious Achilles heel. Just touching that Post-it note had crippled him and left him in agony. If that had

happened in Kohn's presence, he could have done anything to Lucas. Anything.

Just the thought set August's blood on fire. Seeing Lucas like that had made August feel helpless and enraged. He was going to take his time with Kohn. He wanted him to suffer in every conceivable way and had spent the entire day fantasizing about Kohn's face contorting in agony. August might even make an exception with him, leaving his headphones out just to hear him scream.

Logically, August understood Kohn had only managed to get to Lucas because he'd caught him off guard. But emotionally, it infuriated August to think this Kohn could come for Lucas. August's Lucas. But August didn't mind making an example of Laurence Kohn. He'd put his insides on the outside and leave him hanging for all the world to see what happened when they came for someone who belonged to him.

Kohn was testing Lucas, playing with him before he killed him. It didn't matter. Kohn wasn't long for this world. But, in the meantime, August had to keep Lucas safe until he was finished with tonight's assignment.

August usually looked forward to his kills. He'd been looking forward to ridding the world of this particular fucking menace for a long while. It had taken months to vet them and, now that they had, Thomas wanted it handled immediately—wanted August to handle it immediately—before they hurt somebody else.

His father wasn't like August and his brothers. He was the beating heart of their family. Archer said he was the *bleeding*

heart of their family, the one who had a personal stake in every kill, who somehow needed to heal himself with each kill. None of them knew what had happened to Thomas to make him the way he was, but they all knew there had to have been some kind of…incident that had prompted it, prompted him to adopt a bunch of mentally unstable children and train them before turning them loose on the worst of humanity. Nobody just woke up one day and decided to create their own Avengers squad without provocation.

"You're really into him, huh?" Noah asked, dragging August from his thoughts.

"He's…perfect," August said.

Adam flopped back on the couch, body curling with laughter. "Who are you right now?"

"I'm assuming that's a rhetorical question."

Adam scoffed. "Yeah, nobody's perfect, bro, not even Noah."

August cut his eyes to his brother, jaw muscle throbbing. "He's perfect for me."

"Stop teasing him," Noah warned, giving Adam a hard look that had him going from laughing to sulking in six seconds flat.

"Why does everybody baby you?" Adam asked August, as if it was his doing. "Like, you're smarter and meaner than all of us and they all act like you're one insult away from crying yourself to sleep listening to, like…Celine Dion or something."

August sniffed, feeling a little huffy himself. "There's nothing wrong with Celine Dion."

Adam rolled his eyes. "You and your pop divas, dude. It's

pathological."

"Can you watch him or not?" August said, anger edging into his tone.

Adam's mouth curled into a sly smile. "Yeah, okay, we'll watch him *if* you acknowledge that it's weird that you want us to watch your cop boyfriend. Like, I need you to acknowledge that…out loud."

August shook his head. "You don't get it."

"Then explain it to us," Noah said gently.

Adam was right—the whole family did talk to him like they were hostage negotiators attempting to talk him into releasing hostages. Why had he never noticed that before? Was he really that…scary? He knew some people found him jarring and blunt. The way people hid their thoughts and feelings behind a blanket of politeness had always seemed far worse than whatever brutal truth they could tell.

But Thomas had assured him it wasn't true, that his Aspergers and psychopathy blunted him from the damage his words and actions caused others. August could only trust that Thomas told the truth.

August dropped onto the opposite end of the sofa. "The man who's after him, he knows about Lucas's…gift. He's using it to hurt him."

Adam rolled his eyes. "The psychic thing? Again? Do you really believe in that shit?" Adam asked.

"It's not psychic shit. It's psychometry. He has to touch things to pick up impressions. And I know he's telling the truth because I've tested him. I've also seen what happens when his gifts take him by surprise. Kohn has learned to…

manipulate Lucas's talents, imprinting feelings and images on items and leaving them for Lucas to find accidentally. He's playing with him."

Adam scoffed. "Sounds like your boyfriend has a type."

"I would never do that," August snapped.

"We know you wouldn't," Noah soothed, glaring daggers at Adam. "Your brother is just being a dick for no fucking reason. We'll go hang out with Lucas until you get there, just in case something unexpected happens. You don't have to worry."

August felt the knot in his chest ease. "Thank you. He leaves work at four. If you could maybe follow him home, but don't let him know you're there."

Adam snorted. "Seriously?"

Once more, Noah cut his eyes to Adam, giving him a look. "Yes, of course, we will."

"Thank you," August said again, talking directly to Noah that time.

Once he was back in his car, he called Calliope.

She answered on the second ring. "Oh, this is a treat, I never hear from you." There was a second of hesitation, and then she hurriedly asked, "Wait. Everybody's okay, right? You're not calling to tell me anybody's dead. Right?"

"What? No. Do you think I'd be the person they sent to deliver a death announcement?"

"I mean, if everybody else was dead, maybe?" she countered.

"If my family had been slaughtered, it probably wouldn't occur to me to call anybody to tell them so."

"Wow, I'm honored."

It didn't take a genius to hear the sarcasm dripping from her words. "I need a favor."

"What's up, buttercup?"

August should have done this yesterday, but he'd gotten… sidetracked. "I need you to do a deep dive on a man named Laurence Kohn."

There was the sound of nails tapping over keys. "I'm assuming it's not the ninety-year-old Larry Kohn in a nursing home in Boca."

August frowned. "No."

Calliope snorted. "Well, I hope it's not the other one because that guy's a fucking FBI agent."

"Yeah, that's the one," August assured her.

"Oh, come on. You guys are punking me, right? You can't really be asking me to hack the FBI?"

August didn't have time for this. "The man is a serial killer. He has an unknown partner. There's a chance he's actively holding and torturing women right now."

"What am I looking for?" Calliope said around a sigh.

"Kohn is here in town. I need to know what he's doing here, how long he intends to stay, and who he's been in contact with while he's been here. He's still got a badge, so he's either on special assignment or he's relocated. If he's relocated, there's a good chance he's already hunting women in our area."

"What's his MO?"

"In New Mexico, he was hunting on the reservations. Indigenous girls and women. There's no reservation near us, but it's clear he's looking for vulnerable populations. So,

I'd start with high risk girls. But they're not going to be easy to track when sex workers and addicts disappear daily."

Calliope's voice was grim. "Yeah, I'm on it. How deep a dive do you want?"

August gripped the steering wheel hard. "When you're done, I want you to know more about him than his proctologist."

"Done. I'll get back to you when I have anything."

With that, she was gone. August felt somewhat better knowing Calliope was tracking Kohn and Adam and Noah were watching over Lucas.

He doubted Lucas would feel the same way.

August liked to think of himself as a feminist. He didn't really care about the sex organs of who was on the other end of his wrath as long as they deserved it. And Dorothy Bryer deserved it. She was the worst kind of monster, in August's opinion. One entrusted to care for children, both others and her own.

She looked innocent enough. If anybody saw her tied to the metal folding chair, they would most definitely think August was the bad guy. Which he was. But she was so much worse. She was sweating through her Lululemon leggings and matching crop top, her ponytail bobbing as she shouted muffled curses at him from behind her heavily duct-taped mouth.

They usually panicked when the instruments came out.

That was when they knew this wasn't something they were going to charm, bribe, or scream their way out of. They knew they'd been found out. Dorothy, though… She wasn't scared, she was furious. She looked two seconds away from asking for August's manager.

Just for kicks, he pulled the tape from her mouth. "I'm sorry, what was that?"

She huffed out a breath through her nose. "I said, 'Do you have any idea who I am? Who my husband is? You've just kidnapped the wrong bitch, asshole."

August did know who her husband was. Reggie Bryer. Real Estate Mogul. August knew everything about Dorothy because she documented her every thought and feeling online, using social media to garner sympathy over her sick or dead children. Lamenting her shitty genetics or terrible luck. Asking God why he would keep taking her children from her.

"Does your husband have any idea who *you* are?" August asked, running his fingers along the surgical instruments laid out on the sterile metal table.

There it was—the barest hint of fear, a momentary panic they could never hide no matter how devoid of feeling they might be. "Excuse me?"

August grabbed a scalpel, holding it up to the light. "Does your husband know what you did to his children? What you keep doing to his children?"

"You're sick. How dare you bring up my children. You can't even imagine the hell I've been through. My life is a nightmare."

With that, she began to weep, real tears streaming down

her face. August grabbed the other metal folding chair, loudly scraping it across the concrete before he sat before her, straddling the back as he faced her. "You can skip the theatrics, Dorothy. I'm immune to tears or crying or begging. It just gives me a headache."

She sniffed delicately. "You're a fucking monster."

"I know you are, but what am I," August chided, slowly dragging the scalpel across her cotton covered forearm. She didn't even scream, just hissed as the blood bloomed across her snowy white top. She glared at him now, her tears disappearing as fast as they appeared. "That was expensive, you dick."

August thought this would be fun, but Dorothy was just proving to be tedious. "Funerals are expensive, too, but you seem to love planning those. Ironic since black's not really your color."

She strained against the duct tape around her wrists, working them this way and that. He let her tire herself out. When she flounced back against the chair, she glowered at him. "Who the fuck are you, anyway?"

"Why do you do it?" August asked, ignoring her question.

"Do what?"

"Kill them? Hurt them? Drown them, smother them… Why kill poor, defenseless children?"

"I didn't! Both of my children were born sickly. No matter how many doctors they saw or treatments they tried, nothing worked. Why are you doing this to me? I was a good mother."

"Both your children were born sick?" August asked,

feigning interest.

"Yes. That's what I'm trying to tell you. I don't know what you've heard but I swear, I loved my children. I was a good mom to both of them. Please, you have to believe me."

August jerked to his feet and he watched her recalibrate. She thought the tides had turned, that she'd somehow gotten the upper hand. He walked to the table and grabbed the small pile sitting on its surface. When he was sitting down, he held up a photo. A little girl of about four. "Is this the child you loved? The one you were such a good mother to?"

"Yes. Look at her," she sobbed.

August tossed the picture at her, watching it flutter into her lap. "She died of an overdose of allergy medication."

"That's not what the coroner said," she snapped, mouth tightening into a hard line.

"And this child? Your son, Hunter. Six years old. Did you love him, too?"

"Of course, I did."

"Yet, you sat on his chest and held a pillow over his face."

Her eyes grew wide, then narrowed as she sneered. "You can't prove that."

"Did you know there were fibers found in his throat? Something else the coroner just overlooked."

"You're insane."

"Let's say that I believed you. That you loved your two children and it was just bad luck and bad genes that took them out. Say I did believe you…"

He stood. Holding up another photo, another child. "Children have a bad habit of dying around you, Dorothy.

Did they have bad genes, too? Benny Ortega, ten months old, Harry Beckett, age three, Ginger Dunnigan, age five, Flora Eckerd, age two." As he listed each child, he tossed the picture on her lap. In all, there were ten children that they knew about, and probably several they didn't.

She wasn't talking any longer, just seething. She was clearly a psychopath like him. She had no guilt or remorse. She was a shark, cold and calculating. She was already trying to pivot, to plot her next move. Part of him wanted to keep playing with her. He'd thought to torture her slowly, wanting her to feel the fear and anxiety her children must have felt, betrayed by the one person they should have been able to trust above all.

But it would be unfulfilling. She was just an empty husk, barely a person. His phone vibrated in his pocket. He replaced the knife on the tray and reached into his pocket. Lucas.

"One moment," August said to Dorothy. He swiped to answer, "What's wrong?"

Before Lucas could say anything, Dorothy began to shout. "Help me! Help! Please, he's a fucking murderer!"

August sighed, setting his phone down to slap the duct tape back over her mouth. She was back to violently cussing him out. She might be his first victim to chew her way past the gag.

He picked his phone up once more. "Is everything alright?"

"Why is there a woman screaming bloody murder in the background?" Lucas asked.

"Because she's a drama queen," August said, causing an

increase in the muffled voice behind him.

"Are you…killing a woman?"

"I'm killing a child murderer who happens to be a woman. It's the twenty-first century, darling. Equal rights and all that. Now, did you call me to yell at me for killing a woman?"

Lucas gave a huge sigh. "No. I called to yell at you for sending your brother and his boyfriend to babysit me."

August frowned. "Why? What's the problem? Is Adam being a dick? You get used to it, I promise."

"It's not that." August noted that wasn't a no. "I just think it's unnecessary and more than a little embarrassing."

"I told you this morning that I wasn't going to leave you by yourself after what happened with that stupid Post-it note. Noah will keep my brother under control, and I'll be there soon. She's no fun anyway."

A sound like a shriek tore August's attention from Lucas, his head turning just in time to see Dorothy snag the scalpel and swing it wildly. August watched as the sleeve of his black shirt grew wet. August stepped out of her way. "Gotta go," he said, slipping the phone back in his pocket just as Dorothy hit the ground hard.

Her ankles were still firmly tied to the folding chair's legs. That didn't stop her, though. She dragged the chair along as she Army crawled towards August. He cut a wide path around her, coming up behind her like he was approaching a rattlesnake. He placed one booted foot on the hand holding the scalpel, feeling a bit of excitement when she screamed. He'd probably broken her fingers.

"You know," he started, leaning down to snatch the

scalpel from her now useless fingers. "I've been really looking forward to our time together. I could be at home with my boyfriend right now, eating dinner and probably having sex. Instead, I came here to kill you, something I've fantasized about doing since I found out you even existed. But I have to be honest, you've really taken the fun out of this." He put a knee into her back, yanking her head back by her ponytail. "See you in hell, Dorothy."

"Oh, fuck y—" The scalpel cut through her skin like butter, severing her carotid artery and spraying August with warm blood. He sighed, pulling off a glove to reach into his pocket and grab his phone once more, this time dialing Adam.

"Are you almost here? I think your boyfriend hates me."

"You are rather unlikeable. I need a favor."

"What kind of favor?"

"Can you leave Noah with Lucas for an hour and come help me clean up a crime scene?"

Adam groaned. "That Dorothy chick? I thought you were just gonna drown her and toss her in the river?"

"Yeah, well, she turned out to be a lot more trouble than predicted."

"They usually are," Adam commiserated. "How bad is the clean up?"

"Arterial spray bad."

"Oh, come on, man. I hate wet work. Call Archer. Or Atticus. He owes us after the hatchet incident."

August rolled his eyes. Adam was so lazy sometimes. "It was a meat cleaver. Besides, Archer is still at his poker tournament in Vegas, and Atticus is introducing Dad at that Man of the Year thing."

"How many times can Dad win that thing?" Adam grumbled.

"As long as he keeps being hot and rich. All those old ladies on the committee love him. Are you coming or not?"

"Yeah, fine. Like I said, I don't think your new man likes me anyway."

August grinned. "I told you he's smart."

"Yeah, yeah. I'll be there in thirty. Gotta swing by Dad's to grab the van."

"I'll text you my location. Oh, and tell Lucas I'll be a little late with dessert."

Adam didn't respond, just groaned and disconnected the phone. August grimaced as he looked down at the pale face of Dorothy Bryer.

He couldn't believe he'd given up dinner with Lucas for this.

TWELVE
LUCAS

Lucas felt like a child. He was thirty-three years old, sitting on a couch, while a kid barely old enough to buy beer babysat him. Lucas wasn't sure what he'd expected when he thought of August's family, but it wasn't his supermodel brother or his freckle-faced, cherubic boyfriend.

His anxiety spiked when he overheard Adam's side of his and August's conversation, especially when Adam grabbed his keys and smacked a kiss on Noah's forehead, promising to come get him as soon as they were finished cleaning up 'the mess.' What mess? Was August okay? Adam hadn't seemed concerned, more annoyed and slightly amused.

Lucas hadn't asked. Adam wasn't much of a talker anyway. Noah, on the other hand, seemed like he'd been waiting for an opportunity to get Lucas alone.

As soon as the door closed, he turned towards him, pulling his knee up on the sofa and leaning closer. "You get used to it."

Lucas frowned. "Get used to what?"

Noah waved a hand. "The weirdness. The possessiveness. The acting like we're incapable of taking care of ourselves. I have to constantly remind myself that Adam only does it because it's his only way of showing he's concerned about my wellbeing."

Lucas frowned. "August doesn't have any reason to be concerned about my wellbeing. We've known each other for less than a week."

Noah snorted. "You act like time matters to the Mulvaney boys. It doesn't. They're like animals. Once they've locked onto a scent they like, whether it's been ten seconds or ten years, you're theirs. August won't allow you to walk away from him. I know that sounds scary, but being around the family is…never boring. And nobody will protect you like they do."

"Don't I have a say in this at all?" Lucas asked, trying to maintain Noah's casual tone.

A fond smile spread across Noah's face. "He'll tell you that you do. Thomas has drilled societal niceties into all of them— and they know this behavior isn't right—but it's like putting a fresh coat of paint directly over a cracked one. Eventually, the original stuff begins to…push through. You know?"

Lucas had seen it time and again as a profiler. Compulsions couldn't be tamed or forgotten. Sometimes, even years of therapy was no match for the incessant, gnawing need to enact the most depraved fantasies. Eventually, the person had to meet that need and that was when things got messy. But August met that need regularly… Did that make him better?

"What do you think of him? August, I mean," Lucas finally asked.

Noah's gaze slid away from Lucas. "He's funny… Intense. He tries really hard."

That was an accurate representation of August. Intense, funny, but also charming and passionate. It made Lucas smile just thinking about August scrawling silly sayings on his morning coffee cup.

"But you like that, though, huh?"

Lucas's gaze jerked up to see Noah studying him intently. "What?"

"You like being the object of August's attention." Lucas started to protest, but Noah shrugged. "You don't have to explain yourself. I get it. Believe me, nobody understands where you're coming from better than me. Adam is intense in his own way, but he looks at passing as a normal person as a game. He slides in and out of being the bored socialite and the relentless vigilante seamlessly. August…not so much."

This time, it was Lucas who leaned in. "Why do you think that is?"

Noah thought about it. "I think, when you have a brain as big as August's, it's hard to remember the little things and, to him, it's all little things. That's why he smiles when he's not supposed to and then it slips away. That's when he's recalling his training from Thomas. So, it makes him seem off."

The thought of August trying so hard tugged at something inside Lucas. Was he really feeling sorry for a murderer? "He told me he likes it. Likes torturing people."

Noah's tongue darted out to lick over his lower lip. "Does that freak you out?"

"It should, right? I should be horrified by it. I used to hunt guys like him, ruthless killers who enjoyed what they did. August isn't a good guy, not by any standard. Any normal person would run screaming in the opposite direction."

Noah shrugged. "You can't be normal and be with a Mulvaney. It's just not possible. They live equally extreme yet polar opposite lives. They have to be the over-achieving sons of a billionaire one minute and calculating, cold-blooded killers the next. There's no room for screw-ups because the consequences would be a domino effect, ruining everything Thomas has tried to accomplish and landing all of them in prison. Maybe me, too."

"You kill people, too?" Lucas asked point-blank.

Noah's chin jutted forward, his expression guarded, almost antagonistic. "I killed a person, yeah. A man who raped me repeatedly before I was old enough to write my own name. I made it hurt, too. Made him suffer. And no, I didn't lose a second's sleep over it. Maybe that makes me a psychopath, too."

Lucas had struck a nerve. Noah was telling the truth. He didn't feel bad about killing the man, that much was clear, but he was guarded, ready to attack anybody who told him he should feel bad about what he did. Lucas wasn't going to be that person. He'd had a crappy childhood, but the kind that made him feel sorry for his grandfather, not traumatized. He had no idea what it would be like to experience trauma at that level, no matter how long he'd studied it from an academic standpoint.

"You're not a psychopath. Maybe we're not supposed to

say this out loud but not every death leaves a mark, not every person deserves to be mourned. I've interviewed hundreds of killers in my day. I've sat across from every type of murderer you can imagine. People who murdered strangers, family members, co-workers, friends. By and large, the people who are most at peace with their decisions are the ones who killed their abusers. They knew the only way out was through. They do their time with smiles on their faces."

Noah's shoulders slumped, and Lucas felt like he'd passed a test he hadn't known he was taking. Noah studied him closely before asking, "Why haven't you turned August in? You're a Fed. He's a killer. His brothers are convinced you're just gathering evidence on all of us, but I don't believe that. Like, I know August. He's so into you, he'd tell you anything. You could have had this case wrapped up in a bow in a day and a half. You obviously like him, even if he's super weird. But why turn your back on everything you worked so hard for? Didn't it take a lot to become an agent?"

Lucas almost didn't answer. He'd kept his thoughts and feelings about his past to himself. "They turned their back on me. I had a spotless reputation, had a dangerously high level of accuracy with my profiles, and when I finally came clean about how I did it, they not only didn't believe me, they threw me in an institution and threatened to keep me there while leaving a serial killer free to torture women. I guess I learned that good versus evil isn't really black and white. Not every life is sacred. Some people have forfeited their right to keep breathing."

Noah propped his arm up on the back of the couch. "If

you're part of this family, you have to know how to think on your feet, be prepared to move a body, provide an alibi, shoot a gun, wield a knife, remind your psychotic boyfriend why he can't murder a man because he winked at you in a Starbucks. Being the significant other of a Mulvaney is a full-time job in and of itself."

Lucas's gaze dropped to the ring on Noah's left hand. "One you've agreed to take on permanently."

Noah smiled, cheeks pinking, as he looked at the brushed nickel band on his finger. "Yeah, but the decision was easy for me. Adam and I just…get each other. Like, we see each other, flaws and all, and it just works. Our crazy fits. Adam is my family. The Mulvaneys are my family. Being one of them was the easiest decision I ever made."

"I don't have any family either," Lucas heard himself offer. "And the ones I did have weren't exactly going to win any awards."

Noah nodded. "I can't even imagine what my life would have been like if I had the ability to see things or feel things each time I was touched. With my background…I'd be locked in a padded cell for life or not alive at all. How do you do it—keep yourself from losing it?"

It was strange to not have to convince somebody he could do what he did. "I call it shielding, like a partition in my brain I can put up and down at will. But, sometimes, I slip. It's exhausting trying to force my brain to actively not observe something."

"Is that why you like August? Because he's like you?"

Lucas frowned. "How do you mean?"

Noah tilted his head. "You haven't noticed that August has headphones in practically around the clock?"

Lucas racked his brain, trying to remember a time when he'd seen August with anything even remotely resembling headphones. The day they collided. "I never noticed. How does that make him like me?"

"Did you know he has an eidetic memory? He can recall every word he's ever heard or seen without even trying. But he hates it. He said it makes his head too noisy. He plays music almost all the time so he doesn't carry around stranger's voices in his head for the rest of his life."

Lucas shrugged. "He never wears them around me."

Noah once more studied Lucas before saying, "Then he must really like you. Because August values silence over almost anything."

Lucas did his best to ignore the warmth that pooled in his belly at Noah's words. He couldn't let himself get sucked into this twisted fairytale.

Except, he already was.

It was after eleven when Noah rose, telling Lucas that Adam waited for him downstairs and August was on his way up. Lucas suddenly didn't know what to do with himself. Did he sit on the couch? Wait for August to come up? Would he knock? Were they past knocking? He'd never been so struck with indecision before.

August didn't knock, just breezed in the door with a brown

paper bag in one hand and an overnight bag in the other.

"Whatcha got there?" Lucas asked.

August raised the brown bag as he brushed a kiss across Lucas's ear, making him shiver. "The best thing you've ever put in your mouth."

Lucas raised a brow, unable to stop the smirk forming. "Is that so?"

August's mouth hitched up on one side. "That's what the girl at the bakery said."

"Did she say it with a straight face?" Lucas asked.

August paused as if lost in thought. It occurred to Lucas then that he was recalling the conversation—verbatim if Noah was to be believed.

"Is it true you remember every word ever said to you?"

"Did Noah tell you that?" August asked, dropping the dessert on the counter and his overnight bag on the barstool.

"He said you always wear headphones to drown out the noise. I've never seen you wear them."

August brushed his hair aside, removing the tiny earbuds from his ears. "They're not on. I don't wear them around you."

"Why not?"

August frowned in confusion. "Because I want to remember every word you say to me."

It was such a casually breathtaking thing to say. August was somehow insanely romantic without even trying. Lucas crossed the room and slanted their lips together, catching August off guard. He recovered quickly, gripping Lucas's jaw as he plundered his mouth. Lucas's hands ran along his biceps, jumping back when August hissed in pain.

"What? What's wrong?"

"Nothing. I just had a little incident tonight."

Lucas frowned. "Incident? What kind of incident?"

August slipped his shirt over his head, revealing a deep two-inch gash along his arm. "How did that happen?"

August grimaced. "I underestimated her. She caught me off guard while I was on the phone."

Lucas rolled his eyes, tugging August into the guest bathroom and forcing him to sit on the shut toilet lid. "Well, why did you answer the phone in the first place?"

"Because it was you," August said, as if the answer was obvious. "When your significant other calls, you answer."

Significant other. Is that what they were? Their relationship was moving at warp speed. Arranged marriages took longer than dating a psychopath, apparently. "We're not in a relationship."

"Says you," August murmured, flicking his gaze upward, his tone letting Lucas know he found his resistance amusing. "You'll come around."

"Consent is a thing," Lucas reminded, but his tone was light.

"Is this nonconsensual?" August asked. "Do you not want me to keep pursuing you?" Lucas looked back over his shoulder, watching as August grew broody and confused. "Am I pushing you into something you don't want?"

Lucas stopped rifling through his things to stand and sooth August. Who knew psychopaths were so sensitive? He sighed, cupping August's face and tilting it upward. "I want you to keep pursuing me, but I need to feel like it's

not already a done deal. I'm an adult and I have bodily autonomy. 'I licked it so it's mine' isn't a thing in dating."

August's hands came around to grip Lucas's ass, his gaze heated as he said, "I did, though. I want to do it again. Right now." Lucas shivered at the thought of August's tongue probing all the parts of his body, trying not to get swept away by memories of last night. "I'll try to be more mindful of your feelings."

Lucas snickered. "Did you read that in a relationship book?"

There was no humor at all in August's answer. "Yes."

Lucas's heart flip-flopped in his chest. "You did?"

August nodded. "Several."

"Really?" Lucas couldn't help the surprise in his voice.

"Noah thought it would help."

"Did it?" Lucas asked, tilting his head.

"Yeah, but none of them seem to agree on anything."

Lucas quickly went back to looking under his sink so August didn't see the smile that split his face at his disgruntled tone. August had read books on relationships for him. Several. Several? They'd known each other for so little time. When had he found time to read a bunch of books on relationships? Is that why he wrote silly sayings on Lucas's cups?

He gave a triumphant shout when he found the first aid kit buried in the back. He set it on the back of the toilet, opening it and pulling a small bottle free, snapping the seal. He held a wash rag just under the wound as he poured sterile water over it. "This is really deep."

August stared at the cut in disgust. "Scalpels are meant

to do that."

"A scalpel? You let that bitch cut you with a scalpel?" August smirked at Lucas's indignant tone, but he wasn't sure what August found funny about some psycho killer almost slitting his throat. "She could have killed you."

August leaned close, his nose pushing up Lucas's t-shirt to kiss his belly. "It was just her last ditch effort to save her life," he said, his hand sliding up Lucas's jean-clad thigh. "She didn't stand a chance."

Lucas knew the feeling. He sucked in a breath at the feel of August's lips grazing his hip bone and the way his fingers squeezed his inner thigh. "You probably need stitches."

"What I need is you," August countered, hand sliding upward, his thumb tracing the ridge of Lucas's obvious erection. "Seems like you need me, too."

Lucas pressed against August's palm, groaning at the pleasure that bloomed at the sudden pressure. "I need to close this."

"You close that. I'm going to open these," August said, his hands deftly working Lucas's button and zipper open, pushing his jeans out of the way so he could run his mouth along the bulge in Lucas's underwear.

Lucas's head fell back, eyes rolling as August's lips teased at his cock. "I can't focus when you do that."

"I'll be fine," August promised, mouthing a wet spot over the head of Lucas's cock.

Lucas needed to get the wound closed. It could get infected. He threaded his fingers through August's hair, yanking hard enough to make him snarl. "You are going to let me finish closing this up," he said, making his voice as stern as he could with a raging hard-on. "And when I'm done, *then* you can fuck me. Got it?"

August's pupils blew wide as he gazed up at Lucas. "Got it," he said, voice raw.

Lucas smacked a kiss on August's lips. "Good."

He sat on the edge of the tub, using the steri-strips he found to pinch the wound closed and tape it shut. It took the entire pack. Once finished, he bandaged it up before standing. "There. All bett—"

The rest of his sentence disappeared as August tugged him between his thighs, dragged his underwear out of the way and swallowed him down.

"Jesus. Fuck," Lucas managed, hands tangling in August's hair as his knees threatened to buckle. "Not here."

August pulled off, his fist replacing his mouth, working him slowly. "Did you mean it? Can I fuck you?" He bit down on Lucas's hip. "You can fuck me if you want. I like it both ways."

Lucas was having trouble focusing. He liked it both ways, too, but he wanted August inside him. "Bedroom, now."

THIRTEEN
AUGUST

August was way too keyed up. Maybe it was the adrenaline of the night's events, or maybe it was just the thought of burying himself in the tight heat of Lucas's body. Either way, his blood quickened each time Lucas looked back over his shoulder at him. August wanted to throw him down on the bed and lick every inch of him, taste every inch of him, hold him down and fuck him while he made those sexy fucking noises he'd made when he sucked him off the night before.

When they got to Lucas's bedroom, he couldn't stop himself from shoving him up against the door, gripping his face so he could plunder his mouth, biting at his lips, his jaw. "I've thought about this all day. I could barely concentrate on my work tonight knowing you were here waiting for me."

Lucas moaned, squeezing August's ass, dragging him closer until their hips were flush together. Lucas's head thudded against the door, and he bared his throat in an unconsciously

submissive gesture that made August's cock throb.

Lucas trusted him and would let him do anything to him. Literally anything. The thought made August feral, made him want to drag Lucas's clothes out of the way and fuck him against the door until he cried and begged. What did Lucas look like when he was totally helpless? What things could August do to him? Lucas ground himself against August, almost like he could hear his dirty thoughts.

"We can skip the foreplay if you want," Lucas panted against August's lips, shoving his hand down the front of his open jeans, palming his erection. "You can do whatever you want to me. I've been thinking about this all day, too."

You can do whatever you want to me. Lucas couldn't just say things like that.

August lurched away from him, breathing heavily. Lucas startled at August's sudden retreat. "What? What's wrong? What just happened?"

August's heart was racing at the thought of losing it on Lucas, of doing…whatever…to Lucas. *You can do whatever you want to me.* Jesus. "I just… I need you to tie me up. I can't be trusted right now." Lucas took a step closer, but August held up a hand. He couldn't get the thought of hurting Lucas out of his head. "Please."

Lucas examined him closely, his confusion evident. August wouldn't be surprised if he kicked him out and told him never to come back. It was the most logical choice. Any sane person could see he was dangerous. He stood, dancing on a knife edge, as Lucas considered August's request.

Finally, Lucas said, "Get undressed and lie down on the

bed."

August felt woozy from the tension that suddenly left his body. Lucas wasn't kicking him out, and he wasn't dismissing his concerns. He would be safe. Safe from August. Just in case.

He stripped, lying on his back on the mattress, watching as Lucas crossed to his closet, reaching for something on the top shelf, his t-shirt rising up to reveal a thin strip of skin. He fished around until he found what he was looking for, spinning and showing August his find. A set of government issue handcuffs dangled from his finger. He placed the small key on the side table before climbing onto August fully clothed, sitting on his chest to clip one cuff on his wrist.

"Tighter," August demanded.

Lucas rolled his eyes but did as he asked, threading the chain behind one of the wooden dowels of the headboard before cuffing his other wrist. "There. Happy now, grumpy pants?"

August knew Lucas was teasing him, but he didn't care. This was the best way to keep Lucas safe until the impulse to take him apart died down. "Yes. Now, you're safe from me."

Lucas peeled his t-shirt over his head, tossing it on the floor, leaning down to lick a stripe along the center of August's chest. "But now, you're not safe from me." August's breath hitched as Lucas tongued over one flat nipple, tugging it with his teeth, before sitting up again, reaching back to take August's hard cock in hand, giving it a couple of firm strokes.

"You don't have to worry, you know," Lucas murmured,

releasing him to fuse their mouths together in a long lingering kiss before biting over his jaw, nipping at his earlobe as he whispered, "If I wanted to, I could know every single thing you're thinking. You can't catch me by surprise. I won't let you."

August bucked his hips up against the empty air at Lucas's taunt. "I'm not willing to risk it."

Lucas sat back and shrugged, dragging blunt nails down August's chest and belly. "Then I'm free to do whatever I want to you," Lucas said. "Fine by me."

August watched as he stood, removing his jeans and underwear. Naked Lucas was perfection, not overly toned or bulky, no washboard abs, but slightly defined arms and muscled calves like somebody who had spent a lifetime running.

August suddenly ached to touch him, to do all the things he'd thought of before. But now, he was trapped.

Lucas opened the nightstand drawer, grabbing a condom and the lube and tossing them on the bed beside August. He got rid of the pillows, tugging them out from underneath August's head to toss them on the floor. He looked August over for one long moment before he climbed back over him, only this time, he was facing August's feet, his knees braced on either side of August's bound arms, his hard length dangling just above August's lips.

He sucked in a breath as Lucas's mouth closed over his already aching cock, eyes rolling at the wet suction. Fuck. Two could play that game. He lifted his head, taking Lucas in, flushing as his responding moan vibrated along August's shaft to his balls. Lucas spread his knees, lowering himself

so he could fuck into August's mouth in short, shallow thrusts, almost like he worried he might hurt him. August would happily die choking on Lucas's cock.

August tried to keep himself still—tried to give Lucas the same consideration he gave August—but found himself bending his knees, digging his heels into the mattress, thrusting up into Lucas's mouth. Any worry he had that Lucas would be bothered dissipated when he slid his hands beneath August's thighs, swallowing around August's cock until his eyes rolled.

Then Lucas was pulling free of his lips and the heat of his mouth disappeared. Lucas grabbed the lube that had rolled beneath August's thigh, and August watched as Lucas coated his fingers then reached back, giving August a perfect view as he massaged over his hole before pressing two fingers inside.

August had been stabbed more than once, shot in the thigh, had once even had a shuriken embedded into his shoulder thanks to Atticus's terrible aim. But having Lucas right there, inches from his face, fingers working in and out of his tight hole, while August could do nothing? That was true torture.

It could have been his fingers, his tongue. He could have taken Lucas in a million different ways and Lucas would have let him. Had clearly wanted him to. And now, he was making August pay. Making him suffer for not having enough faith in his own self control. He was making a show of it, too, rocking back on his fingers, whispered curses falling from his lips each time he pushed back in.

"Lucas…" August said his name like a warning. He couldn't break through steel but, with enough motivation, he could probably break the headboard.

Lucas looked over his shoulder at August. "What? You didn't trust yourself to do this. So now, I have to prep myself all alone."

"You're not alone," August said, tone bordering on sulky.

"What's the matter? You wanna play, too?" Lucas teased, slipping his fingers free and wiping them on the sheets. He grabbed the foil packet and tore it with his teeth. August sucked in a breath when Lucas rolled it onto his leaking cock, slicking it with lube. When Lucas rose up on his knees, August said, "Turn around. I want to see your face."

Lucas complied, turning to face him, straddling August's hips, reaching behind him to grip the base of his cock, pressing it against his entrance. They both groaned as Lucas lowered himself down, taking August all the way to the root in one swift movement. "Oh, fuck. You're even bigger than you look," Lucas managed, giving a few experimental rolls of his hips.

August could barely talk. Each minute movement sent shocks of lightning along his nerve endings. Lucas placed his palms on August's chest and began to slowly work himself up and down. "Fuck, you feel good," Lucas moaned, quickening his pace.

"Christ, this is going to be over fast if you keep doing that," August warned.

Lucas leaned over him, pressing words against his lips. "Fine. Your legs are free. You do the work."

August didn't even wait for Lucas to finish speaking, just braced his heels on the bed and fucked up into Lucas, but it wasn't any better. If anything, it was worse. August couldn't slow his thrusts, not when Lucas was so hot and tight and wet.

"Touch yourself. I want to feel you come with me inside you."

Lucas gripped himself with one hand and braced his other on August's chest. He couldn't take his eyes off him. He was sexy as fuck, especially when he was completely unaware of anything but chasing his own release. His breaths quickened, and every other thrust had a low whine falling from his lips.

Something occurred to August then. "Did you mean it?"

"Mean what?" Lucas asked absently, his hand moving in time with August's thrusts.

"Can you really feel what I'm thinking, what I'm feeling, while we do this?"

Lucas hesitated, then nodded. "If I let myself."

"Do it. I want you to know how good you make me feel."

Lucas's hand fumbled, and August froze, worried he'd ruined everything. But then Lucas closed his eyes, rocking himself on August. They both moaned at the same time. Lucas sucked in a breath, his movements quickening once more. August let him control the pace, and he couldn't take his eyes off him. Each time August felt a charge of excitement, Lucas moaned or whined or whimpered, which only served to wind August up even more. It was the world's most erotic feedback loop, each of them feeding off

each other's pleasure.

Lucas wasn't even touching himself anymore. He leaned back, his hands on August's thighs as he rode him hard, devastating August's already tenuous control, tension building between them with each downward motion. "Oh, fuck. Oh, fuck. I can feel you. I can feel it like a physical touch."

If Lucas could feel him, then he had to know he wasn't going to last much longer. "I'm close."

"I know. Me too," Lucas managed, somehow working himself even faster.

Heat coiled at the base of August's spine, and then his orgasm hit, sending shock waves of pleasure over him. He came with a hoarse shout, filling the condom, goosebumps erupting along his body. Lucas's knees clamped hard around his hips, his breaths growing more frantic, more ragged. Finally, he wrapped a hand around his flushed and leaking cock, giving one or two pulls before he was crying out, coating August's furry chest and belly with his release.

August sucked in much-needed breaths as Lucas collapsed on top of him. "Holy fuck. That was… That was amazing. I wish you could feel what I felt. It was…mind-blowing."

"Just think, you could have been doing that all along," August said, annoyed with himself for even bringing up Lucas being with other men.

Lucas folded his arms on August's chest, dropping his chin to his forearms. "You don't get it. I've never done anything like that. Nobody believes I can do what I do. So, they think their thoughts are safe. Usually they are, but sometimes, I slip, and when I do, the results are pretty

bleak. But you… You just let me in, you *invite* me in, and it's so hot. You're so fucking hot because I can trust that your thoughts won't hurt."

August didn't know what to say to that. He'd been called a lot of things in his life, even attractive, but nobody had ever called him trustworthy and they'd never called him hot, especially not while looking at him like Lucas was. Before he could think of something to say, Lucas was reaching for the key, unlocking August's wrists and working the blood back into his hands and fingers.

"Shower?" Lucas asked as August got rid of the condom.

"Yeah, sure."

"Then we should order food. I'm starving. Did you eat after you…you know?" He made a stabbing motion like he was in a Hitchcock film.

August couldn't help but laugh. "No, there was no time after we got everything cleaned up. She was a pain in the ass even after she died."

Lucas took August's hand and led him into the bathroom, turning on the water. When they stepped under the spray, Lucas frowned at August. "Are you okay?"

He wasn't. A single thought hit him like a blow to his diaphragm. "You can't leave me."

Lucas blinked rapidly, water droplets catching on his eyelashes. "What?"

August cupped Lucas's face, forcing him to meet his gaze. "I know you think this is crazy. And I know some part of you thinks Kohn is going to kill you, so none of this matters anyway. I know that's why you're so casual about

bedding a killer."

Lucas opened his mouth like he was going to protest, but August shook his head.

"Don't. Don't lie to me. I know you think you have a clock ticking down over your head, but it's not true. I won't let that happen. If it comes down to random strangers or you, I'll choose you every time. I'll literally burn this world to ash before I let somebody hurt you. I don't care who suffers because of it. I know that's intense and weird but I need you to know I mean it. You're not going to die, and I'm not letting you go. If you're going to leave me, you're going to have to kill me first. Please, kill me first."

August snapped his mouth shut, turning away from Lucas, cursing his inability to be normal for five fucking minutes. It felt like an hour had passed before Lucas's arms came around him from behind, his lips pressing against the nape of his neck. "I need you to know that is literally the most fucked up thing anybody has ever said to me after sex, including the one time a guy said I looked just like his older brother…after we fucked. Sadly, I already knew that because I saw it…you know, with my mind."

August wanted to laugh but he couldn't. He was waiting for Lucas to tell him to get out, to call him a psycho, a lunatic. "I just needed you to know. I feel bad about it. Well, I would feel bad about it if I was capable. I know I should feel bad about it. But I also know me. I don't care that we barely know each other. It's just you. You're the one for me, and if I can't have you, I'd rather not exist anymore."

Lucas turned August around, wrapping his arms around

his neck. "I have no idea how I'm supposed to feel about that. Ironic given my profession. If I had a patient tell me their significant other had said that to them, I'd tell them to run fast and far in the other direction and that they were in an abusive relationship. But here I am, not going anywhere. I'm not afraid of you. And maybe I do feel like I'm on borrowed time, but that doesn't make this any less real to me...whatever this is."

"You're not afraid of me?" August asked, heart thudding heavily against his ribs.

Lucas's brows went up, a half smile forming. "*Of* you? No. Afraid for everybody else, yes. I can't let you burn the world down just for me."

August studied Lucas's face, pushing his wet hair out of his eyes. "You say that like you have a choice."

"Fine," Lucas said around a sigh, reaching for the soap. "But that doesn't mean we're getting married. We're not in a relationship. Not yet. We haven't even known each other a week."

August frowned at Lucas. "What does that have to do with anything?" he pouted. Then asked, "Then what are we?"

Lucas pressed the soapy cloth to August's chest, taking his time to scrub him thoroughly. "Roommates at whatever asylum we both end up in if things go sideways with Kohn."

August's pulse returned to normal when he realized Lucas wasn't running away, that he was just teasing him. "We can buy matching straitjackets."

Lucas slid the washcloth lower with a grin, cleaning August's balls like he planned on eating off them later. "Do

they make couture straitjackets?" Lucas asked.

August leaned down and kissed him, pressing himself into Lucas's hand. "Of course. Only the best for the Mulvaneys."

FOURTEEN
LUCAS

Cricket smiled when Lucas and August entered the coffee shop, smirking when she saw their fingers threaded together. This morning, her hair was acid green and she wore purple lipstick. She waved hello and immediately started to make their usual orders as they took a table near the door. The place was completely empty. Still, Lucas couldn't help but note how August took the seat facing the door. It was such a cop thing to do. Ironic considering August was anything but.

Once their order was complete, August snagged it from the counter, dropping too much money into Cricket's tip jar. He placed Lucas's coffee and muffin on the table as he returned to his seat, tangling their legs together. They didn't talk much, but it was a comfortable silence filled with glances that made Lucas blush like a fucking school girl thinking about what they'd done just hours before.

Lucas slowly dissected his chocolate chip muffin, tearing it into tiny pieces before popping them into his mouth. August had chosen a cheddar jalapeño scone, which he was

eating with a delicacy Lucas found amusing, like he was concerned about getting crumbs on his jeans and t-shirt.

As they ate, Cricket watched them carefully, her gaze darting from them to something behind the counter, to the door, and back again. It wasn't that she was behaving any weirder than usual, but something in her behavior was making Lucas uneasy, which in turn was making August scan the restaurant for whatever perceived threat might be lurking.

When August's phone rang, he turned it over to view the screen, immediately picking it up when he saw who was calling. He placed the phone between them and hit the speaker button. "Morning, Calliope."

August putting it on speakerphone seemed like a weirdly intimate gesture. Lucas rolled his eyes at the ridiculous thought, earning a confused look from August. Lucas waved a hand to let him know to ignore him.

"How's the arm?" Calliope asked in lieu of a greeting.

August's mouth formed a hard line. "Who told?"

Calliope chuckled. "Who do you think? Adam texted me before you two had even left the warehouse. You let that bitch get a hold of a scalpel? That's not like you."

"Thank you. That's what I said," Lucas interjected, giving August a superior look.

There was a long pause, and then, "Oh, my God. Are you him? Are you Lucas? *The* Lucas?" Calliope asked with the same reverence and awe she might give a celebrity.

August smirked at him, taking a sip of his coffee.

Lucas leaned closer to the phone. "Um, yeah. Hi."

"Hi. *Hi*," she said again. "I've heard so much about you. Is

it true you're psychic? I totally believe in all of that. Astrology. Tarot. Ghosts. My mother knew when people were going to die before they did. She said she used to look at their faces and instead of their normal face, she'd see a skull instead. It started when she was a kid, in church no less—"

"Calliope," August interjected, "was there a reason you called?"

Lucas liked her instantly. Unlike August's cocky brother, Adam, Calliope seemed more like Noah, more…human. Friendly. Excited to know him. It was an odd feeling after being surrounded by hundreds of people—from doctors to co-workers—who thought he was crazy.

"Can you get to your father's house? I want to walk you through what I found, but I think you need to see it on the big screen."

August flicked his gaze to Lucas, who shrugged. "I can be there in an hour or so."

"*We* can be there in an hour or so," Lucas corrected, giving August a hard look so he knew he wasn't going to debate this with him.

August studied him for a long moment. "*We* will be there shortly."

Calliope sounded giddy as she said, "He's going to meet the family? Already? You work faster than Adam."

August sighed. "Calliope…"

Lucas smiled. August had a way of using people's names like a warning. He'd done the same thing last night when Lucas had him tied to the bed. His whole body flushed at the thought. He'd had August Mulvaney tied to his bed, had experienced what was probably the single most erotic and intimate moment of his life to date…and there was literally nobody to tell.

"Ugh, fine. Do you want me to let your father know you're coming?" Calliope asked, defeated.

"No. It's fine. I imagine, if he's home, he'll find his way to us eventually. He has a sixth sense about these things. And, whatever you do, do not tell the others. Lucas doesn't need to be overwhelmed by the rest of the family."

"Aww," Calliope simpered.

August disconnected with an eye roll, then looked at Lucas. "Are you sure you're up for this? My father hazed the shit out of Noah when Adam brought him home the first time."

Lucas's chest squeezed. "He can't be worse than the people I thought were my friends. I need to see this through. I've wasted too much time running scared since I got out. Who knows what Kohn's been doing or how much blood I have on my hands because of it."

August frowned. "You didn't do any of this. You tried to warn others. You tried to do the right thing and they punished you for it. This is on them."

When August stood, Cricket called out, "Um, Lucas?"

Something in the way her voice wavered made his original uneasiness ramp up a notch. "Yeah?"

She hesitated, then reached under the counter and retrieved a box. "I know you said to call you if I saw that man again, but…" She trailed off, her face pale.

There was nothing ominous about the box, but she held it

gingerly like it was a bomb. It was just a black shoebox with an elaborate red ribbon around it and a small white tag.

She came around the counter, chewing on her bottom lip. "Um, this was outside our door this morning. It had your name on it. It wasn't August's writing. Something about it gave me the creeps, but I wasn't sure if it was from that guy or not. I was going to show you when you came in but you just looked so happy. But now that you're leaving…what should I do with it?"

Lucas's stomach dropped, but August took it from her calmly and gave her a reassuring smile. "We'll take it from here. If you get any more packages like this, give us a call. Don't touch them, just call me." He fished a business card out of his pocket and handed it to her. "Lucas is going to be staying with me from now on."

"What?" Lucas asked, head snapping up.

August set his jaw like he was ready to fight if necessary. "You heard me. He's toying with you. You're not going to play some cat and mouse game with a serial killer."

Cricket gasped. "Serial killer? He said he was an FBI agent." She frowned, muttering to herself, "That badge looked so legit."

"He is a serial killer and it *is* a real badge," August said with a matter-of-fact tone that floored Lucas. "So, you can imagine how dangerous he is. If you see him, call me. No matter what time of day or night. Understand? Don't call the cops. Call me."

Cricket's eyes went wide, and she nodded, clearly spooked.

Lucas probably shouldn't find this bossy and authoritative August as attractive as awkward and stilted August, but he did. The man was a dozen different people all rolled into one sexy, brainy package and Lucas's psychotherapist heart was there for it. He would never be bored with August.

Cricket swallowed audibly, her hand crumpling August's card in a death grip. "Am I going to die or something?"

August gave her a surprisingly gentle smile. "You're not his type. People will care if you go missing."

A myriad of expressions played across Cricket's face as she was at once relieved but also horrified at the implications of his statement. Nobody wanted to think their safety came at the expense of somebody less fortunate.

Lucas raised his hand to touch her arm but then thought better of it. He didn't need any accidental transference. He was anxious enough as is. "It's going to be okay."

Cricket gave him an incredulous look. He got it. He wasn't sure he actually believed his words any more than she did. But he had to keep telling himself it would be okay.

Until it wasn't.

Thomas Mulvaney's home looked like something out of a movie. Sprawling grounds with lush landscaping. A garage big enough to fit Lucas's apartment five times over. A giant house that looked like it could easily hold the college's entire social sciences department with no trouble.

August didn't knock, just pushed open the door, nodding

at a young woman in a polo shirt and khakis pushing a vacuum cleaner across a Persian rug, her ponytail swinging as she moved. All throughout the house were other cleaners, dozens of them. How many people did it take to upkeep a house of this size?

August paid little attention to any of them, giving a head nod to anybody who frowned in their direction, but otherwise dragging Lucas through the house without justifying his presence. Lucas supposed just understanding the complicated layout of the place had to give some indication he belonged there. Lucas hadn't been in a house this big since he worked a case where a corporate mogul had fallen victim to a serial arsonist, and that house had been missing most of its walls by the time they'd arrived on the scene.

August led him down a narrow corridor to a solid door with a keypad. He dialed the code without worrying about Lucas watching over his shoulder. Maybe the code changed daily or something.

Once inside, they entered what looked like a boardroom. The room August had showed him in his mind the night he'd broken into his apartment and said he was Batman. There was a large table, screens that encompassed two walls, a murder board on a third wall…and four men staring at him from where they were seated around the enormous conference table.

August sighed, setting the shoebox on the table. "Why are you all here?"

The older man stood, giving Lucas a friendly smile. Thomas Mulvaney was even hotter than his pictures,

objectively speaking. Lucas tried to recall if he'd ever read how old the man was, but nothing came to mind. He could have been anywhere from his late forties to early fifties, but he was fit and well-dressed and walked with the confidence of a man who was used to going unquestioned.

"Lucas, this is my father," August said begrudgingly, like he only did it because it was expected. "You know my brother, Adam. The redheaded one who looks like he smelled something bad is my older brother, Atticus, and the one who looks like he just rolled off a pirate ship is my brother, Archer. This is Lucas."

Thomas reached out and took Lucas's hand without waiting for him to reciprocate. He was instantly hit with a barrage of images. A much younger Thomas crying over five caskets. A man looking at a little boy through an observation window. Thomas fighting with a much younger man with russet hair and haunted eyes. Thomas telling those gathered around the table to be nice to Lucas, and their many objections. Lucas snatched his hand away, a shiver running through him.

Thomas tilted his head, gaze sharp. "What did you see?"

Lucas hesitated. Had that been a test of some kind? August had said they'd hazed Noah. Was that what was happening now? Was Lucas earning his way into the meeting? There was no way Thomas had intended Lucas to see everything he had. The first few images had felt…intimate. Too intimate to share out loud. "You telling the others to be nice to me because it might set August off. Adam sulking because you were mean to Noah when he first came here.

Atticus complaining about somebody named Kendra never being allowed to be in the loop."

They all stared at him, then swung their gazes to Thomas as if waiting for him to pass judgment on Lucas. Thomas just smiled and gestured to the row of empty chairs. "Have a seat, Lucas. Please," he added, almost as an afterthought. Lucas continued to stand, reading the room as hostile despite Thomas's sudden change in demeanor.

"Why are you all here?" August asked again.

Atticus snorted. "Because you have Calliope spying on an FBI agent for this man—a former FBI agent, a *stranger*—and didn't feel the need to tell the rest of the class."

August was fuming. "And, instead, she snitched and helped stage this little intervention?"

Thomas sighed. "Calliope didn't tell me anything I hadn't already heard from the boys. And she knew not telling me was a greater risk than pissing you off."

"You told her not to do the background check on Laurence Kohn?" August asked. Lucas's heart sank. He thought they were finally getting somewhere.

Thomas frowned. "No. I let her do the investigation. I just asked her to do another background check of my own. On your friend here."

Yeah, this wasn't going to end well. He shouldn't have dragged August into this. Wait, had he dragged August into this, or had he invited himself in? Lucas couldn't even remember anymore.

August's affect went cold. "I didn't think I needed to tell you I was utilizing Calliope for a personal matter. And I

definitely didn't think you'd run a background check on my boyfriend without even talking to me first."

Atticus dipped his head towards Adam, stage whispering, "Did he just say boyfriend?"

"Uh-huh," Adam confirmed, leaning forward, like he was anticipating a fight. Archer reached for a highball glass filled with amber liquid, clearly bored.

Thomas was eerily calm. "You asked Calliope to investigate a federal agent. That affects us all."

"So, is this an ambush?" August asked. "If Calliope didn't actually find anything, we'll go. We have jobs. I'll make sure we do our own investigating from now on."

He grabbed Lucas's hand, tugging him towards the door.

"August, stop." August froze at his father's harsh tone. "Calliope did find information about your agent."

August didn't turn around. "She can forward it to me at my apartment. It will minimize any blowback on you."

Lucas had never experienced August this…livid. He wasn't showing any outward sign of anger, but Lucas could feel his rage like a living thing, filling Lucas with heat from the point where they touched. August didn't like his father's lack of trust in him, and the images he projected to Lucas were almost cartoonish images of increasing violence as August processed his fury.

Thomas's voice was firm but not unkind. "August. Sit. Now."

Lucas leaned into August's space, pressing his lips to his ear. "Don't start a war over me. Hear him out. We're already here."

Lucas tugged him back to the two seats at the end of the table, relieved when August followed without a fight. Once they were both seated, Lucas asked, "What did you find about me? I should at least be able to explain myself, no?"

Thomas gave the barest hint of a smile. "To start, I wanted to know if you were mentally unstable, or if there was any way you truly were clairvoyant. I thought, perhaps, it was a clever way to trick my son into thinking you already knew all our secrets. That you were undercover."

"And now?" Lucas said, guarded.

"After reviewing your record with the FBI, your rapid mental decline, and your medical charts from the facility, I made some phone calls to a few trusted friends in the profession and concluded that nobody spends that kind of time in a mental health facility to sell a good cover story."

"So, you believe him?" August asked.

"He just said he thinks he's truly crazy, not undercover. Not a glowing endorsement," Atticus said.

Thomas flicked a gaze to his oldest son. "Atticus, quiet."

The large man began to sulk. The Mulvaney boys didn't like being questioned and they certainly didn't like not getting their way. They were like murderous toddlers, willing to defend their toys and their status as Daddy's favorite with violence. The criminologist in Lucas wanted to sit with each of them and see how they ticked. But that wasn't why they were there.

Thomas looked at Lucas. "I believe you can do what you say you can, and I believe you've been set up. I'll reserve my judgement on anything else until we hear what Calliope

has found."

Thomas hit a button on the conference room speaker. "Calliope, we're all here."

The screen directly in front of them lit up, but there was no information presented. "Sorry, August," she said sheepishly. "Okay, here's what I know. Laurence Kohn transferred here permanently about two weeks after Lucas took the job at the university. He actually settled in before Lucas officially moved here. He lives alone as far as I can tell, is working a desk job as a supervisory special agent, and pays his bills on time. His computer is pristine, his bank records boring. On paper, he's clean enough to squeak."

"Did you find anybody who might be his partner?" August asked.

"Yeah, that's the thing, his phone records are the only thing that stand out as strange. He receives an obscene number of calls from burner phones. At first, I thought maybe this partner was just overly cautious, tossing burner phones after limited use, but then I realized the numbers overlap. He's getting repeat calls from burner phones, but they're all coming from different people."

"Human traffickers?" Archer enquired.

Lucas shook his head. "Kohn was torturing these women. Traffickers don't damage their merchandise. Traffickers use drugs and debt to control their victims. They don't mutilate them unless keeping them becomes a liability. These women were taken solely for his perverse pleasure. There's too short a window between when they're taken and when the bodies are discovered."

August turned to Lucas. "But you said only three bodies were recovered, despite several young women going missing. Could there have been a reason he didn't keep them? Maybe they'd caused too much trouble? Maybe the others were trafficked, but these women were…a warning? Or, like you said, a way to taunt you?"

"Maybe. But it just feels…off. Wrong somehow. I can't explain it. If he was trafficking them, he'd have to be hiding his money somewhere, no?"

Archer shifted in his seat. "If the transactions are taking place on the darknet, he could be using cryptocurrency. It's the preferred currency of the underworld."

"So, we have nothing? For all intents and purposes, he's just another upstanding citizen," Lucas said, disgust leaking into his tone.

"Except, we know he's not. He's fucking with you. That Post-it note wasn't just a warning, it was a clue," August said. "He wants to play with you, drag you into his twisted fucking game. Whatever is in that box, I guarantee it will be something that forces you to experience something terrible for another piece of the puzzle. We know he's guilty. Just let me fucking kill this guy. Nobody is going to miss him."

Lucas shook his head, his gaze locked on the shoebox. August was right about the box. Kohn was fucking with him. "What if he's taken more girls? We don't know there aren't other women out there being tortured."

"Lucas is right. Girls are going missing here," Calliope said, drawing everybody's attention back to the speaker in the center of the room.

"Who?" Thomas asked sharply.

A cursor appeared on the screen as Calliope said, "I can't tell you who, but I can tell you where."

"What do you mean?" Thomas asked.

A map appeared on the screen. "Do you see this six block radius?"

"Yes," Thomas confirmed, looking at the blocks she'd highlighted in pink.

Calliope was rapidly typing even as she spoke, like she was somehow multitasking. "It's our version of skid row. This place houses the greatest number of our homeless population, addicts, and sex workers. As you can imagine, there's a lot of overlap."

"Okay?" August prompted.

"There's a certain number of indigent people who regularly go missing. Strangely, the statistic remains fairly static. Two weeks after Laurence Kohn moved into the city, that number began to spike...steeply. People are disappearing from this part of town at an alarming rate." Missing person posters began to fill the screen, overlapping each other until no one person stood out. "If I get rid of the men and those found dead, all of these women and young girls are left."

Lucas could feel his breakfast creeping back up his esophagus. "Calliope, is there any overlap in profiles? Can you cross-reference details of their lives? Their features, characteristics? Anything that denotes a pattern?"

"I can try. It's going to take time. This population tends to live off-grid, whether they mean to or not."

"In the meantime, maybe we should just do it the old fashioned way," August suggested.

Lucas frowned. "Meaning what?"

"Let's just tail him," August suggested.

Lucas shook his head. "We have lives. We can't just follow the man around day and night."

August's brows knitted together. "Not us. We'll put a GPS locator on his vehicle. Bug his house."

Adam scoffed. "I don't recommend breaking into an FBI agent's house."

Thomas sighed. "Yes to the GPS tracker. No to the breaking and entering." At August's incredulous look, Thomas said, "For now."

August huffed. "Fine."

"Calliope, let's make this the priority. Put Noah's other cases on the back burner, see if you can narrow down the most likely victims as Lucas suggested, and also see if you can find any reference to Kohn owning any form of cryptocurrency."

Nails resumed their clicking. "I'll do my best, but if it's not Bitcoin or Ethereum, if it's one of these lesser known currencies, it's going to be nearly impossible."

"Do your best," Thomas said. "Keep me in the loop. Nobody does anything without my say so. Understand?"

August's nostrils flared but he gave a single nod. "Calliope, send me what you have on Kohn. I want to get a tracker on his car today."

"Got it."

With that, she was gone. Thomas looked at Lucas. "You

need to make peace with the fact that you might never get the proof you need. If we can't find his victims, there may come a time when you have to decide between a few missing women and a world full of potential victims."

"I don't know if I can do that," Lucas said, choking on the thought of leaving these women to die somewhere.

"Then we'll do it for you," Archer said before shooting the rest of his drink.

"Yeah, there's a clock on this operation," Thomas said. "If we can't nail this down in the next week or so, we're going to take him out. We have no choice."

Lucas scrubbed his hands over his face. He understood their logic, he did. They couldn't hunt for these missing women forever. They didn't even know who they were. It would be like chasing ghosts, maybe literally. At what point did he just let the Mulvaneys do what they did?

And could he live with himself when it was over?

FIFTEEN
AUGUST

August looked for Lucas after his first afternoon class ended. A bored freshman lingering in the auditorium said Lucas had left for the library twenty minutes ago to make copies of a rubric for a term paper. August frowned at that. Why wouldn't Lucas just use the copiers for the faculty?

The library was a red bricked, three-story, gothic monstrosity with arched windows and entryways. When he entered, students frowned at him like he wasn't welcome. He paid them little mind, grateful for the silence since he'd forgotten his headphones on his desk. He passed conference rooms and sound-proofed cubbies made just for studying as well as three checkout desks manned by students.

There were copiers on each floor, but August bypassed the ones on the first floor as they were visible from the entryway and there was no Lucas. He wasn't on the second floor either. On the third floor, August headed to the most desolate part of the library, the section filled with how-to manuals and technical guides.

Even if August hadn't known where the copiers lived, he could have just followed the sounds of Lucas's frustrated curses. August smiled, picking up his pace. He rounded the corner just in time to watch Lucas kick the copier once, then again.

"This copier is notoriously temperamental. That's why it's back here in no man's land."

Lucas startled at August's voice but recovered quickly, voice sullen. "Of course, it is."

When Lucas smacked the top of the copier once more, August tugged him away, pulling him deeper into the stacks. "What's wrong with the faculty copier?"

"It's out of order." Lucas glared at the machine beside them as if it had broken the other copier.

"Why not use the one outside your office?"

Lucas blew out a breath through his nose. August hadn't ever seen him so on edge. "Because every time your friend sees me she tries to pump me for information about the two of us."

"Bianca?" August asked.

Lucas shrugged. "I guess. You two seemed cozy the day we met."

There was just the slightest hint of...something underneath his voice. Surely not jealousy. "Are you... Do you think I have a thing with my co-worker? Me? Do I seem the type?"

Lucas was uncharacteristically sulky. "How would I know? We barely know each other."

August studied him carefully. "What's going on? You were

fine when we left my father's house. Now, you're pouting and beating up office equipment like it owes you money."

"I just can't stop thinking about how more women have gone missing. Because of me. I spent weeks just trying to pretend none of this was happening. I was selfish and stupid, and now, more people are going to suffer and die because of me."

August cupped Lucas's face in his hands, backing him into an aisle full of ancient books with yellow pages. He could smell their age. "You did everything you could. You got yourself thrown into a psychiatric facility trying to save those women, trying to take a killer off the streets," he reminded him.

"I should have lied. I should have found another way to let them know it was him. I could have…" Lucas trailed off, hand flailing helplessly.

"Could have what? Manufactured evidence? Caught him in the act? He doesn't work alone. They would have killed you and never looked back. You did the right thing."

Lucas clenched his teeth together until the muscle in his jaw ticked, swallowing hard before he said, "You would have just slit his throat and been done with it. No, you would have killed him slowly, made it hurt, then killed him, and these new women would have never run across him."

August shook his head. "Because I've been programmed to kill. I don't investigate people, I don't have to prove anything to anybody. Noah, Calliope, and Thomas find the cases, they find the evidence. I get a file folder and a plan. Then I do what I do." August examined Lucas, hoping to

see some of the strain leave his face, but it only seemed to grow worse. "Lucas, you've been given a gift. You can see the best and worst of people with a touch. You can do something less than one percent of the population can do. You're kind of miraculous. And even though my father didn't say anything, I guarantee he's already thinking of how he could use you in the family."

Tears rolled down Lucas's cheeks, his face growing hot beneath August's hands before he wiggled from his grip. "You're just saying that to make me feel better."

August scoffed. "I'm saying that because it's true. I'm the last person anybody would come to if they wanted to feel better."

Lucas sniffled, wiping at his face, dropping his head back against some old books. "You seem to be the only thing that does make me feel better anymore."

August's brows knitted together. It was a compliment, but it was said with such misery it confused him. "That's a bad thing?"

Lucas gave a humorless laugh. "I'm sleeping with one serial killer and playing head games with another. We haven't even known each other a week, but when I feel like there's a hole in my chest, you're the only person I want to call."

Something about Lucas's words sent a rush of fierce possession through August, some deep primitive need to claim what was his right there. Lucas wanted to call him, just him. He was Lucas's person. He surged forward, crashing their mouths together, groaning when Lucas's lips softened, then yielded beneath his with a sound of surprise.

August crowded him up against the stacks, growling when he could feel Lucas's cock hardening against his hip. He dragged his lips away to kiss along his jaw before tugging the shell of his ear with his teeth. When his hand went to Lucas's belt, he snatched August's wrist. "What are you doing?" he whispered.

August frowned in confusion, glancing down at his hands. "I'm opening your pants. Why are you suddenly whispering? I assure you, nobody's coming into this section of the library. The only reason anybody comes to the third floor is to read periodicals, and those are way on the other side." Lucas gazed warily over August's shoulder, but his fingers loosened on August's wrist.

"We can't do this," Lucas said, though it was half-hearted.

August nosed behind his ear. "You know you want my mouth on you right now," he murmured. "Think about it. Picture me on my knees, your cock on my tongue, my lips working over you, sucking you down, working you until you come down my throat."

"Jesus, August…"

August's cock throbbed at the pleading in Lucas's tone. "You said you like me on my knees for you. I like it, too. Let me make you feel better. Let me taste you."

This time, when August undid Lucas's pants, he didn't protest, but his breath quickened and his hands fisted at his sides. August dropped to his knees, practically purring at the way Lucas combed his fingers through his hair, gazing down at him, lips parted and pupils blown wide.

"Fuck, I really do like you on your knees for me," Lucas

managed, his tongue darting out to wet his lower lip.

August pushed the tails of Lucas's shirt up and kissed his belly before tugging Lucas's pants and underwear just far enough out of the way not to hinder him. With Lucas freed, August ran his tongue up the underside of his length. Lucas gave a low groan, his head thumping hard against the shelf.

August smiled, teasing just under the head of his cock before sucking it into his mouth, tongue playing with his slit until he tasted the bitter tang of his pre-cum.

August hummed his approval, then took him to the back of his throat. Lucas's hoarse shout echoed in the quiet of the library. August didn't stop, just reached up to slap his hand over Lucas's open mouth. August sucked him in long, hard pulls, working him with purpose. Lucas lost his mind behind August's palm, his muffled moans and whines driving August crazy.

He could have done this all day if they were anywhere else. He craved the heavy weight of Lucas's cock on his tongue, the taste and scent of his skin, the way the hair at the base tickled his nose. He could revel in every part of Lucas forever and never get tired of him. But he couldn't draw this out. There wasn't time. He had a class in fifteen minutes and he was guessing Lucas had other things to do as well. When Lucas began to fuck himself between August's lips, he relaxed his throat, letting Lucas chase his release.

The closer Lucas got, the noisier he grew. Some twisted part of August wished he could take his hand off, wished he could let the world hear how good they were together, how good he was at keeping Lucas satisfied. August wanted the

world to know Lucas belonged to him, that they belonged to each other.

Lucas's hips stuttered, his hands tugging hard on August's hair as he gave one final long moan behind his hand, then flooded August's mouth. He swallowed it all and then some, doing his best to savor every drop.

By the time he dropped his hand from Lucas's face, he was sagged against the shelf, sucking in heavy breaths. August carefully tucked Lucas back into his clothes, his own erection painfully obvious in his slim fit trousers.

Lucas pulled August to his feet and attempted to open his pants, clearly determined to take care of it for him. August batted his hand away. "No. You can return the favor tonight. I'll be fine. This was about you."

"Thank you." Lucas threw his arms around August's neck and kissed him deeply before dropping his cheek to August's shoulder.

Warmth spread through him. He wrapped his arms around Lucas in return, surprised when he didn't immediately break the hold. He just clung to him. August found he enjoyed having Lucas bundled in his arms. He smelled like soap and spicy cologne, and the heat of his body bled through August's clothes in a way that made him feel content. Suddenly, thoughts of all the things they could do together later in the privacy of August's apartment flooded his head until he shook them away.

He needed to be less turned on, not more.

"Are you okay?" August asked when Lucas seemed determined to just stay in August's embrace all afternoon.

"I just need you to let me do this a little while longer. I can't usually hug anybody because my shields slip, and then I just learn all of their cringey thoughts."

August rubbed his cheek against Lucas's hair. "But not me?"

Lucas shook his head against August's shoulder. "No, not you. You're just worrying about making sure I'm not late to my next class and thinking about how much you like this and some surprisingly dirty things you want to do with me tonight. Which I'm totally on board with, by the way."

"You can get all that just from hugging me?" August asked.

"Yeah. Your thoughts are very clear to me. Clearer every time we touch, if I'm being honest."

"Is that a bad thing?" August asked.

"Only in that I don't want it to suddenly disappear," Lucas admitted.

August squeezed him tighter. "It will only disappear if you run."

"I'm right here," Lucas said softly.

It was on the tip of August's tongue to make him promise, but he didn't want to deal with the fallout if Lucas refused. "I should get to class. Do you want to walk down with me? I can show you the copier that works."

Lucas stepped back and gave a hesitant nod. "Yeah, I have to have these for my next class."

August held out his hand, relieved when Lucas took it. Some part of him had thought he would refuse, that he wouldn't want others to see that they were together. Truly together. Which they were. Even if Lucas didn't know it yet.

Shit, could he read that, too?

"Yes," Lucas said, amused.

"Sorry."

Lucas snorted. "No, you're not."

August smiled. "Okay, I'm not, but I would be if I could be."

Lucas rolled his eyes, but there was a lightness to him that hadn't been there a few minutes before, and that was all August cared about.

After they left work, Lucas was eerily quiet. He kept glancing back at the shoebox in the backseat like it was a wild animal that might attack him if he turned his back on it for too long. August assumed Lucas's afternoon class had gone okay after their library encounter, but he didn't want to break the silence in case it hadn't. He just wasn't sure what the right answer was in this situation.

The relationship books he'd read said it was customary to ask about a significant other's day, but given how theirs had started, it seemed absurd to drop a question so mundane. Still, he didn't want him to think that he wasn't attempting to do all the things real boyfriends did. When he looked at Lucas, August wished he could feel the same worry and empathy that a normal person would, instead of just this insatiable curiosity to poke at him, to know what it was he was thinking or feeling.

Thomas would tell August that people weren't lab rats to

be experimented on. But August didn't think of Lucas that way. Not really. But he didn't know how he was supposed to give him what he needed—like the relationship books said—if he didn't test Lucas to see what worked best for him. Thomas would tell him to just talk to Lucas.

He managed to hold his tongue until they began to creep along the cars parked outside a clean, gated apartment complex. When August had said he was going to place the GPS tracker on Kohn's car, Lucas had insisted on coming with him. He didn't mind the company, but he was concerned there might be an accidental encounter that could compromise their element of surprise. Still, he couldn't refuse him. He just liked being in his presence.

August pulled up to a call box outside the complex and clicked through the directory, starting with A. It took two tries before somebody answered the phone and pressed a button to open the gate for them without question.

"How did you know that would work?" Lucas asked.

August pulled forward. "I didn't. After a few duds, I would have just had Calliope hack the gate. But people are notoriously lackadaisical about letting people inside their communities. They assume they're there for a reason or rationalize by saying it's not like their doors are unlocked."

Lucas nodded but fell silent once again. They crept slowly through the maze of apartments looking for Kohn's building. Lucas nodded to a two-story walk-up on the left. "Over there. It's that one."

August scanned the parking lot. The spaces weren't assigned. "Now, we just have to find his car."

Lucas continued to stare out the window. "What if he's not home?"

"Then we wait."

"What if he's out there hurting somebody else?" Lucas said again, anxious.

August sighed. "Then there's nothing we can do about it."

Moody silence returned. August backed his borrowed car into a parking space and turned off his lights. His Mercedes cost over a hundred grand. While it was a fairly upscale development, his car would have stood out and the last thing they wanted was to be noticeable. Instead, they'd taken his father's Ford pickup truck, one of several cars he owned.

They were better off looking for Kohn's car on foot. It shouldn't be too hard to find a Black Lincoln Navigator in a sea of Toyotas and Hondas. It did beg the question of why Kohn drove a car that was bound to stand out like that while living in such a nondescript apartment complex.

When he glanced over to see Lucas staring out the window into the darkness, he finally asked, "Can I touch you?"

Lucas glanced over at him, startled. August winced at the abruptness of his question. "You don't have to ask," Lucas said. "I told you, I'm not afraid of your thoughts."

August didn't want to tell Lucas that there might come a time when he was not only afraid of August's thoughts but disgusted, maybe even horrified. But that was a discussion for another time. He slid his hand over Lucas's thigh, squeezing. "Are you alright?"

"No. But I will be. I think. It's just hard to not feel responsible for those missing women."

August shook his head. "You have to stop—"

Lucas cut him off, pointing as he said, "August…" August followed his finger to see a black Navigator coming around the corner, heading towards the exit. "He's leaving."

August waited a good thirty seconds before he turned on his lights and crept out of his parking space. "Good. Let's see where he's going."

August did his best to keep his distance while they were winding their way back out of the complex. He turned onto the main road just in time to see Kohn making a right at the street light ahead. He sped up so he didn't lose him, making sure to keep a few cars between them so as not to alert Kohn of his tail.

When they entered the highway headed north, Lucas looked at August in confusion. August had no answers, so he concentrated on the road. He could lose Kohn at any exit if he wasn't careful. Lucas's hands fisted in his lap, his face tense as he squinted through the windshield.

They drove for a good half hour before Kohn took an exit in the middle of nowhere with only an obnoxiously large truck stop that touted showers, entertainment, and a twenty-four hour diner. August followed, but when Kohn parked outside the diner, he circled around to the convenience store before backtracking. By the time they parked, Kohn was sitting at a booth in the back.

August once more backed his truck into the parking lot facing the window before extinguishing his headlights. Kohn sat alone at a booth. August could see why Lucas was surprised the man had flirted with him. He was tall

and muscular, his brown hair shaved into a high and tight military cut. He looked...unapproachable. He sipped a coffee for approximately fifteen minutes before another car pulled up. A souped up black and silver Mazda RX-7 purred into the spot directly beside Kohn's Navigator. Somebody had sunk a lot of money into that car.

"Who's Mr. Fast and Furious?" Lucas asked.

The man was tall and broad, with tattooed muscles, a white tank top, and saggy well-worn jeans. He strode confidently to the back booth where Kohn sat, sliding into the seat opposite and flagging down a chunky silver-haired server, who gave him a disgusted look.

"Do you think that's him?" Lucas asked in a rough whisper, as if the man might hear him. "His partner?"

August distractedly noted that Lucas had a tendency to whisper when he grew nervous. "You tell me."

"He doesn't fit the typical profile. Look at him, he's confident, moves with authority, doesn't seem to defer to Kohn in any way." Lucas shook his head. "Maybe I've got this all wrong. It doesn't make any sense."

August didn't say anything, just continued to watch the two. When the car beside the stranger left, August crept his truck into the space beside it. The windows were tinted. A man like that was bound to have a security system on his car. He had an idea. He hopped from the truck and moved to the car's window, using his phone to snap a picture of the VIN number just below the windshield.

Once he was back in the pickup, he hit a button on his phone. The ringing filled the cab as Lucas frowned at him.

Calliope answered on the second ring. "'lo?" she said around a mouthful of something.

August figured he could skip the politeness. "Is there a way to bypass a car's alarm in, say, the next five to ten minutes?"

"Do you have the VIN number?" she asked.

"I just sent a picture."

"Hold please."

They listened to her type for a solid minute. "The vehicle is owned by Vasili Kudashev. Age sixty. Russian import/export guy."

August frowned, gaze returning to the man in the booth. This was definitely not a sixty-year-old Russian. August supposed the man inside could have stolen it, but he also doubted a sixty-year-old man was going to be into street racing, and that car was most definitely used for racing. "Does he have a son?"

More typing. "Um, no. He has a daughter and a grandson. Daughter is thirty-eight, grandson is fifteen."

August shook his head, trying to make the pieces fit. "I need to get into that car. Tell me you can turn off the alarm."

"Hm, looks like he put a five thousand dollar unhackable alarm on that car." August blew out an irritated breath, but then she said, "Luckily, this system relies on an app. An easily hackable app. Give me ten minutes and you can have total control of his vehicle. Hell, you can drive away with it if you like."

With that, she was gone. They sat, watching the two men talk emphatically about something, Kohn jabbing his finger against the table as the man across from him dipped

French fries into a milkshake like the two were on a date.

August received a text that said: **Car's all yours.**

"Keep an eye on them. Let me know if our friend starts to leave."

Lucas didn't answer, just nodded, gaze glued to the two figures inside. August didn't waste any time. He went in on the driver's side, looking around for anything that would give any clue as to who this new player was. His registration was also made out to this Vasili, but the insurance was with a company named D&G Ltd. August knew a bullshit company when he heard one. He flipped through the owner's manual, hoping something might come loose, but there were no papers. He was just about to close the glove box when he noticed a piece of paper wedged in the back. It was an invoice from an auto parts store. The customer name was Devon Nicholls.

Lucas rolled the window down. "We gotta go. She just brought the check."

August did his best to replace everything exactly as he'd found it, closing the door and creeping back behind his truck just as Devon Nicholls pushed open the door of the diner. August made it back inside just as Nicholls deactivated his alarm system. Or, at least, thought he had. He didn't even glance in their direction. Just hopped in his car and tore out of the parking lot fast enough to leave tire marks on the pavement.

Inside, Kohn was settling the check, chatting with the server who had looked at Devon Nicholls with such disgust. Lucas reached for the GPS locator so fast, August didn't

even have time to process what he was doing. He jumped from the truck, ducking down as he raced across the empty parking space to Kohn's Navigator.

Like a horror movie, August watched as Kohn strode towards the front door. He looked to Lucas, who was fixing the tracker high up in the wheel well where it wouldn't be noticed. Shit. August left the truck, his brain running through a million scenarios. If Kohn had seen him, they were fucked.

August rushed towards Kohn, spinning him around. "Oh, sorry, man. You wouldn't happen to know if there's a payphone in there, would you? My phone died and it's an emergency."

Kohn blinked at him in confusion. "What? No. I don't know."

From over Kohn's shoulder, he watched Lucas close the truck door silently. "Yeah, sure. Sorry. Have a nice night."

August had no choice but to enter the restaurant and wait. Luckily, Kohn seemed to lose interest in him immediately, leaving the parking lot as quickly as his friend.

Once back in the truck, he turned on Lucas. "You're crazy. You could have gotten yourself killed."

Lucas gave him a pissy look. "He wasn't going to kill me in the middle of a diner parking lot. He's having too much fun leaving me presents. I just want to know where he goes from now on."

August sighed, hooking his hand behind Lucas's neck, tugging him close enough to slant their lips together. Lucas didn't resist, but he did look confused when August released

him. "What was that for?"

August shrugged. "For being you, I guess. Can we go home now?"

Lucas nodded, exhaustion etched on his face. "Yes, please."

SIXTEEN
LUCAS

When August had said home, somehow Lucas hadn't expected it to be August's home, even though he'd said as much that morning. Had it only been that morning? It was strange how his days stretched longer and longer but part of him still felt like he was hurtling to some unknown finish line that filled him with dread.

August's apartment building was definitely luxurious. The building itself was tall and shiny with huge floor to ceiling windows and a lobby as big as any hotel's. When they came to a halt at the entrance, August left the keys and came around, opening Lucas's door for him before nodding at the valet. They passed an actual uniformed doorman. Lucas didn't even know buildings still had doormen.

August took his hand as they entered, completely oblivious to the shocked expressions on the staff's faces. Had August never brought somebody home with him? The thought of that filled him with a sort of smug satisfaction. In the elevator, August stood behind him, his arms around

his waist, his chin hooked over his shoulder as they seemed to keep climbing higher and higher.

Lucas stared at their reflection in the mirrored doors. They were so different in every way. Dark and light. Apathy and empathy. Too much and never enough. Still, Lucas craved August's touch, his obsession, the safety of knowing somebody was on his side. Did it make him a bad person for taking what August offered so willingly?

When August pushed in a code on the keypad next to his door, Lucas had no idea what to expect when it opened. He'd imagined August's surroundings would be minimalist, tidy, lots of white space, maybe stacks of books. Guys like August tended to be rigid in their routine and in their decor. They often color coded things right down to their underwear.

What Lucas found was anything but sparse and minimalist. August's entire apartment was black. The walls, the furnishings, the cabinetry. Even the rug on the wooden floors. But there were strange hints of warmth. A dark wood mantel with plants spilling over the edge. Light fixtures made of wood wrapped with black cords attached to bare bulbs that dangled over the enormous dining table and the stark white countertops in the otherwise black kitchen.

Somehow, the black paint, the raw wood, and the plants made the cavernous space seem more organic. Lucas had forgotten that August wasn't the face he showed the world. Well, he wasn't only that face. This was the darkest part of August, the real part. The one who didn't think anything of having jars of what looked like remains lining bookshelves next to skulls covered in crystal, small antique figurines,

and books that looked moments from disintegration.

"This is a very dark academia aesthetic, Mr. Mulvaney," Lucas teased.

Lucas tried to take it all in. While the color palette was very monochromatic, there were several pieces of art, ornate gold mirrors, and a strange collection of trinkets. But the piece that snagged Lucas's attention was the collection of swords, knives, and other weapons arranged over the fireplace like an art installation.

Lucas's gaze went wide. "Are those actual weapons?"

"You don't like it?" August asked, frowning. "Noah and Adam thought you'd find it too much. We can change it to your taste if you like. The black just makes it possible to cut the noise."

"The noise?" Lucas echoed, beginning to prowl the space.

"Harsh lights, sound, too much color, it all makes my head noisy. Makes it hard to think. I find the absence of color soothing."

Right. August didn't like being overly stimulated. It made sense with all the things going on up there. "I like it. It's very…you."

"I like being surrounded by my favorite things. My father calls them my treasures. Things I found over the years that I immediately took to. Things I refused to part with, no matter what."

"Like me?" Lucas said, regretting the words almost immediately.

The way August's gaze snapped to him, raking over Lucas with possessiveness, made him harden immediately. "Yes.

Exactly like you."

"Are you going to put me on one of your shelves?"

August shook his head. "No, I much prefer you in my bed."

Lucas prowled closer. "I'm pretty sure I still owe you from this afternoon."

"As much as I want to cash in that IOU, I think maybe we should deal with the shoebox in the room."

Lucas swallowed hard, glancing over at the box. "I know I need to handle it. I know. It just hurts. I know that doesn't make me sound very tough or manly, but the pain isn't just physical. It's…psychic. I don't just feel their physical pain, I feel their emotional pain, their exhaustion, their terror, every regret they've ever had in that moment."

August leaned forward and kissed his forehead. The gesture was so spontaneous, it made Lucas's heart skip. "About that. I have an idea. But you would need to trust me."

"I do trust you," Lucas said, surprised that he meant it. Maybe not surprised. It was clear Lucas would never be the object of August's temper or rage, but that didn't mean he was trustworthy. But Lucas did trust him. With his life. And his heart. And, apparently, with his head.

"Let's go in the bedroom." August grabbed the box from the table and led Lucas to another lush room.

This room was also dark, the walls a dark green, like some exotic plant found deep in a rainforest. The sheets were a stark white but the coverlet a patterned black velvet. Like the other room, it had wood accents, broken up only with the plant life surrounding the space. He hadn't expected August to have plants or anything that required care. "Do

you take care of all these yourself?"

August nodded. "They're good for oxygenation and purification. Why?"

Lucas looked at the healthy greenery. "Plants require a certain amount of babying."

August scoffed. "Keeping plants alive is a formula. As long as I know the steps required, I can give them what they need. And with a photographic memory like mine, I always know what they need."

Lucas chewed on his bottom lip for a moment before he asked, "Is that what you do with me? Apply the formulas you found in your relationship books?"

August set the shoebox in the center of the bed. "There's no one simple formula for you. I'm constantly having to test the theories and see what you respond to best."

Lucas studied August, his stomach dipping at his blunt explanation. "So, I'm like a science project?"

August sat on the edge of the bed and dragged Lucas between his spread thighs. "What you are is mine. It's my job to make you happy. I lack the capacity to do so on my own. I can't love. I can't feel guilt or empathy or remorse, any of the things that might help me understand what you need. All I have is research and context clues, which I'm not very good at interpreting. But I can give you what you need. I'll do whatever it takes. But I can't do it without help. Testing my theories is all I know."

Lucas's heart skipped at August's explanation. He carded his fingers through August's hair. "You're surprisingly sweet for somebody who 'lacks the capacity' to make me happy

on your own."

August wrapped his arms around his waist and just held him like he had earlier in the library.

After a few minutes, Lucas pulled away. "What was your idea?" Lucas's eyebrows shot up when August stood and began to undress. "I thought we were dealing with the box first?"

August smirked. "We are. I just figured you'd want to be comfortable for this next part."

When August was in his underwear, he looked at Lucas expectantly. He sighed and stripped down, crawling onto the bed, careful to avoid the shoebox, as he settled between August's legs, his back to August's chest. "Now what?"

"You can pull sensations from me, right? Use me as a buffer. Like I do with my music and the rest of the world. I'll be your psychic headphones."

Lucas snickered at the ridiculousness of the statement. "Psychic headphones?"

The idea was silly. There was no way something like that would work. Except, it already had in August's office when he'd showed him his frozen lake. "Fine, but if there's a severed foot or hand in there, all bets are off."

August lifted the box, testing its weight, giving it a slight shake. "It doesn't feel like a severed appendage," he said with an authority Lucas didn't dare question.

"Okay," he said finally. "How do we do this?"

August circled his arms around Lucas's torso, his palms running along his chest and belly. "Did you find the lake soothing?"

Lucas let his head drop back against August's shoulder.

"Yes."

"Then just close your eyes and focus on me."

Lucas let his lids flutter closed, shivering instinctively when the icy wind of August's psyche hit him. Lucas wondered if everybody could conjure this level of white noise at will or if August's genius gave him an almost supernatural edge over the rest of the world. Or maybe it was his psychopathy. Either way, Lucas found it easy to melt into his head.

Just like before, August stood behind him on the bank of this frozen lake, holding him just as he did in real life. Everything was so real, Lucas thought he could reach out and feel the drops of water pooling off the barren tree branches to form icicles. The wind whistled but Lucas didn't feel cold anymore, just serene.

He wasn't sure how long they stood there, but when August set the shoebox between Lucas's splayed legs, it suddenly joined them in this snowscape. His stomach dropped as his hands hovered over the box.

August pressed his words against Lucas's ear. "I'm right here. Just remember I can't see what you see so you'll have to talk me through it."

Lucas nodded, almost afraid to speak. He flipped the lid off the box, unable to hide his surprise when he saw the object within was just a shoe. Part of him knew it was never *just* anything with Kohn, but he'd expected something more gruesome.

It was a sky-high platform shoe made of clear acrylic, like if Cinderella had become a stripper. There was a butterfly

charm hanging from a chain that dangled from the back, at the heel. Lucas swallowed hard, hand hovering over the shoe, willing himself to pick it up.

"You can do this. Focus on what doesn't belong. Remember? You're ready this time. This isn't anything new to you. You've done it a thousand times before."

August was right. This wasn't anything new. Kohn had caught him off guard last time. He was ready this time. He picked up the shoe, sucking in a breath as the first image hit him. "A woman. She's leaning into the window of an old truck. It smells like loose nicotine and stale beer. She has on a cheap pink wig, like for a Halloween costume. And a blue cotton dress. These heels. Now, she's in the truck. Bench seat. An old radio is playing classic rock. He lights her cigarette. She's laughing. She's not afraid of him at all." He hissed as electricity jolted through him. "Pain. Blackness. He must have knocked her out."

The next images were like a strobe light, throbbing in and out of focus. He groaned as a wave of nausea washed over him. "I'm right here," August promised.

Lucas leaned back against him, stepping out of his memories to look out over the peace of August's lake.

After a moment, he plugged back in, only, this time, he was her. "Something metal is pressing against my back. It's like a grate digging into my skin. My arms are over my head, my shoulders ache. It smells like sweat and blood and urine. And fear. Does fear have a smell? I can see him. He's right there. He's wearing a...bag on his head, with the eyes and mouth cut out."

"He's fucking with them? Using it to heighten their fear?" August asked.

"It should be ridiculous but it's terrifying. When he takes a girl, she doesn't come back. I know I won't be coming back. He's usually dressed casually, but now, he's shirtless and wearing leather pants, like some kind of medieval executioner."

August's hand petted through Lucas's hair. "Putting on a show, maybe?"

"I'm scared. And so fucking thirsty. I just want some water. I ask for it but he ignores me." Lucas whimpered. "He's not dragging it out for my benefit, he's moving around, busy, like he's performing some kind of ritual or routine."

"What's he doing?"

"He's leaning over…adjusting something in the corner of the room maybe. He's not even paying attention to me, just making himself busy. I can't see what he's doing. He has all these…tools on the wall. Homemade. Crude. Terrifying. He hasn't used them on me yet, but I know I'm next. I know this is the end for me." He couldn't stop the sob that escaped. "My mom. She won't know what happened to me. She'll think I left her to take care of herself. She'll be worried when I don't come home."

"Shh," August soothed.

"He flips a switch and the whole room is bathed in red. I'm so scared, he's kneeling in front of me…"

"What's he doing?" August asks.

"He's… Jesus. He's taking off her shoe. He's doing this for me. This is for me. He wanted me to see all of this."

Lucas launched the shoe off the bed with a snarl, knocking the shoebox away and wrenching himself from August's grasp to pace in front of August's bed. "I'm so fucking sick of this shit. Why doesn't he just come after me directly? Why is he doing this? You should just fucking kill him. No, fuck it. *I* should just kill him. I want to kill him, August. I want to watch him writhe in fucking agony. I want to watch him bleed. I want it to hurt. I need it to fucking hurt."

August was there suddenly, holding his face. "We can do that. We *will* do that. I swear to you. I can show you a million ways to make him scream."

That shouldn't have been hot. There was nothing sexy about what he'd seen but he was jacked up on adrenaline and fury. And August was there. "Fuck me," Lucas whispered. "I know I said I'd take care of you but I need you to make this stop. I feel like I'm going crazy."

"Fucking you isn't exactly a hardship," August promised before crashing their lips together, pulling back to say, "I don't have anything for you to subdue me…"

Lucas shook his head. "No. We're done with that. You don't need it. You're not as scary as you think you are."

August's nostrils flared as he spun Lucas around, dragging him back against him before sinking his teeth into his throat. "Yes, I really fucking am."

"Then show me," Lucas taunted.

Lucas prayed August didn't refuse, couldn't handle anything less than whatever brutality August was willing to give him. He wanted to be punished. He wanted to drown out the visions still swimming in his head. He wanted

August to fill him up, hold him down. No, he fucking needed it, *needed* him to fuck the anger and rage and nervous energy out of him before he lost his fucking mind.

August threaded one hand in Lucas's hair while the other one plunged into his underwear, wrapping around his rapidly hardening cock. "Last chance."

Lucas canted his hips, fucking into August's fist. "I'm not changing my mind."

August's hand slipped free and Lucas mourned the loss. When his underwear pooled around his ankles, he stepped free before August's hand settled between his shoulder blades, bending him over until he was forced to brace his hands on the comforter.

Fuck.

August draped himself over Lucas, biting at his ear. "Fuck. You look good like this. Bent over, vulnerable. What was it you said? Completely at my mercy?"

Lucas shivered but not from fear. August's fingers were tugging at his balls, massaging them between his fingers, slipping farther back to tease roughly over Lucas's hole.

Then he was gone, leaving him completely exposed. Lucas watched him in his periphery as he stalked to his side table and grabbed something before returning, dropping to his knees behind him.

Lucas sucked in a sharp breath as August's teeth sank into his ass cheek. August gave a satisfied rumble, then soothed over the marks with his tongue. The pain/pleasure of it was dizzying, making his cock throb, pre-cum oozing obscenely onto August's pristine black comforter.

Before Lucas could recover, August spread him open and laved over his hole with a laser focus that had him moaning long and low, pushing back on August's nimble tongue. "Oh, fuck."

August locked his hands around Lucas's waist, dragging him closer, fucking his tongue against his entrance, licking and sucking at it like he couldn't get enough.

"More," Lucas begged, voice ragged. "Fuck me."

Lucas wasn't sure August heard him at first, but then his mouth disappeared and two slick fingers impaled him in one hard push. Lucas couldn't stop the rough sound that fell from his lips. "Stop being fucking gentle. I'm ready. I want your dick, not your fingers."

August was on his feet in one graceful move, his fingers never leaving Lucas's body. His hand came around Lucas's throat, pulling him upright, just as he slipped his fingers free. Before Lucas could say a word, August impaled him on his cock in one hard thrust, driving the air from his lungs and forcing him up on the balls of his feet. "What was that?" August growled against his throat.

Lucas couldn't speak with August's fingers gripping his throat and his hips pistoning in and out of him in a brutal rhythm that robbed him of thought. This was what Lucas needed. August wasn't hurting him, he was…possessing him. He was inside him and all around him. He controlled the pleasure he felt and the air he breathed.

Suddenly, August's hips faltered. "Fuck."

The sudden change in August's tone scared Lucas for some reason. "What's wrong?"

"I forgot the condom."

Something loosened in Lucas's chest. "I'm negative."

"Me too," August swore. "But I'll stop."

Lucas paused for only as long as it took to process August's words. "No. Don't stop." Then, more forcefully. "Keep going. Seriously, fuck me."

The change in August was instantaneous. He pulled free of Lucas only long enough to push him onto the mattress and follow him down, forcing Lucas's legs apart with his own so he could drive back into him as he pinned him to the bed, surging into him relentlessly.

"Fuck, I wish you could feel how fucking hot and tight you are inside. You're so fucking perfect," August muttered, voice strained with exertion.

August planted a hand between Lucas's shoulder blades, pulling almost all the way out before driving back in, the head of his cock scraping along Lucas's prostate with every pass. Lucas couldn't speak, couldn't think, couldn't stop the helpless cries falling from his lips. Each thrust set his soul on fire, made his dick throb where it lay trapped between his belly and the blanket.

August's full weight fell heavy over him once more. "It's okay, you know. It's always okay. If you want to know what I'm feeling, what I'm thinking. Do it. You can be in my head if you want."

Lucas didn't hesitate, just let go of his already tenuous control, a harsh groan falling from his lips as deep drugging waves sucked him under until he was just pure sensation. He could never explain the spine tingling, toe curling

euphoria that glowed hot along every fucking nerve ending. He was being fucked and, somehow, fucking at the same time. A three way between two people.

He could feel the primal, near feral possessiveness August felt as he drove into him as much as he could feel the actual pleasure coursing through August as he chased his release. A release that would have him emptying himself in Lucas's body. He could feel how much that thought excited August and therefore excited Lucas, too. The intimacy of the experience made his chest tight and his cock ache, overwhelming every part of him.

August was close, so close. Lucas could feel it like a coil winding tighter and tighter inside him, could hear it in August's sharp breaths and feel it in the spikes of pleasure peaking through him, the way he held him tighter and buried his face against Lucas's throat.

August's hips fell off rhythm and then he was coming hard, spilling inside Lucas, both of them giving harsh shouts as August's teeth sank into the tender flesh of Lucas's shoulder.

August shivered on top of him for a moment before slipping free of his body and rolling him over, clearly intent on taking care of him, unaware that he already had. His brows shot up in surprise as he saw Lucas's spent cock. "Did you…"

He'd come untouched, somehow taking August's pleasure as his own. "Yeah, who knew that was even possible."

August kissed him deep, licking into his mouth. "That's so fucking hot."

Lucas chuckled, suddenly exhausted in his bones. "I'm glad you think so."

"You can't fall asleep. You haven't eaten," August chastised.

Lucas's lids were at half-mast, his words slurred, brain sluggish. "I'll eat tomorrow…"

Whatever August said was lost on Lucas as he was already being dragged down into a deep sleep.

SEVENTEEN

AUGUST

August was up early, per usual. He did his time on the treadmill, then took a shower, smiling when he saw Lucas hadn't moved an inch. He was still on his back, naked, arms thrown up over his head like he'd surrendered to sleep, snoring deeply. After yesterday, he'd clearly needed the rest.

Once August dried off, he carefully settled over him, kissing his slack mouth. Lucas didn't even open his eyes, just his legs, letting August settle between them, wrapping his arms around August's neck. He let Lucas feel how hard he was. He moaned at the sensation of August's hard cock against his own.

"Morning," Lucas rasped against August's ear. "You smell good."

"So do you," August promised, burying his face against Lucas's neck to rock against him with intention.

"I sincerely doubt that," Lucas countered, opening his legs wider to get August closer, as if letting him know he was on board with whatever they were doing.

"Did you sleep okay?" August asked, continuing the slow roll of his hips.

"Yeah, I can't remember the last time J slept so hard." Lucas brought his legs up to hook around August's thighs, heels brushing the backs of his legs with each lazy movement.

If this was what having a person of his own felt like, August could see why Adam was so protective of Noah. August couldn't get enough of Lucas. He was warm and sexy and—despite his claims—smelled incredible. Just his scent drove August crazy. "I like you in my bed," he managed, hating that he couldn't better articulate how much of an understatement that was.

"I like me in your bed, too," Lucas said, breath hitching as he rose up to meet August's downward motion. He ground himself against Lucas, harder this time, just to hear his low moan. "Mm, fuck. Do that again."

August chuckled, gently tugging on Lucas's earlobe, repeating the motion. "Like that?"

"Just like that," Lucas gasped, his words almost a plea.

August captured his mouth in a kiss that lingered, his arms coming around Lucas's shoulders to hold him steady as they lazily worked against each other. "Do you have classes this morning?" August asked against his lips.

"One this afternoon. You?" Lucas asked.

"I have one this morning and another this afternoon, but I'll have my TA teach it. Let's just stay in bed all morning."

"We can't. Can we?" Lucas asked, breathless but hopeful.

"Oh, we definitely can."

After that, there wasn't any more talking. There was

nothing frantic about their movements until they were moving faster, panting harder, working against each other until they came one after the other.

Even then, they made no effort to move. August lay collapsed on Lucas, cum drying uncomfortably on their skin. He definitely needed another shower, but he was just going to bask in the afterglow a little bit longer, then talk Lucas into joining him.

"Do you want to order breakfast in?"

"Meh," Lucas said. "Let's just stop by Cricket's on the way to class later. I don't want to move."

August's phone began to chirp and vibrate along the side table. He groaned, extending his arm to snag it, swiping to answer without looking. "Yeah?"

There was a moment's hesitation. "Are you okay?" Calliope asked. "You sound out of breath. Did I catch you on the treadmill?"

August could feel Lucas shaking with laughter beneath him. "Yeah. Just finished. What's up?"

"Kohn arrived at work, so he's not out murdering any helpless women. But that guy you asked me to look into last night, Devon Nicholls, I got the info you asked for."

"Go ahead," August said, rolling off Lucas when he gently pressed a hand to his chest.

Calliope made a terse sound before saying, "So, this guy is the opposite of clean. He's been in and out of jail since he was *twelve years old*. Started with petty crimes, shoplifting, boosting cars, then he graduated to bigger stuff, like assault, domestic violence, and arson. He appears to be part of

some street racing gang, which I didn't know was a thing. An offshoot of the Aryan Brotherhood. And we all know how great those guys are. But he and his little band of thugs are local, involved in everything from drug dealing to gun running. And they are super unapologetic about it, if their social media accounts are anything to go by."

"So, why is a Nazi gangbanger driving the car of a squeaky clean Russian import/export guy, and why is he meeting with Kohn in the middle of the night?" Lucas asked loud enough for Calliope to hear.

"Oh," Calliope said, as if putting the pieces together. Her tone perked up at Lucas's presence. " Morning, Lucas."

"Morning," Lucas said, a small smile forming on his lips when August rolled his eyes. Calliope treated Noah like that as well. Like they were instantly a new addition to their little 'people with feelings' clique.

"As to your question, my guess is Mr. Russian isn't as clean as he wants the world to think he is. These guys usually like to keep themselves six degrees from the action," Calliope said. "They usually pay well, though, and Devon Nicholl's has a lot of money going in and out of his accounts despite not having paid taxes in years."

"That's a dangerous game," August said.

"Nah, federal time is a country club to these types. They're just as comfortable in jail as out. But what does that have to do with Kohn being a serial killer?" Lucas asked.

"I don't know...yet." Calliope continued to type as she talked. "But Nicholls has a bunch of sock puppet accounts."

"Sock puppet accounts?" August echoed.

"Dozens and dozens of fake online identities. Some of them are taking me pretty far down the rabbit hole of the darknet. I'm going through them all looking for any kind of slip up. These douchebags eventually get lazy. Hopefully, I'll find something to connect the two."

August looked at the sudden worry etched on Lucas's face, squeezing his thigh before saying, "Let me know when you do."

As soon as they disconnected, August rolled towards Lucas, dropping his head on his chest. "I swear, sometimes, it's like she's speaking another language."

Lucas's hand found its way into August's hair, scratching blunt nails over his scalp in a way that had him pushing up into his fingers like a cat. He never liked touching, but he couldn't get enough of Lucas's hands on him.

"Why don't you just read a book on coding and become a master hacker in an afternoon?" Lucas asked. "Then you'll speak her language."

August smiled. "It's already too crowded in my head. Besides, I still haven't figured out this whole love language thing. It's confusing. And that's coming from somebody who learned to speak Russian in a week."

Lucas's heartbeat accelerated beneath August's ear. "You don't have to keep stressing over my love language, whatever that is. You seem to speak fluent me."

August shook his head vehemently. "I don't, though. That's the problem. I am not like Adam or Atticus. My autism makes it impossible for me to pick up on the context clues like they do. That's why people think I'm…

weird. I need a book, a manual, a guide. I don't want to screw this up."

"You're not screwing this up," Lucas assured him. "I've… I've never in my life felt as comfortable as I do around you. Do you know what it's like to live in constant fear of touching people? It's exhausting. I don't have to be afraid with you. There's no deep, dark secrets."

August dropped a kiss on Lucas's chest. "I just want to make you happy."

"Why?" Lucas asked.

August frowned at the abrupt question. "What?"

"Why do you care so much about screwing this up? Psychopaths can't love, can't form love matches. Wouldn't you forget me eventually or, at least, become indifferent?"

August hated the strange shock of fear that rocketed through him at the thought. It wasn't said with any malice, more an academic curiosity with a tinge of anxiety.

Still, the thought of losing Lucas was something August couldn't quantify. "I would never forget you. And I certainly wouldn't become indifferent. I've spent just a few days with you and the thought of not seeing you every day is… It makes it hard to breathe." August swallowed hard, squeezing Lucas tighter. "You can't leave."

Lucas gave a heavy sigh, and then his lips were brushing the top of his head. "I'm not leaving."

"Ever," August said bluntly.

Another kiss landed on his head. "I'm right here."

Silence stretched between them for a long time before Lucas asked, "Did you really learn Russian in a week?"

"I learned to speak it in a week. Mastering writing it and speaking it conversationally took me almost a month."

There was another long pause before Lucas pressed, "Why Russian?"

August shrugged. "When I was nine, I became obsessed with Tolstoy. I wanted to read his works in his native tongue."

"You wanted to read Tolstoy at nine?" Lucas said, voice filled with wonder.

"I had already read Tolstoy. I wanted to read it again, in Russian."

Lucas snorted. "Wait? Didn't Tolstoy write in English?"

August smiled at that, tipping his head slightly to look up to where Lucas reclined on his pillow. It was so nice talking with somebody who cared about these things. "Yes. Tolstoy was a polyglot like me. He spoke English, French, and German, in addition to Russian. But he could read in a dozen other languages. I just fixated on this idea that I should read his books in Russian. I get hung up on these thoughts sometimes, and I can't let them go until I've done it. So…Russian."

"Is that why you have a degree in Russian Literature?"

August smiled. "No. I have a degree in Russian Literature because my father said I needed to look more well-rounded. To look like I had interests outside of the hard sciences."

Lucas snickered this time. "So, you thought you'd just minor in Russian literature. You couldn't just take, like, a film class or something?"

August shrugged, putting Lucas's hand back onto his head, hoping he would get the message. "I spoke Russian.

It seemed easy enough."

His lids fluttered as Lucas's fingers once more began to comb through his hair.

"Did you really get inducted into MENSA when you were six?"

August hesitated before saying, "No."

Lucas's fingers paused. "No?"

August sighed. "No. I was four. My father told people I was six."

Lucas's fingers slowed. "Why? Wouldn't that have been more impressive at four?"

"It's a long, convoluted story, most of which isn't mine to tell."

Lucas's fingers went back to scraping over August's scalp. "I have time. Tell me what you can?"

August only hesitated for a moment. "My father is like me in a lot of ways. He came from an…unstable home environment. Only, when they learned he was gifted, they brought in tutors to homeschool him, locked him away from his friends and siblings so he wasn't distracted from his studies, used him to impress their rich friends. He was attending college in Scotland when they died. He was fourteen."

Lucas curled in closer. "What does that have to do with your age?"

"Thomas had his doctorate before he was old enough to drink. He was obsessed with psychology, like you. When he met a woman doing groundbreaking research on sociopaths, he wanted to test her theories, wanted to know if there was a way to…fix people like me. But he knew, to do that, he'd

have to have total control over our environment like she had, and no review board was going to give approval of a study like that. And he didn't want us to feel like we were growing up as actual science projects. He wanted us to feel...supported, to have the affection he never got."

"Makes sense," Lucas said, though his tone was hesitant, like it didn't entirely make sense.

"As you can imagine, no adoption agency was going to hand a bunch of damaged children to a man who was barely more than a child himself. So, he went about it through slightly shadier means. His money bought him access to people who had an interest in his research and who also weren't fond of committee oversight. Kids disappear from the system all the time. My father helped us reappear without questions."

"So, how old are you, really?"

August shrugged. "Thirty, I think. Maybe thirty-one. I never knew my actual birthday."

"Do you remember anything about your original family?"

August nodded. "That's the curse of an eidetic memory. I remember everything. My mom was...very sick. She was schizophrenic. She thought I was some kind of supernatural creature because I was far too advanced for my age."

"She was unmedicated?"

August ran a finger over Lucas's belly. "I imagine so. She was truly afraid of me. That much was obvious. She felt bad about it. She didn't want to hurt me. She just feared me. She gave me books and food, a lamp to read by, but other than that, she tried to forget I existed. Sometimes, I could hear her sobbing outside my door."

"How are you so calm about it? That sounds like a horrible experience."

August smiled at the distress in Lucas's voice. "I'm sure, from a psychiatric standpoint, had Thomas not intervened, I'd be on the other side of one of your investigations. But I never felt sad or scared. Understimulated, tired of reading the same thing over and over again. Tired of being dirty. But the silence was actually nice compared to all the sights and sounds I deal with today."

"Still…"

"By the time she tossed me in that room, I could speak and read. I was barely two. I imagine, for a woman as sick as she was, that was terrifying. She did the best she could."

"How did you believe I was clairvoyant so easily? Knowing how disturbed your mother was? Did you ever just think I was crazy?"

August shook his head. "There was no faking the terror on your face when you touched me. Besides, I study science that, ten years ago, people had firmly labeled science fiction. I can't do my job without knowing that just because I don't understand it that doesn't mean it's not real. Truthfully, I was far more willing to believe your amazing solve rate was supernatural versus actual profiling which is, at its core, truly just an educated guess."

August grunted as Lucas shoved him off and pounced on top of him in one smooth motion. "An educated guess? An educated guess?" Lucas asked, pinching at whatever skin he could reach, as August tried to catch his surprisingly quick

hands. "Do you have any idea how much schooling I did to learn how to make those 'educated guesses'?"

August laughed, finally snatching Lucas's wrists and holding them hostage as he looked up at him. "I said educated. You guys use predictive modeling. It's just a combination of statistics and knowledge of the human psyche that allows you to guess what kind of suspect the police are looking for."

Lucas scoffed. "Our profiles are correct, on average, about sixty-six percent of the time. You can't fight the numbers."

August made a face. "True, but they've only led to an arrest in approximately two point seven three percent of cases, so..."

"That's because we can only intercede if we're invited in," Lucas said, voice pouty.

August had never heard Lucas sound huffy. He found his slightly sullen expression adorable. It made him want to kiss the pout of his lips. "If you work with us, you'll always be invited in."

"Work with you?" Lucas echoed.

"Yeah, my family. I was serious when I said my father is probably already thinking of ways he can use what you do to help us."

Before Lucas could respond, August's phone rang once more. Calliope again. August frowned, swiping to answer. "What's wrong?"

Calliope made a sound almost like a wounded animal. "I found something. Oh, God. I found a lot of...something."

"What did you find, Calliope?" Lucas asked, still perched

on top of August.

"So, remember the sock puppet accounts? Well, I was just going through each one, scanning emails for anything that might be of interest, and I found a link. So, I clicked the link and…" She made another troubled whine. "I think I know what's going on and it's so, so much worse than a serial killer."

"How the fuck is that even possible?" Lucas asked.

"Can you guys just get to your dad's house? We're going to need everybody. Or, at least, whoever's in town. This is bad. Bad. Bad. Really, just so fucking bad. I need to bleach my eyeballs badly. "

"Can you not just tell us?" August asked, tone sharp.

"Look, I don't know why you're so cranky. I'm the one who just had to wade waist deep into the darknet. I'm only explaining this once. So, get to your father's house and then I'll tell you what I found. If you don't like it, too bad."

With that, she was gone. They both sat staring at each other in confusion for a solid minute before Lucas said, "I guess we're going to your father's house?"

"I guess we are."

"I need clothes," Lucas said, realizing he hadn't brought any.

"I need coffee," August countered.

Lucas climbed off of him. "Stop by my place and then visit Cricket?"

"Deal. But first, shower."

EIGHTEEN
LUCAS

Lucas headed up the stairs of his place on autopilot. He couldn't think of anything except whatever it was Calliope had found that would somehow explain how the puzzle pieces fit together. Some small part of him was irritated that it took Calliope less than a day to figure out an answer he'd been searching for for months. August kept reminding him that Lucas had no help and limited resources, but it stung just the same. Those women could have been spared.

August was hot on his heels when he reached his door. He went to put his key in the lock when the door swung open an inch or two, like somebody had left without latching it all the way. Lucas frowned over his shoulder at August, who immediately stepped in front of him like a shield, pushing the door open all the way.

Lucas's gaze swept the room, looking for anything out of place. Nothing appeared to have been touched. Could he have just left the door unlatched? No. Because somebody had disabled his alarm. How would they have done that?

Called the alarm company and given their badge number, Lucas realized.

"Is there anything out of place? Something that wasn't here when you left?"

Lucas shook his head. "I don't think so."

"Don't touch anything."

"I'm sure he didn't leave prints behind," Lucas muttered.

"Kohn could have imprinted on anything in this apartment. Just don't touch anything without mentally preparing yourself."

Shit. Lucas hadn't even thought of that. "He's really not even the slightest bit concerned that I'm going to stop him. This is just a game to him. He's fucking with me."

"He's a psychopath. A good one, if he managed to fool an FBI psych evaluation. None of this is on you. And, I promise, when we get him, you can be the one to kill him, as fast or slow as you like."

Knowing August, that was probably a pretty large romantic gesture. Part of Lucas thought there was no way he could torture another human being, but another part of him thrilled at the idea of hearing Kohn scream. The things he'd done to those women? They deserved their revenge.

August did a quick sweep of the apartment while Lucas stood staring, fantasizing about watching those women rip Kohn apart. When August came back, he pulled Lucas against him briefly, then kissed his temple. "Go get dressed. Keep your guard up. Pack a bag. You're not coming back here."

Ever? Lucas found the prospect less daunting than he imagined. He dressed on autopilot, opting for his nicer

jeans and loafers, a t-shirt, and a zip front cardigan. The nice thing about being a college professor was the bar was pretty low attire-wise. Last week, one of his students had attended his class in Rick & Morty pajama bottoms and a faded Van Halen t-shirt. Nobody really gave a shit, which was perfect considering Lucas's current state of mind.

Once dressed, he threw a bunch of clothes into an overnight bag and met August in the living room. "I reprogrammed your alarm with a new code. Kohn will be dead before he catches up with it. Besides, he did what he set out to do. Let you know he could get to you whenever."

Lucas swallowed the lump in his throat, feeling like he might choke on the rage coursing through him. August took his hand and led him out of the apartment, firmly shutting the door behind him.

Downstairs, Cricket was perched on the back counter, looking at her phone, her now fire engine red hair in two strange buns on either side of her head. She looked up when the bell over the door chimed, perking up when she saw them. "Hi, guys. Your usual?"

August added several more coffees to the order, presumably for his family. Lucas felt a slight shiver of trepidation at the idea of meeting even more of his family members. As she went to work, Lucas perused the pastries behind the glass.

"Enjoy it while you can," Cricket said wistfully.

"What?" Lucas asked.

"This place is shutting down. We can't compete with the Starbucks down the street. So…end of the month I'm out of a job."

Lucas frowned at that, but August nodded. "Can you put a mix of the pastries in a box? We'll take them to go. Also, call me and I'll see about finding you a new job. With my family, there's bound to be somebody looking to hire."

Cricket's eyes went wide. "Really? Thank you."

August nodded, unbothered, but Lucas's heart did a weird somersault in his chest. How was this man somehow the sweetest person he'd ever met without even trying? Was Lucas just so far gone that everything August did seemed perfect?

He turned around to gaze out the window, his gaze snagging on a lime green Toyota Supra parked a bit farther down the street. "August." August snapped his head around at the alarm in Lucas's tone. "Look."

August followed Lucas's gaze. "Cricket. How long has that car been parked there?"

Cricket paused what she was doing as if considering his question. "I'm not sure, but there's been all kinds of tricked out cars parked on the street this week. I think maybe there's going to be some kind of car show or something."

Lucas turned on her. "Have any of the drivers come in here?"

Cricket froze. "I-I'm not sure. Hardly anybody comes in here anymore."

Lucas kept pressing. "Anybody who looks like a skinhead? Somebody with some shady tattoos?"

She shook her head. "Definitely not. I would have noticed. Are they killers, too? I thought you guys were college professors? Are you, like, secret agents on the side or something? Am I in danger?"

Lucas wanted to assure her that she wasn't but he had no idea what the fuck was going on. "They aren't after you. They want me. If they come in here and ask about me, tell them anything they want to know."

"What do you mean?" she asked in confusion.

"It probably won't come to that. They'll probably just keep spying on me from a distance. But if they want to know where I'm staying, tell them I'm staying with my boyfriend. Give them August's name if you have to. Tell them you don't know anything else. Text us when they leave. Do your best to stay where people can see you from the street."

Cricket's fair skin grew chalky. "Maybe I should just go home sick."

"You could do that, too," August agreed. "It might be safer."

She glanced to where her phone sat on the counter. "Yeah, I'm going to call the owner."

"Do you want us to wait with you?" Lucas asked.

Cricket shook her head, gaze nailed to the car down the street. "No. I'm fine. I'll lock the door if the driver tries to come inside."

August picked up the cup holders filled with coffees, so Lucas grabbed the pastry box. "Chances are, he'll try to follow us when we leave."

Cricket heaved a heavy breath. "No offense, but I fucking hope so."

When they entered the Mulvaney secret lair, Lucas stopped

short. He wasn't sure what he expected, but it wasn't all the people packed around the table. The usual suspects were there—August's grumpy brother, Atticus, and his alcoholic brother, Archer. Adam was there, too, sitting with Noah on one side and two identical looking men on the other. Thomas was the only one standing.

August slid the pastries down the table and set the coffee between them. Lucas watched in surprise as they set upon the treats like sharks in a feeding frenzy, elbowing each other out of the way to snag what they wanted from the box. All but Atticus, who turned up his nose at the sugar, taking the black coffee and retreating as far from the melee as he could manage.

"I wanted that, dick," one of the twins said as Adam snatched a donut from his fingers and stuffed the entire thing in his mouth.

"'The' you should be fasser," Adam managed around the fried dough.

Noah rolled his eyes at the others, giving an apologetic look to Lucas before snagging a cheese danish from the corner of the box, breaking it into pieces to eat.

Archer took the lid off his coffee and dumped the amber liquid from his glass into the cup. There were twelve steps in that man's future.

When they'd finally settled back into their chairs to eat, Lucas asked, "Um, can we get started? I'd really like to know what Calliope found."

"This one's kind of bossy," the other twin said. "Didn't see that coming."

August glared at the two men. "Lucas, the rude one is Avi, the other is Asa. You know the rest of them. Is Calliope ready?"

Lucas gave a hard look from one to the other before dismissing them entirely, turning to Thomas. "Has she said what she found?"

Noah shook his head. "Not yet. We just got here ourselves."

"Calliope, are you there?" Thomas asked.

"I'm here." She still had a hard edge to her voice. "I wish I wasn't but I am. Anybody with a conscience might want to skip the refreshments. This one's grim."

Noah looked longingly at his pastry before pushing it away. Lucas didn't feel like eating anyway. None of the others seemed bothered by Calliope's warning.

"What did you find?" Thomas asked as August and Lucas finally took their seats.

"A red room," Calliope said in a rush.

"A what?" Lucas asked, relieved to see nobody else seemed to know what she was talking about.

A picture popped up on the screen before them. It took a minute for Lucas to truly understand what he was looking at. It was almost comically horrific, like a poster for some slasher film. There was a woman on a medieval rack, face contorted in agony, and a man in leather pants and a bag over his head wielding a curved blade. The entire picture had a red overlay and the words 'five days' blinked over it.

"This is a red room," Calliope said, as if that somehow explained everything.

"We have eyes, Calliope," Adam said, earning an elbow in the ribs from Noah. "What?" he stage-whispered.

"What's a red room, Calliope?" Lucas asked patiently.

Once more, she made a whine, like she struggled to even get the words out. "A red room is pay per view darknet torture porn."

A shock went through Lucas's whole body. "What?"

Calliope took a deep breath and let it out, saying her next words slowly. "A red room is where people pay to watch and participate in the rape, torture, mutilation, and murder of unwilling participants," she clarified, her voice shaking. "As you can imagine, these rooms only stay open for a specific amount of time, and they're incredibly lucrative. Usually, they're filmed overseas because it's harder to track them down. But I think these are happening right here."

"You're telling me that these women are being kidnapped so that people can pay to…torture them?" Lucas said, suddenly grateful he'd heeded Calliope's warning.

He'd imagined it would be bad, horrible even. He'd seen the bodies, had witnessed first hand the torture endured by these women, but knowing that it was not only for one sadistic bastard's compulsion but…as entertainment? As profit? Lucas's vision swam, his head spinning. He couldn't breathe. Those girls… All of those girls were dead? How many people had watched? Participated? Committed atrocities from the fucking comfort of their own fucking homes?

Lucas could hear August talking to him, but he was too busy practicing dragging air into his lungs and blowing it back out. He was going to pass out. He needed his meds.

Suddenly, hands were on his face, holding his head up, but it wasn't August. It was Noah. "Lucas. Focus on my voice. I think you're having a panic attack."

"My pills. I have my pills in my pocket," Lucas managed, his mouth suddenly a desert.

Noah reached for Lucas's jean pocket, but August slapped his hand away. "I'll do it."

Lucas saw Noah raise his hands, as if to show he wasn't touching Lucas, before his vision swam again. This time, it was from the sweat pouring into his eyes.

His heart hammered in his chest, and some part of him worried he was having an actual heart attack. He was going to be humiliated later, but, right now, he needed to focus on pulling himself together. This wasn't helping anybody. He swallowed the pills August pressed between his lips.

Noah was in his face again. "You're okay. Just practice breathing with me. In for five. Hold for five. Out for five. Again. You got this."

The attack felt like it took forever, but it lasted probably less than ten minutes or so. He flushed when he noticed everybody looking at him. "Sorry," he muttered. "I haven't been sleeping much lately."

Noah nodded encouragingly. Thomas gave him a sympathetic smile. August had a death grip on his hand. The other's just watched him carefully.

Archer pointed to Noah with the scone in his hand. "That's alright, the little one puked the first time he sat in on a meeting."

Noah shot up his middle finger. "Sorry, child sex

trafficking makes me sick. Two weeks ago, you drank an entire case of cheap red wine, destroyed our bathroom, vomited everywhere, then passed out in it. The housekeeper almost called the cops because she thought she'd stumbled into a crime scene."

Archer rolled his eyes. "She was being dramatic. She overreacted."

"It looked like the hallway scene from *The Shining*," Atticus added.

Avi snickered. "Yeah, I saw the pictures on TMZ. It was pretty fucking gnarly."

"Is this an intervention, or can we kill some people?" Archer asked.

Lucas shook his head at their banter, wiping his hands over his face. "What do we do?"

"We kill him, obviously," August said.

Asa picked up a pen and tapped it on his chin. "But who's bankrolling this? Like, if this Kohn guy is just the executioner, they'll find another one if we kill him, no?"

Thomas nodded. "Asa's correct. Who's bankrolling this operation, Calliope?"

"If I had to put my money on anybody, it would be the squeaky clean Russian," August said.

"The Russian? Is that some kind of codename?" Atticus asked.

August briefly filled them in on what had happened at the truck stop and what Calliope had found about Devon Nicholls.

"So, we're saying the Russian has ties to a group of street

racing skinheads, who are torturing and killing women for money?" Noah said.

"It seems that way," Calliope agreed. "I have to do more digging, but I'm guessing that's the narrative."

"Tell me we're taking them all out," Noah said.

"There's no *we*," Adam reminded. "You're benched. I can't focus when you're there."

"I'm going," Lucas said, giving August a hard look. "Don't even try to bench me. I passed training at Quantico. I can deal with Kohn. You promised."

"We take Kohn first," Thomas said. "Torture what info you can out of him. Find those girls. This room opens back up in five days. We need to make sure they don't have time to go shopping for a new victim."

"If he confirms the street gang is involved, we'll go in and take them out, too. But we do this one step at a time."

They all nodded.

Thomas looked at each of them, gaze sharp, tone borderline threatening. "This needs to be clean. We're about to kidnap a Federal agent. We can't afford any mistakes. In the meantime, I want everything you can find on these gangbangers. Where they hang out. How many there are. We have to be strategic. The last time we took out a large group of people, the investigation took a little too long to go cold. No repeats of last time."

Lucas blinked at the implication. How often did they go in and eliminate multiple targets at one time? Were they truly talking about casually taking out an entire gang of Nazis?

When they were back in the car, Lucas finally asked,

"Don't you guys ever worry you'll get caught?"

August frowned. "Worry? We don't really worry about anything. We're incapable. It would be inconvenient to get caught. Especially for me. Prisons are noisy, dirty, the lights too bright. My father would be the one who suffers and I won't have that."

"What do you mean?"

August briefly took his eyes off the road. "He has a reputation to uphold. He's proud of our family name, our legacy. In a different world, he'd be proud of the invisible part of our lives, too. But we don't live in that world. Calliope does a good job of manufacturing alibis, faking social media posts. But the truth is, the sheer absurdity of a man like my father using his own children to exact revenge on strangers is what keeps us safe. It's too impossible to fathom."

It was true. Lucas wouldn't have believed it either if he hadn't seen it. "Do you really think this will work? That we have a shot at kidnapping Kohn and forcing him to tell us where those missing girls are?"

When August looked over at Lucas again, a chill rolled over him. It was unnerving to see August without the mask. "He'll talk. They always do. But you need to know that this can sometimes be a long and very bloody endeavor. I understand if you don't want to subject yourself to it. I don't mind doing this for you."

The idea of August getting to be the one to make Kohn scream left Lucas feeling cheated in a way that should have concerned him more. "I don't want you to do it for me. I want you to show me how to do it myself."

This time, it was August who looked startled. "You want me to teach you how to torture somebody?"

He did. He really did.

"Yes, please."

NINETEEN
AUGUST

"The key to torturing somebody is figuring out what scares them personally."

Lucas sat on August's black couch in a pair of worn gray sweatpants and a faded Quantico t-shirt, a small smile on his face, watching as August paced the room like he was at the front of the lecture hall and not his own living room.

"With some people, it's cultural, with some it's psychological, others physiological. We've come a long way since the blood eagle and the Judas cradle, both of which were surprisingly ineffective techniques when it came to extracting information. Now, we've learned that, sometimes, all it takes is total sensory deprivation. For others, it's sensory overload. With some, it's humiliation. So, knowing your victim is important."

Lucas raised his hand until August stopped to look at him. He was being such a brat tonight. "Yes?"

Lucas's smile spread to a full grin. "I appreciate this brief introduction to Torture 101, but I'm a criminologist. I

understand the psychological component of torture. I just want you to show me how to enact said torture."

"Enact said torture?" August echoed.

Lucas laughed. "I've taken the class, Professor. I just need the lab. Show me how to make somebody suffer."

August snickered at the analogy but also at the way Lucas's use of the word *professor* went straight to his dick. They would definitely be exploring that later.

He padded barefoot to the weapons artfully arranged on his wall, choosing a small wicked-looking dagger. It was ancient, hand crafted, expensive, and sharp enough to flay the skin off a man with enough precision so as not to damage the tissue beneath.

He crossed the room with his prize, straddling Lucas's lap, knees on either side of his thighs. "But that's the thing," he explained, carefully running the flat side of the blade along Lucas's perfect jawline. "One man's torture is another man's kink. Take me, for instance." He twirled the blade in his hand. "You can't torture me with a knife because I like the pain." August dragged the blade over his forearm, hissing as the edge opened up a shallow one-inch gash, beads of blood forming instantly. "It's an endorphin rush."

Lucas gazed up at him, studying his face. "When I was stabbed, I didn't really feel any endorphins, just the searing pain of my lung collapsing."

"There's a difference between a controlled cut and intent to kill," August reminded. "But my kink isn't everybody's kink. This is more about finding out what works for your target."

Lucas shook his head. "I don't care about how to hurt

him… I want to know how I can turn off my emotions. I know you don't have that problem, but how do I keep my humanity from sneaking in and making me feel sorry for the piece of shit when I'm hurting him?"

August ran a thumb along Lucas's full bottom lip. "I don't know how to tell somebody how not to feel because I never do. When I'm hurting somebody, I'm only concerned about two things: my mission and the rush I get from their pain."

"So, there's nothing I can do?" Lucas asked.

"I wouldn't say that," August said. "The key isn't turning off your feelings, the key is to focus on your needs. Be selfish. Care only about what you want. Let go of your fear. Be a bit of a hedonist. Do the deep, dark things you think about in your mind but would never dare say out loud to anybody. Do it and don't apologize for it."

August's gaze widened when Lucas took his arm and licked over the wound, collecting the droplets on his tongue. "Like that?"

August's cock twitched at the sight of blood smeared across Lucas's mouth. Yeah, this lesson was going sideways quickly. Lucas gazed down at August's erection, now obvious between them.

August gave him a reassuring smile. "Well, that was unexpected."

Lucas reached up and pulled him down for a kiss that tasted of salt and copper. "I have my own kinks, too, you know. I wasn't always a total headcase. Once upon a time, I was just a normal red blooded guy with all the same twisted little idiosyncrasies as the rest of the world."

"Do tell," August teased, plunging his tongue into Lucas's mouth.

"Shouldn't we be focusing on the torture?" Lucas asked, even as he returned August's kisses with enthusiasm.

August slid his hands beneath Lucas's shirt, playing with his nipples until he bucked his hips upward with a moan. "August…" he whined.

August teased and tugged at the tight peaks. "Actual torture is more of an on the job training activity. We'll use Kohn as your class project. In the meantime, I think we should work on exploring this side of you. Your selfish side."

"How do you know I have a selfish side?" Lucas asked, his thumb running over August's cock, now tenting his loose fitting pants.

August captured Lucas's lips once more, talking in-between deep, drugging kisses. "Everybody has a selfish side, a dark side. Some part of themselves they wouldn't dare explore because they're afraid of what the world might think of them. You know that, though. Don't you? This is your job. Studying the darkest parts of people."

"But what if I like it?" Lucas asked, running his tongue along the seam of August's mouth. "What if I like that deep, dark part of me too much?"

August took Lucas's hand and slipped it inside his pants. "Then who better to explore that with than me? I lack the capacity to judge you. Your kinks might not be mine, but nothing you say can truly shock me."

Lucas sighed against August's lips, his hand working his cock, thumb teasing the head in a way that had August's

eyes rolling behind his lids.

"Do you really like knife play?" Lucas asked. "Do you truly like the way it feels when somebody cuts you?"

August nodded. There was no reason to lie to Lucas. He already knew August's darkest secrets. He canted his hips, working himself lazily into Lucas's tightened fist.

"Can I try it?" Lucas asked, breathless.

August arched a brow. "Cutting me?"

Lucas's tongue shot out to sweep over his lower lip, a hard glint in his eye that August wanted to explore further. "Yeah."

August nodded. "Let's go to bed."

In the bedroom, August set the knife on the side table, undressing while Lucas leaned against the wall and watched. August could see he was also hard, the front of his gray pants damp in one spot. Once he was naked, Lucas walked up to him, turning him towards the bed, trailing his lips along his shoulder. "On the bed."

August shivered at Lucas's terse instruction. He did as he asked, lying across the comforter on his stomach, settling his arms overhead, not overly concerned about getting his white sheets messy. After all, that was what bleach was for.

Lucas kneeled between August's legs, squeezing his calves, before running his hands up the back of his fuzzy thighs to cup his ass. Then he was straddling August, sitting on his butt, bending down to trail his tongue along his spine. "How do you know you like being cut? Have you let other people cut you before?"

August liked the weight of Lucas on top of him, liked the

illusion of helplessness. "Not in a long time and never with anybody other than just a…professional."

August watched Lucas stretch to wrap his hand around the hilt of the knife from the side table before running his fingers along the unmarred flesh of his back. "What if I cut you too deep?"

"Then I'll require stitches. You can't cut me deep enough to kill me as long as you avoid any major arteries and my spinal cord, of course. I'd like to be able to walk when this is all said and done." He could feel Lucas's hesitation. "This is supposed to be you giving in to your darkest fantasies, not mine. If you don't want to do this, we can find—"

The first cut was shallow, right across the muscle of his shoulder blade. August's cock throbbed at the sudden rush of chemicals pumping into his brain. He grunted, then moaned as Lucas dragged his flat tongue along the wound. "Was that okay?"

August cleared his throat. "More than okay. Stop worrying about me, and just do what you want."

Lucas sucked in a breath. "That's a lot of power."

"That's the point. When you're torturing somebody, you're in complete control of their mind and body."

"I do like the idea of being in total control of your body."

Lucas hesitated another minute, then began to make a few more shallow slits. They were harmless, no more than paper cuts, but they were enough for August to roll his hips against his mattress, looking for friction, as blood droplets rolled lightly down the slope of his back. "Are you carving your initials into my skin?"

Lucas ran his fingertips along the cuts, then began to form letters on the blank canvas of his skin, writing M-I-N-E in August's blood. Fuck, that was hot. He caught August around his throat, craning his head back to feed bloody fingers into his mouth, leaning down to rumble against his ear, "And if I was? If I carved my name into you? Then what?"

August sucked his fingers, almost high off this side of Lucas, off knowing he was willing to be as sick and twisted as he wanted with him. He pushed back against Lucas's hard length, now firmly pressing against the cleft of his ass, only a thin layer of fabric between them. "Then you'd better fuck me after."

The sound that left Lucas was almost animalistic, but then he was grabbing the lube they'd left by the bed, moving back to yank August's hips up. When Lucas impaled him on two slick fingers, he rolled his hips back on him eagerly, not the slightest bit concerned about how needy he looked.

Lucas fucked his fingers into him harder. "Tell me you're ready because I need to be inside you."

"I'm good," August swore. "Do it."

Lucas pulled his fingers free, shirt flying as he shoved his pants out of the way. August sat up, no longer content to wait, grabbing Lucas's cock and pressing it against his entrance before sinking down onto him in one fluid movement until he was buried.

After that, there was no more talking. They were just moving together, the scent of blood and sweat and sex mingling in a way August found intoxicating. He couldn't get enough of Lucas's hard cock driving into him. He rolled

his hips downward on every upward thrust.

One of Lucas's hands found August's nipple, the other wrapped around his hard, aching cock. August's head fell back against Lucas's shoulder. He'd never experienced anything like this. It was hot and raw and sticky, blood and pre-cum mingling as Lucas jerked August roughly. There was nothing about this that should have been sexy, but he'd never been so hard in his life.

Lucas mouthed at the wounds he'd left and August found himself hoping Lucas had carved his name into his flesh the same way he'd imprinted himself in August's psyche. He was already so close to the edge of his climax. Lucas pounded into him with intention, his hand working over him hard and fast, his breath panting in August's ear. Then he was coming, his body spasming as goosebumps rose along his skin.

"Holy shit," Lucas growled as August's release spilled over his tightened fist. He pressed his palm between August's shoulder blades, pushing his chest to the mattress, hands digging into the flesh of his hips to drive into him with intention. Then he was blanketing himself over August, shouting his cry into his skin as he emptied himself inside. Lucas didn't seem like he was in any rush to free himself from August's body, so they just lay like that, joined until Lucas's spent cock slipped free on its own.

"That was…" Lucas said, then trailed off.

"Messy?" August offered around a laugh.

Lucas's nose trailed across the nape of August's neck. "I was going to say hot. But we do need to clean up. And

probably change your sheets. It looks like a crime scene in here. Kind of smells like one, too."

It was a few more minutes before August could bring himself to move. They showered, both of them taking their time, enjoying the scalding water. Lucas was extra gentle as he cleaned August's slashes. He'd had far worse injuries than the meager cuts of the tiny dagger, but he found he liked Lucas babying him just like he had the other night. It was a foreign feeling, having somebody act as if they needed to care for him. As if he was worthy of that care and consideration.

When they were dried off, Lucas dabbed each cut with antibiotic ointment and carefully bandaged them. Only once they were back in bed did he allow August to take control again, forcing Lucas into little spoon position so he could press his nose against his damp hair.

After a while, Lucas said, "If I can't do it…if I start to let my conscience get the best of me…I'm going to need you to do what I can't. I'll probably hate myself for it, but I need you to do it anyway. Those girls deserve justice."

August pressed a kiss to Lucas's shoulder. "You can do it. But if you choose not to—for whatever reason—I've got you. I've always got you."

"What if he refuses to talk? Torture has a notoriously low success rate."

"We'll get the information we want with or without him. There's nothing he can tell us that Calliope won't find eventually. But he's earned his time at the end of my knife or whatever other instrument I decide to go with. This is

what I do. It's what I was built for. He deserves everything he has coming to him."

"I just really want to be the one to do it."

"Then you will be."

Lucas's voice trembled. August didn't know if it was rage or fear…or both. "The things he's done…they've *all* done. I want them to pay. Even the ones who just watched. Anybody who profited off the suffering of those girls, they all deserve to suffer in the most medieval ways imaginable."

"You need to get some sleep," August reminded him gently.

"They're fucking monsters," Lucas whispered, almost to himself.

"Yeah, but you've got me and I'm the monster other monsters fear."

TWENTY
LUCAS

Lucas was quiet the following morning. He couldn't stop staring at the small bandages covering August's wounds as he dressed. Lucas had done that. He'd taken a knife and carved a part of himself into August's skin. Would it scar? Would it be a permanent reminder of their night together?

He should feel guilty about that, right? August had said he'd liked it, had even come first, but some part of himself couldn't help but wonder if it made him no better than Kohn. He'd liked August's pain, his submission; it had brought out some weird animalistic instinct Lucas hadn't even thought he'd possessed. Worse still, he couldn't wait to do it again.

The bed sank as August sat beside him. "Stop."

Lucas's gaze darted towards him, startled. "What?"

"Stop running last night through your head, second-guessing what we did and dissecting who you are as a person. I can literally see you trying to gear up for a good brood. What we did last night was one hundred percent consensual.

It doesn't make you a bad person if you enjoyed it. There's a football field size difference between our sex play and Kohn brutalizing women for entertainment. You know that."

Did he?

"Are you okay?" Lucas asked, changing the subject as he traced the bandages on August's shoulder.

August frowned. "Why wouldn't I be? Oh, you mean the scratches on my back? You could have done more damage with your fingernails. Which I'm also fine with, in case you're wondering. But I'm better than fine. I actually get a little turned on every time one of them twinges. If I could teach class without a shirt on so everybody could see what you've done to me, I would. I like wearing your marks. And if you were being honest, you'd admit you liked it, too."

Lucas turned, slotting their mouths together in a kiss that lingered, then pressed his forehead to August's. "I just hate waiting. I understand needing a plan of attack to take out some vicious gang of skinheads, but waiting to take Kohn off the street is…frustrating. I just want this over. I want to know these women are safe, and if they're not, I'd at least like to know there won't be any other victims."

August kissed him again. "I know. Just be patient a little bit longer. I promise you it's almost over."

"And then what?"

Lucas hadn't meant to ask the question out loud. It was just one of those things that had been bouncing around in his brain for days. A question that made him feel even more guilty for worrying about his love life when people were dying.

 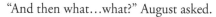

"And then what…what?" August asked.

Lucas started to stand. "Nothing."

August pulled him back down. "Not nothing. What do you mean 'and then what?'"

"What about us? What happens when this is over?" Lucas blurted.

August waved a hand. "We move in together, get married, live a life most people could dream of." August's face changed, his expression darkening. "Unless you don't want that." Lucas's brain ground to a halt, but August continued talking. "If that's what you're saying, I'm going to need you to table that discussion until after we settle this Kohn issue because I cannot go into this thinking I'll never see you again or I won't come back out."

Lucas had known August would say something like that. He'd known, deep down, that August was serious when he'd said he'd never let Lucas go. Ever. And he needed that. In the deepest, darkest part of him—the one August said everybody had—Lucas needed to know August would never stop fighting for him. He needed to hear the words. More than once. Maybe every day. That dark part of him needed to see the desperation in August's eyes at the thought of losing him, and maybe that made Lucas the sadistic one, but it was like pushing on a bruise or tonguing at a cavity. He needed to know August ached as much as Lucas did.

Lucas swallowed hard. "You know how crazy this is, right? To outsiders, we look insane."

August shrugged. "To outsiders, you are insane. I am, too. Who cares what the world thinks?"

"I know you're right. I guess I'm just tired of being stared at, you know? I always feel like a sideshow freak," Lucas admitted.

Other than his brief time at the FBI—back before everybody knew his secret—he'd always been an outsider, an outcast like his mother. Not even his own grandfather had wanted him. As much as he loved basking in August's intense obsession, it made him feel like there was a spotlight shining on him all the time.

"Once you're a Mulvaney, it's not going to be any better. I'll shield you from it as much as possible, but people are going to dig into your past. They're going to know about your dismissal from the FBI. They might even find out about your psychometry. People are going to be curious about you because my family is in the public eye."

"How do you do it? How do you guys do what you do without the rest of the world finding out?" Lucas asked. Surely, there had to have been at least one outsider who asked the right questions.

"We're not just killers…we're illusionists. Calliope creates fake social media posts, geotags them and everything. She Photoshops pictures, gets creative if needed. And, in a pinch, we have some very powerful people determined to see my father's experiment remain successful. Powerful allies create very strong alibis."

Lucas gave a hesitant nod. "I'm going to need time…to figure this out…to process—" At August's mutinous look, Lucas cupped his cheek. "Not us. We don't make sense, but I'm not in a place where I'm going to question my gut, not anymore. I know this works. Crazy or not, whatever we are works for us. But the rest of it, the public eye thing…your family… I just need time to figure that out."

August's shoulders sagged. "Yeah, that makes sense. I understand that. What time is your first class?"

"Ten thirty. You?" Lucas asked, leaning in to trail kisses along August's scruffy jaw.

"Not until one, but I have mentor meetings with my grad students starting at eleven."

"Good, you have time to feed me," Lucas said, catching August's mouth in a lazy kiss.

"You keep kissing me like that and we're not going to have time for anything but me throwing you on this bed and feeding you my dick."

Lucas pulled back to look at him, startled by August's words. They both burst out laughing. "I need coffee and a chocolate chip muffin the size of my face."

August stood, pulling Lucas up with him. "You just want to stop and check on Cricket, don't you?"

Lucas smiled. "Part of me hopes she isn't there. She seemed pretty determined to not come back. But I'd also like to make sure there's no souped up cars still parked outside my apartment. It worries me that they didn't follow me to your place."

"If I had to guess, it's because they already know you're staying with me and somebody is already here, watching us."

The thought made goosebumps raise along Lucas's skin. August tried to rub them away. "Relax. We have an advantage. They don't know we know about them. They

still think you believe Kohn is a serial killer with a partner, not part of a larger conspiracy. By the time they realize what we know, it won't matter."

"I know you're right. I just want to know the world is safe from these heartless pieces of shit."

August gave him a reassuring kiss on the head, then they both finished dressing. When they were walking out the door, Lucas noticed August wearing an amused expression. "What?"

August's smile widened. "It is somewhat amusing that these so-called skinheads all drive foreign cars, no?"

Lucas grinned. "Most of their gear is probably made in China, so..."

August locked the door behind them. "Let's go get breakfast."

Lucas was relieved to find there were no tricked out sports cars parked outside the coffee shop. He was less relieved when he realized every single parking spot was taken. It would be ironic if the bad guys couldn't find parking for their stalker mobiles. But that also meant Lucas and August couldn't find parking either.

From the outside, everything in the tiny coffee shop seemed calm. The lights were on, the sign in the window was flipped to open. Lucas couldn't see inside with the tint on the windows, but he felt the knot in his stomach loosen slightly.

"Why don't you just circle the block a couple of times

and I'll go grab our breakfast?"

August frowned. "I think I should go in with you."

"I'm just going to grab our food, check on Cricket, and then we'll be on our way. They're not going to attack me in broad daylight in a wide open coffee shop."

August eyed him warily for a solid minute before slowing on the street to let Lucas out. He leaned over the console to smack a kiss on August's cheek. "I'll be right back."

Lucas jogged across the street, avoiding the few cars on the road, grateful their schedules allowed them to miss out on morning traffic. It was odd to be worried about taking down Nazis one minute and the flow of traffic the next, but it was just one more weird thing in Lucas's life. If he had to make a list, the weird far outweighed the normal at this point.

When he pulled open the door, the bell overhead jingled as usual, but there was no shout of greeting from the back. The seating area was empty, but that was nothing new. Lucas moved forward, listening for any sign of life from the back. It was eerily silent.

"Hello?" Lucas called. "Cricket?"

Lucas crept closer to the counter, brow hooking upward when he saw her phone charging beside the industrial coffee maker. "Cricket?"

When she didn't answer, he moved behind the counter, no longer worried about etiquette. Cricket's phone was fully charged. It must have been there for a while. Her purse was tucked away in a small cubby beneath the pastry boxes, alongside her pale blue sweater.

When he stood, his gaze landed on something that made

his blood freeze in his veins. A delicate gold hoop, covered in blood. Shock rocketed through him. Cricket's nose ring. Fuck. He didn't stop to think, just slapped his hand down on top of it, sucking in a sharp breath as visions assaulted him.

Cricket perched on her usual spot on the counter, listening to music, and a man strode in wearing ripped jeans and a yellow shirt with *Don't Tread on Me* in black block letters sitting above a coiled snake. She pulled her headphones free of her ears, eyeing the man warily as he approached the counter. "Can I help you?"

"You know guys don't like when girls add those crazy colors in their hair or do that weird shit with their makeup, right? In the animal kingdom, creatures who look like you are a warning, telling mates to stay away. Telling them they're venomous."

Cricket smirked. "Yet, here you are."

"I'm just saying, men want a woman who's modest."

"What makes you think I'm looking for a man?" Cricket countered.

She never got to hear the man's answer. A shooting pain racked her body, and then she was collapsing, the man on the other side of the counter coming around to help another man holding a taser. Kohn. He reached down and snatched the ring from Cricket's nose, tossing it on the counter. "Get her into the van. I'll meet you back at the yard."

Lucas yanked his hand away, heart hammering in his chest. They took Cricket. He pulled his phone free from his pocket. He was about to tap his name when a familiar voice said, "Hey there, stranger. Miss me?"

A heavy dread settled over Lucas like a lead weight. He turned slowly, unsurprised to see the gun trained on him or that Kohn held the weapon. "Where is she?"

"Your little pink-haired friend? Or was it blue? Or green?" Kohn asked around a laugh. "She's safe. For now. The clients have a pretty specific type, but I think, just this once, they'll make an exception. They love watching me break the tough ones."

Lucas's nostrils flared. "I'm going to fucking kill you."

Kohn seemed decidedly unbothered. "I was hoping you and I could…reconnect. How did you like my gifts?"

Lucas had known, at some point, he'd be this close to Kohn again, but he'd never imagined it would be by surprise. Not since he'd met August. He'd made Lucas feel a little too safe. "I found them unoriginal," Lucas taunted.

Kohn barked out a surprised laugh. "Nice to see you can still keep your sense of humor. I'll try to do better in the future."

Lucas darted his glance to his phone and back. Had he hit send? Was August outside? "How much longer are we going to play this game? What is it you get out of this? Did you think I wouldn't find out about your little Nazi friends and their red rooms?"

Kohn arched his brow. "I wanted you to know. I gave you all the clues. I just wasn't sure if you were capable of putting it all together on your own without the power of the FBI behind you."

A strange lightness overwhelmed him. Kohn had no idea who Lucas had behind him. He had an army of

psychopaths and the Mulvaney name. Lucas wasn't a victim anymore. Lucas tapped his temple. "I have something the FBI doesn't."

Kohn's lips curled up in something resembling a smile. "It doesn't matter, though, does it? Nobody will ever believe you. But you still have time to just walk away. This has been fun, but it's growing tedious. Still, I don't want to kill you. You're such a marvel. A freak of nature."

"What about those women? Their lives were worth living."

Kohn rolled his eyes. "They were junkies. Whores. Sub-humans. Burdens of society. Nobody misses them. Most people didn't even notice I'd culled them from the herd."

"So, they're all dead?" Lucas asked, a sadness he'd never experienced before settling over him.

"All but your colorful little friend. Our clients are getting picky. They're tired of the broken ones. They want to watch me carve up ones who look like them, who look like the girl who rejected them at prom, the one who thought she was too good for the nerdy guy, too cool for the loser who played *Dungeons and Dragons*. They want their revenge, and I'm the one who lets them live out their fantasies."

Lucas forced himself to breathe. Kohn wanted him to lose his shit, wanted him to do something stupid. So, he just stayed silent, hoping the look on his face conveyed the level of hatred he had for the man.

"If you walk away now, nobody needs to know about your past. I'd hate for your nerdy professor boyfriend to learn what a headcase you are. Does he know about your little breakdown? About your time in the nuthouse? I bet

his rich family would shut down your romance quick if they knew who you really were. Then you'd be all alone again. Totally helpless. I like helpless. It looks good on you."

At that moment, August rounded the corner, coming through the back just as Kohn had. He pressed a wand to Kohn's neck and his whole body jerked comically before he collapsed, the gun slipping from his fingers as he fell. Lucas picked up the fallen weapon, kneeling over Kohn's still twitching body, noticing the stain at his crotch. He'd wet his pants.

He leaned down to make sure Kohn could hear him. "You look so helpless. It looks good on you." The man made a low groan, but Lucas stood. "What the hell did you hit him with?"

"A cattle prod."

"He's got Cricket."

"I know. I heard. Looks like the plan's changed. Time to improvise."

August handed Lucas his keys. "Go get the truck and pull it into the alley. Open the back. You'll see a keypad. The code is 1-8-4-2. Inside, you'll find zip ties. Bring them to me."

"What are we going to do with him?"

"Exactly what we'd planned on doing to him tomorrow. Torturing him for information."

Kohn gave a long moan at that, trying and failing to sit up.

August slapped his face. "Hey, can you hear me? Settle down or I'm going to shove this so far up your ass that when I press the button it will bake your organs."

Part of Lucas wanted August to do it, to just end it

then and there. But they still had Cricket. Those maniacs had Cricket. He moved on autopilot, following August's instructions to the letter. Once Kohn's wrists were secured behind his back, August sat him up using a handful of his hair. Lucas got a small thrill when the man screamed in pain.

"You don't know how bad you just fucked up. If they don't hear from me in the next five hours, they're just going to start the show without me. Let me go and I'll tell you where to pick up the pieces of your little friend when we're done with her. Hell, if you find me a replacement, maybe I'll even leave her in one piece."

"August…" Lucas said, not even sure what he wanted to say.

August's face went blank. It was like a switch had flipped, all of August's humanity disappearing in a blink. The hollowness in his eyes, the complete lack of emotion on his face, gave even Kohn pause when August got in his face.

"Do you think I'll need five hours to break you?" he asked.

Lucas couldn't help the smile that formed on his face. For the first time since Kohn had entered Lucas's life, the man looked truly horrified. Like he'd looked into August's eyes and saw the bleak fate that awaited him.

"I'm going to get him in the car. Call Noah and my father and let them know what's happened."

Lucas's gaze darted to Kohn. "Shouldn't we be worried about using names in front of him?"

"He won't live long enough for it to matter." He slapped Kohn's face. "But how much pain's involved…that's up to him."

Lucas picked up the phone and began making calls.

TWENTY-ONE
AUGUST

"Why do I even bother to say things like 'no mistakes'?" Thomas asked over the speaker of August's truck, then sighed. "It's like you boys take it as a personal challenge. A way to spite me. Have I not given you everything?"

August rolled his eyes. "You're being very dramatic, Dad. Did Archer get you drunk again?"

"He did not. I'm just tired of cleaning up after you boys for the last six months. You're all getting sloppy. Distracted. You would never have made these kinds of mistakes last year."

"Atticus makes mistakes monthly, yet you still let him be your favorite," August reminded, uncertain as to the reason for his father's suddenly poor mood. "Did Aiden call you? You always get grumpy when Aiden calls."

"I told you that nobody does anything without my say so. Yet, somehow, here we are with you driving down the freeway with a federal agent hog-tied in your backseat in broad daylight."

Lucas gazed at August with wide eyes, clearly unnerved

by Thomas's irritation. August knew it was just his father's way of processing things that didn't go the way he'd wanted. "He had a gun pointed at Lucas. What should I have done? Just let him shoot him?"

"It's too late for should haves. But what you should have done is called me before you barged in there and cattle prodded a federal agent."

August sighed. "As you said, it's too late for should haves. We're at the old denim factory. I'm probably going to need help with the clean-up once I get the information I need."

Lucas kept glancing over his shoulder to where Kohn was out cold in the back.

They sat parked between two cement buildings. The old factory was good for privacy. It was an abandoned sixty-thousand square foot space surrounded by a grouping of smaller, equally empty, buildings. The only people they ever had to contend with were the occasional vagrants and they would run at the first sign of trouble.

Thomas muttered something under his breath before saying, "Text me when it's done and I'll send in reinforcements."

Once they dragged Kohn inside, August rigged a chain over a metal beam, securing it around the solid steel cuffs before Lucas helped him truss Kohn upwards, stopping only when his toes barely scraped the ground. August cut Kohn's clothing free, kicking the fabric out of the way. Kohn was sweating profusely, and he reeked of urine and fear. He was conscious but pretending he wasn't. August let him maintain his illusion for just a bit longer.

Lucas had retreated to the side of the room, leaning

against the wall, his arms folded over his chest. He wasn't sure if Lucas could handle what was about to happen, but knowing Cricket's life hung in the balance would likely keep him from completely caving to Kohn's inevitable mental breakdown. August opened the duffel bag he kept hidden beneath the panel in his Mercedes. He unrolled his knives, smiling when Kohn scoffed as if they were inferior to the grotesque instruments he'd fashioned himself.

August didn't need to rip off body parts to break Kohn, but he would if he had to. He was just getting started. He took a set of small earbuds and shoved them deep into Kohn's ears. Once the speakers connected, he keyed up his death metal playlist and turned it on, cranking the volume up as high as it would go, watching Kohn's face contort as the music assaulted him from the inside out.

"Fuck you," Kohn spit, fighting to stand on his toes, trying to take the weight off his shoulder joints. "You think some loud music is gonna break me?" he screamed. "Fucking amateur."

August snatched a knife from the display, crossing the room. Lucas gasped as he grabbed the man's nipple, pulling it away from his body before slicing it clean off, tossing it to the floor as Kohn screamed. August flinched at the noise.

Lucas crossed the room and pulled something from his pocket. August's air pods. "I saw them in the center console and figured you could use them. I know the screaming bothers you."

August wrapped his arms around Lucas, dragging him in for a deep kiss, swallowing his cry of surprise. Kohn

grunted in disgust.

"It's just headphones," Lucas said.

August shook his head. "It's not just headphones. I don't know what love feels like, but I imagine it's like the feeling I'm having right now."

Lucas's face went soft, his smile radiant. "That's the sweetest thing anybody's ever said to me after cutting off another man's nipple." August chuckled. "Are you going to keep slicing off body parts until he talks?"

"No. That was just for fun. I'm going to give him about thirty minutes with the headphones, and then we're going to really get started."

"So, what are we going to do in the meantime?" Lucas asked, letting his hands slide down to cup August's ass.

"Mr. Blackwell, are you suggesting we fool around while there's a man being tortured five feet away?" August teased, already backing Lucas up against a large metal cylinder that dominated the space.

"I mean, you once told me that you could get me off in thirty minutes or less," Lucas reminded him.

There was the sound of boots scuffing over the concrete floor, then a voice called out, "Keep it in your pants, you little perverts."

Lucas shoved August away from him like they were kids caught making out in a janitor's closet. Asa and Avi appeared from the back of the building. Lucas frowned when he saw Avi swinging a two-liter bottle of soda.

August rolled his eyes. "What are you two doing here? I told Dad I needed help with the clean-up. We haven't

even started."

Avi raked his gaze over Lucas in a way that made August contemplate gouging his eyes out, especially when it lingered at his crotch. "Strangely, Dad thought you might need some backup just in case Ms. Cleo here doesn't have the stomach for the blood and guts."

Lucas shot Avi his middle finger. Avi blew him a kiss. August gave Asa a look that let him know he better get their brother in check. As usual, it was ignored.

Asa walked to where Kohn dangled, giving the man a push, watching as he swung. "This him?"

August nodded.

"He doesn't look like much," Asa mused.

Kohn spit on him. Asa calmly wiped the spit from his cheek with the back of his hand before reaching between Kohn's legs, gripping his balls and twisting with enough force to make all of their testicles attempt to climb back in their body. Kohn opened his mouth in a silent scream, then promptly threw up.

"Gross," Avi muttered.

"Um, what is the two-liter bottle for?" Lucas asked.

Avi looked down at the bottle in his hands. "Oh, this? I thought we could test the soda bottle theory."

"Soda bottle theory?" Lucas echoed apprehensively.

"Mm, you'll see."

"Well, I was going to give him another few minutes with the death metal, but what the hell? Might as well get started. He looks pretty worse for wear," August muttered.

"You said he was mine," Lucas reminded, looking back

and forth between the twins.

Asa laughed. "Okay, psychic-friends-network. You wanna play? You can play." He yanked the headphones from Kohn's ears. "You gonna tell us where the girl is?"

"Fuck. You," Kohn wheezed.

Asa snickered. "I was hoping you would say that." He looked to Lucas, crooking his finger. "You ever waterboarded anybody?"

Lucas gave Asa the absurd look his question deserved. "No. I've never had the opportunity."

"Well, now's your chance. Only we're going to use soda."

Lucas frowned again. "I don't follow."

Asa handed him the bottle. "Don't worry. I'm going to walk you through it. Take the cap off."

Kohn scoffed, swollen eyes glaring in Lucas's direction. He did as Asa instructed. Asa gave a look in August's direction, making sure he was okay with where this was heading. "When you're ready, put your thumb over the top and shake the shit out of it. We want to build that pressure good and high."

"And then what?" Lucas asked, putting his thumb over the top but not agitating the soda.

"Then it's up to you. If you're feeling particularly spicy, you can jam the top of the bottle up against his asshole and give him an enema he'll never forget. But you could also rupture his intestines and he'll bleed out without giving us the necessary information. So, instead, once you get that soda good and shaken, you're going to put that thing right up to his nostril and let it go."

August was certain Lucas would refuse, but the slow smile that slid across his face made August proud.

"Hold his head up."

"Woohoo!" Asa cried, wrenching Kohn backwards by his hair, steadying his swaying body with his own. "This is gonna be epic. Do it."

Lucas shook the two-liter until it appeared to be nothing but froth, pressing the bottle to Kohn's nose. "Last chance."

"Fuck you, you little bit—" Lucas took his finger off the top, sending a water cannon of pressurized carbonation into Kohn's nasal passages and down his throat. The man's eyes bulged, soda spewing from his mouth even as he made gurgling sounds and his body convulsed.

When the bottle was empty, Lucas tossed it aside, but there was no way to question Kohn. He was still hacking, his body trying to forcibly expel the soda from his lungs.

"That was everything I thought it would be," Asa said, gazing at the mess beneath Kohn. "What should we do now? I brought hedge clippers. We could start playing this little piggy with his chunky little sausage toes?"

"What about it, Kohn? All you have to do is tell us where Cricket is. Then you'll at least meet the devil with all your toes."

"They're going to carve that bitch up and leave pieces of her scattered along the freeway for you to pick up like trash," Kohn rasped.

Before August could react, Lucas turned and grabbed a blade from the table—one August never bothered with—a clunky looking meat cleaver, much like the one his brother

had once plunged into a pedophile's skull. Before any of them could even guess at his plans, he dropped to his knees and swung, ridding Kohn of four out of five toes in one go.

Kohn's screams echoed through the hollow building, making August's ears ring. He was going to have a migraine for days after this.

"Nice," Avi said, voice full of admiration. "Now, do the others."

"No. I'm done fucking around with him," Lucas snapped. "Tell me where she is or the next things I take are your fucking balls, followed by your dick."

"He'll definitely bleed out from that," Asa said, earning a glare from Lucas. "What? I'm just saying."

"We could cauterize the wound?" Avi suggested.

"If he's not going to talk, I don't fucking care if he bleeds out. I want him to bleed out. Let him fucking die trussed up like the fucking pig he is."

"Here, use this one. It will slice through him with far more precision," August said, handing over a small paring knife. To Kohn, he said, "What's it going to be?" When Kohn didn't answer, Lucas pressed the blade against his balls until his face contorted and he began to make animalistic sounds between bared teeth.

"He asked you a fucking question," Lucas snapped. After another thirty seconds passed, he scoffed. "Fine, have it your way."

Lucas tugged down on Kohn's testicles, likely to make it easier to cut. "Wait!" Kohn shouted. "Fuck. Wait. Just… just fucking wait."

"Where is she?" Lucas asked again.

Kohn's whole body sagged. He'd accepted that he wasn't walking away from this. "There's a junkyard on the corner of Bramford and 2nd Street. In the back, there's a shipping container. If she's still in one piece, you'll find her there."

"That wasn't so hard, was it?" Asa said, patting Kohn's red face.

"Who the fuck are you people?" Kohn muttered. "I thought you were a fucking college professor."

"I am," August said, bored. He pointed to Avi. "And he's a fashion designer." Then Asa. "And he's an architect."

"But together, we fight crime," Asa said in a mockingly cheerful tone.

Avi grinned at Kohn's frown. "Millennials. We're all about the side hustle."

Asa snickered, but Lucas just continued to stand there, staring down at the knife in his hand. "You butchered those women," he said, almost to himself. "You raped and tortured them, destroyed their bodies, did unspeakable things. For money. For entertainment. Because it got you off."

Kohn shook his head. "Hey, I only did what the audience wanted. It's them you should be pissed at. They paid to play. I'm just the sword. I didn't care about those bitches one way or the other."

"That's not true. You very much enjoyed what you did," Lucas said. "I felt it. I saw how excited you got, felt how much you enjoyed their pain, their torment. You wanted them to be not just scared, but broken, hopeless. Some of them were fucking children. I know you liked it. You made

sure I knew. Remember?"

A slick smile spread across Kohn's face. "Yeah. Yeah, I fucking did."

Lucas's hand flicked upwards, and then Kohn gave a strangled wheeze as blood poured from between his legs. Lucas's lip curled in disgust as he dropped what was left of Kohn's manhood on the floor. The man was chalk white now, his life draining rapidly, but he was still conscious when Lucas said, "I enjoyed that, too, you demented fuck."

August pulled Lucas back. He was coated in blood, and there was a near feral look to him. He gently took the knife from his hands and gave it to Asa. "Can you two handle that while I try to clean him up?"

"The showers in the old locker rooms work. I dropped the go bag from your trunk in there, too."

August nodded, already pushing him towards the back of the building. Once they made it back there, he turned on the water, undressing a near catatonic Lucas and setting him beneath the scalding spray. He didn't try to wash himself, just stood there staring at his feet, maybe watching Kohn's blood circle the drain.

August called Calliope and relayed the information they'd gleaned from Kohn. "I need eyes on that red room. I'm almost positive Kohn was talking out of his ass, but just in case, make sure the clock hasn't run down."

There was a series of rapid-fire typing. "They're still counting down, but Kohn wasn't lying about them pushing up the timeline. They're planning on opening the room tonight. We got three hours."

"Can you get satellite images of the yard? I'm guessing this is where Kohn's little band of Nazis hangs out. I imagine, on a show night, they're all in attendance. Can you get somebody to recon the space so we can go in and clean house?"

"I'm on it."

August grunted his approval. "Let me know how quick we can get in there and get her out."

"Wait. How's Lucas?"

August sighed. "I honestly don't know."

TWENTY-TWO

Lucas moved on autopilot. His training as a psychologist told him he was disassociating—avoiding a reality where he'd castrated a serial killer in a warehouse—but mostly he was just…processing how little he cared about what he'd done to Kohn. He should care about cutting off pieces of another human being, no matter how much that human deserved it.

But he just…he just didn't.

He hadn't relished the man's pain as he'd imagined he would, but he hadn't been disgusted by it either. It had been a means to an end. He had information they needed and Lucas had been determined to get it. He wanted his friend back. If something happened to her because of him, he didn't know how he was going to move past it.

They were back at Thomas's house, back in their Batcave. On the large screen was a satellite image of one of the largest junkyards Lucas had ever seen. He was doing his best to focus for Cricket, but his thoughts kept tunneling away until the room and everyone in it seemed light years

270

away. August sat beside him, throwing worried glances in his direction every few minutes or so, as if gauging exactly how close to the edge Lucas was. He wanted to tell him he was fine, that there was nothing to worry about—because there wasn't. But if that was true, why did Lucas have this slithery feeling in his stomach?

The screen came alive as Calliope's voice filled the room. "I'm assuming we're all here?"

Lucas looked around at the others. Everybody was there except the last brother, the one who lived on the other side of the country. Aiden? He was always suspiciously absent. There was a story there, but Lucas wasn't sure he'd ever know it.

"Monk has eyes on the shop here," Calliope noted. A thick red circle appeared around the building at the front of the compound. "He says there's currently seven men visible, all of them sporting side arms and rather large knives strapped to their legs. He knows all this because the two large bay doors are open."

Adam groaned. "That's gonna complicate shit."

"Who's Monk?" Lucas asked nobody in particular.

August squeezed Lucas's hand. "He's who we call when we need to outsource surveillance. He's a former black ops soldier, and he doesn't ask a lot of questions."

"How many other people know about you guys?" Lucas asked.

August shook his head. "He doesn't know who bankrolls his jobs. He deals exclusively with Calliope and gets paid in cash. He doesn't care who wants the info or why."

"Oh," was all the enthusiasm Lucas could muster for

what was an otherwise smart move for Murder, Inc.

"Do we know for sure there's only seven of them?" Avi asked.

"No," Calliope said. "They periodically get up and head to the back, but the same people who go out are the same people who come in. But we can't assume there's nobody else back there who isn't also equally armed."

"So, they could be holding Cricket in the back of the building," August said.

Lucas's stomach curdled as he let his imagination run wild with what those men could be doing to her with every visit. "We need to go now."

"Things don't go well when we rush assignments," Noah said from the chair beside him. "I know you're worried about her, but they aren't going to fuck with her off camera. These sick fucks pay a lot of money to watch. As long as the clock is still counting down, she's okay."

Trepidation burrowed into Lucas's chest. "Yeah, but we're down to ninety minutes."

"So, stop interrupting so we can come up with a plan," Adam offered, rolling his eyes.

Lucas leaned back, nodding. "Sorry, go ahead."

Another red circle appeared over a rectangular shape. "This is one of two shipping containers on the property. This one could possibly be Kohn's mobile torture chamber. But, unfortunately, there's also this one back here. Either of these could be what we're looking for. She could be in either, or neither. There's no way to know until boots are on the ground."

"Is there a side entrance to the building?" Thomas asked.

Arrows began to appear. "There's a door here, which is—I'm assuming—an office, and there are the two open bay doors that, according to Monk, are operational. Then there's a door that leads directly into the junkyard. The yard itself has ten-foot fences with razor wire. There might also be dogs."

"God, I fucking hate dogs," Atticus muttered.

Noah's face contorted in disgust. "What kind of monster hates dogs?"

"One who got bit on the ass by a boxer during an assignment and needed stitches and two rounds of antibiotics," Archer murmured, taking a sip of something clear—more than likely with an alcohol content.

"I hope you mean the dog breed," Noah said.

"As if Atticus would ever lower himself to bed a mere boxer. He's saving himself for an heiress," Asa said around a laugh.

"Enough!" Thomas shouted. "Just be aware that there may be guard dogs on the premises."

"You're not going to hurt the dogs, right?" Noah asked. "Right?" he reiterated at their silence. He turned to level a glare at his fiancé. "Adam Mulvaney, if you hurt a dog, don't bother coming home."

Lucas felt some level of amusement at the way Adam's jaw dropped. "I—Wha—We don't even know there are dogs!"

"I can't believe you'd even consider hurting a dog," Noah said, brooding.

Adam looked to the others, flummoxed. "How am I

in trouble for hurting invisible dogs? What is happening right now?"

"But if there are dogs?" Noah prompted.

"If there are, we'll make sure they're not hurt," Adam muttered obediently.

"Not one hair on their fuzzy little heads," Noah repeated vehemently.

Archer snickered. "You're so whipped."

Adam flicked him off. "You're just mad you curl up with a whiskey bottle every night."

"Jesus Christ. Can we just get on with it?" Atticus asked, pinching the bridge of his nose.

"We still have no way in," Avi reminded them. "What's our best bet?"

"We could scale the razor wire, hit 'em from the back," Asa suggested.

"No," August said. "We go in through the front." He stood, walking to the screen. "We position Asa and Avi here and here, on either side of the bay doors. Lob flash bangs in and lower the doors while they're blind. The rest of us go in during the melee. Lucas and Atticus can advance into this back area, clear the rooms, then sweep the yard. Then we find Cricket and torch the place on the way out. After, have Calliope deliver evidence to the cops implicating the squeaky clean Russian."

It was a good plan. Complicated given the logistics, but it was clear August and the others had executed a large scale massacre before. The only one looking even slightly concerned was Noah. Lucas was almost positive he was still

worried about the dogs that may or may not exist within the junkyard.

"Why am I babysitting?" Atticus asked.

"Because you kind of suck at killing," Adam reminded him.

Atticus seethed. "Are you never going to let this meat cleaver thing go?"

"It's not just the meat cleaver, bro. You're just...unlucky," Asa said.

Avi nodded. "It's true. You look like an overgrown leprechaun but you got screwed out of the luck part. Bad shit just follows you. Embrace it."

"Fuck all of you," Atticus said, pouting.

Lucas glared at Atticus. "I'm a trained FBI agent. It's not like I don't know my way around an extraction."

Archer snickered. "You're an egghead, poppet. Embrace it."

"Yes. When was the last time you had to qualify on the gun range?" Atticus asked.

"When was the last time you did?" Noah countered, holding his hand out for Lucas for a fist bump, which Lucas begrudgingly returned. He appreciated Noah having his back without asking for receipts. Atticus wasn't wrong. Lucas hadn't had to qualify with a weapon because he rarely had cause to carry one in his line of work. It had been a while since the academy. But he had no doubt he could do what needed to be done.

"Fine. I'll go with Lucas. Atticus is with the others," August said. "I won't be able to focus with you out of my sight anyway."

Lucas's heart flip-flopped in his chest, and he couldn't

shake the feeling he was blushing.

"We have a plan. Does everybody know what they're doing?" Thomas asked, once more cutting through the banter.

"Does it even matter, Pop?" Asa asked. "It all goes to shit at the last minute anyway."

"It's true," Avi parroted. "The objective stays the same. Get the girl, kill the bad guys, destroy the evidence. Don't get caught. Lather. Rinse. Repeat."

"Don't get dead," Thomas said drolly. "Dismissed."

The moonless night was on their side, as was the near deserted location. During the day, the area was bustling with dozens of manufacturers creating everything from storm shutters to neon signs. But once the sun went down, most people went home, blanketing the neighborhood in darkness.

The building was ancient. Pieces of concrete had worn away in chunks, and the once orange trim was now a rust color. There were giant cracks and divots in the parking lot, but it didn't stop the men from parking their overpriced cars in front of the open doors, allowing them to work on them as they talked and drank with their friends.

To the casual observer, they were just a bunch of drunken fools, laughing a little too loud, partying a little too hard. But inside the doors, tacked up on one of the side walls, was a Nazi flag right next to the American flag. The men wore runes inked on their skin, symbols stolen from the Norse Vikings and co-opted to represent hate. Even from across

the street, their casual use of slurs carried.

Lucas checked his watch. There was only forty-five minutes until their little show began. He raised his binoculars, scanning for Asa's and Avi's heat signatures, making a frustrated sound when he saw nothing. "What are we waiting for?"

"People are getting into position. I know you want to get Cricket out of there but we only get one shot at this."

"I know," Lucas muttered, raising the binoculars to his eyes once more just in time to see the twins closing in on either side. They were dressed head to toe in black, wearing balaclavas that hid their faces. They carried guns with silencers in one hand and a canister that resembled a can of shaving cream in the other.

Avi held up two fingers, letting them know they were clear to cross the street. They met Atticus, Archer, and Adam at the corner, hunkering down on one knee. "Remember, when they give the signal, you go straight to the back. Find Cricket and get out. If you run into somebody you don't know, shoot to kill."

"And if we run into Cujo?" Atticus grumbled.

"Run," August suggested.

Atticus glared at August. "Great advice."

"Ready?" August asked. They all nodded. August pressed the comms button. "Ready?" he whispered to the twins.

They gave a single nod as one.

"Go."

After that, everything happened at once. They rolled the canisters into the group of men, and, as expected, it took

a few moments for them to process this was an attack. By then, the twins were rolling the doors down, slamming them shut and locking them with heavy black devices.

Adam kicked in the office door just as a man stumbled into the room, holding his eyes. Adam dropped him with a headshot before they broke into two groups—Adam, Atticus, and Archer moving into the garage with the twins, August, and Lucas advancing forward, August in the lead.

Lucas kept his gun raised but his hand off the trigger, some part of him secretly concerned he'd accidentally shoot August in the fray. While their weapons were silent, the responding gunfire was deafening.

In the hallway, a man came running from a back room, running headfirst for August. Lucas pulled the trigger, catching the man in the shoulder. August's hands moved so quickly Lucas didn't even see the cuts he made, only the aftermath of blood bubbling from the man's lips. They stepped past him, moving deeper into the building, kicking open doors and clearing them as quickly as possible.

At the final door, they found themselves spit out into the junkyard. There were cars stacked like metal towers on either side, creating a dizzying maze of twisted metal. August pulled his gun but kept his knife in his non-dominant hand as he swept the space for stragglers.

When they took another turn, Lucas was certain he'd never be able to backtrack his way out of the place, but it didn't matter because they'd found what they sought. The shipping container.

August pointed two fingers at his eyes, then in the

opposite direction, clearly telling him to keep watch as he disengaged the metal lock, swinging the door open, weapon raised. The smell hit Lucas first. Even without looking, he knew there was a corpse in the container. He couldn't help himself. He had to look. He had to know if they were too late. August hopped up into the trailer, turning the girl so her face was visible in the barely-there glow of the filthy security light sitting high on a concrete pole in the center of the metallic sea.

Lucas's stomach unknotted when he realized it wasn't Cricket, but his relief was short-lived. A girl was still dead, somebody who shouldn't have had to endure that level of horror. She'd been there for some time. Rigor had set, then passed, her body starting to give in to the gases that released after death. August closed milk white eyes with his gloved hand.

These men were so cocky, they literally just left the bodies where they fell until they were ready to dispose of them. Fucking pricks. He'd seen a million cases, had interviewed hundreds of serial killers, but it had always been so abstract. None of it had really penetrated until Kohn, until this. The level of venomous hatred coursing through him felt lethal. Fuck.

Lucas's gaze darted upward to August's. "She's not here. Where the fuck is she?"

Lucas's eyes widened as August raised his arm and fired. He spun around to see a man get knocked off his feet.

"My guess is she's wherever that guy just came from," August reasoned.

August dropped from the container, motioning for Lucas to follow, like that wasn't already the plan. They turned down another narrow passage lined with crushed metal, sweeping left to right, Lucas checking their six as they slowly advanced in the only direction possible.

A piercing shriek cut through the space followed by, "Get the fuck off me, you stupid motherfucker!"

There was a grunt and a groan. "Ow. Get back here, you crazy cunt."

August and Lucas bolted towards the girl, running directly into a terrified Cricket, whose hands were zip tied so tightly her wrists appeared purple. When August caught her, she looked back and forth between the two of them with wild eyes. Lucas quickly remembered she couldn't see their faces.

"It's us. It's us. You're okay."

A tall heavyset bald man lumbered around the corner, wheezing and limping. Cricket gasped, backing herself into Lucas as she realized he was the lesser of two evils. August jabbed his knife into the man's carotid and twisted before pulling it free. The man coughed, spraying blood as he fell.

Lucas turned Cricket to face him. "Are there any more like him coming?" Cricket shook her head, appearing dazed. "Then let's get the fuck out of here."

"Wait! No," Cricket shouted, yanking herself away from Lucas and taking off for where she'd come from.

Lucas threw a confused look at August, who shrugged and ran after her. They found her trying without luck to unlatch the second shipping container lock.

"Help me," she snapped.

Lucas jumped into action, letting August keep watch this time. Inside, three girls huddled together, all of them filthy, half-dressed, and extremely malnourished. "They're alive," he mumbled to himself. He looked to August. "What do we do?"

"Free them," August said, nodding to the keys dangling from a hook just inside. Lucas's hands shook but he managed to get them loose, helping them out of the shipping container.

August cut Cricket's zip ties, rubbing her wrists. "You know who we are, yes?"

She looked back and forth between the two of them and then nodded.

"Nobody else can know. The others are dead. This building is about to go up in smoke. When I say so, I need you to take the girls and run. Do you understand?"

Once more, she nodded, watching them both intently.

August fished a phone from his pocket. One of several burner phones the Mulvaneys seemed to have on hand. "Get somewhere safe from the flames and then call 9-1-1. Tell them you don't know what happened but that a group of men with Russian accents attacked the men inside while you were being transported and that you managed to free the others and get away."

Cricket just stared at him until August shook her gently. "Do you understand?"

"Yeah," she managed, nodding slightly. "I understand."

He handed the knife to Cricket. "Let's go."

Back in the shop, August stored the girls in the office until

they were ready to start the fire. They found Atticus sitting on a turned over bucket, dabbing at a bite mark on his leg.

"What the fuck happened to you?" Lucas asked.

"I fucking hate dogs," he snarled.

They'd gathered the bodies and stacked them in the garage, dousing them in fuel. Adam was crouched in the corner. "What's he doing?" Lucas asked Asa.

Before Asa could answer, Adam stood, moving to reveal his find. "Guys, meet Lightning." A dog with a smooshed face and more wrinkles than fur snorted, then drooled.

"That was their guard dog?" Lucas mused as the mutt panted heavily, licking at Adam's hand.

"I'm going to bring him home to Noah," Adam said excitedly.

"That thing is not going in the Volvo," Atticus vowed, pointing at the bulldog.

Adam rolled his eyes. "Whatever. I'll ride back with the twins. They go home with dogs all the time."

"We good?" August asked.

"Yeah, all we gotta do is light the fire," Archer said, pulling free a match and a lighter.

August nodded, filing back into the office to speak to Cricket and the girls. "Go. Now. Find someplace safe from the fire. In ten minutes, call the police. Got it?"

She nodded, motioning to the girls, who skirted past August and Lucas like they were the bad guys. It made sense to be wary of men in face masks, Lucas supposed. Especially after what they'd been through.

Cricket was the last out, but she turned back at the last

minute to look at August. "You're still going to help me find a job, right?"

A smile spread across August's face. "Most definitely."

"Okay, be careful."

With that, she was gone. They lit the match as they were walking out the door, Adam carrying his newfound friend. They'd almost made it to the car when the explosion happened, shaking the ground hard enough to knock them all off their feet.

August stood, helping Lucas to his feet. "Yeah, we gotta go. Right now."

Lucas didn't breathe again until they were back at Thomas's house.

TWENTY-THREE

August found Lucas in his childhood bedroom, perusing his things like he was in a museum. He'd been quiet since they returned home. After they debriefed Thomas about their mission, Lucas had just sort of broken away from the herd with Noah, who seemed over the moon with Adam's ugly four-legged present. Noah must have shown Lucas which bedroom belonged to August.

"You can touch if you want. If you have a deep need to dive down the rabbit hole of seven-year-old August's brief love of fencing or my fascination with space."

Lucas shook his head. "None of these things are you."

August wrapped his arms around Lucas's waist, relieved when Lucas relaxed against him. "How so?"

"You keep everything you care about with you. Your treasures. The important things are all lining the walls of your apartment or tucked away in boxes somewhere in your house. You don't like the things you covet out of your sight."

"Still putting that profiling brain to work, huh?"

Lucas gave a humorless laugh. "Is it over?"

"The twins took care of Kohn's body. The fire at the junkyard is out, but it will take months for them to piece together what happened with what's left. The rumor right now is meth lab."

"Any word on Cricket?" Lucas asked.

"She's already been released from the hospital. The other women were severely malnourished, and suffered some minor injuries, but none of them had made it to the main event. They are being held for fluids and observation. Atticus is still limping around like he went up against a great white and not a bulldog with sleep apnea."

Lucas snorted, but any trace of humor quickly disappeared.

It made August uneasy. He didn't know how to approach Lucas when he was in this strange mood.

"Are you alright, Lucas?" August asked.

Lucas craned his head around, expression pained. "Oof. I don't like when you say my name."

"What?" August asked, dumbfounded.

"When you say my name, it feels like you're chastising me or something. Like…I don't know. It's just weird. You need to come up with some kind of term of endearment for me. Just not baby. It always sounds sleazy to me."

August snickered. "That's what Adam calls Noah when they're having sex, so yeah. No thank you."

"Your family is disturbingly close for a bunch of psychopaths," Lucas mused.

August pulled his phone free, hooking his chin over

Lucas's shoulder so he could type in front of him.

"Did you just Google terms of endearment?" Lucas asked.

August scoffed. "Why do you ask questions you already know the answer to? What do we have on the list… Babe? Honey? Love? Sweetheart? Dove? Pet? Sugarplum?"

Lucas wrinkled his nose. "Ew. No. Too syrupy."

August smiled. "Aren't terms of endearment, by their very nature, supposed to be syrupy?"

Lucas pulled a face. "I suppose. But we're not really syrupy people. We're scientists. Professors," Lucas reminded, as if that fact had escaped August.

August ran his nose along Lucas's cheek. "Oh, I know. I very much like when you call me Professor. Just so you know."

Lucas pressed his ass back against his now half-hard cock. "Good to know, Professor."

August buried his face in his neck. "Don't be a tease or I'm going to fuck you against the door of my childhood bedroom."

"Don't threaten me with a good time," Lucas shot back.

August contented himself with placing open mouth kisses along the column of Lucas's neck, then the shell of his ear. Lucas reached behind him to wrap his hands around the backs of August's thighs, pulling him closer. "No. You will not distract me until we solve the problem at hand. What about *umnishka*?"

"Russian?" Lucas asked.

"Mm."

"What does it mean?"

August grinned. "Technically, it means clever one, but

it's often described as a teacher being proud of his student. Like I'm saying, 'that's my boy.'"

Lucas hummed, turning to loop his arms around his neck. "You want me to be your clever boy? I think you might have a genuine student/teacher kink, Professor Mulvaney."

"Are you still trying to head shrink me, Mr. Blackwell?"

"The head on your shoulders is not the one I'm interested in at the moment," Lucas murmured against his lips.

"As much as I'd like to explore this further, you never answered my question. Are you okay?"

Lucas shrugged, pulling away enough to look up into August's face. "No. I'm tired, and I'm hungry, and I want to stand under a hot shower for three days."

"Is that all there is to it? You're just exhausted and in need of food and a bath?"

"In a few hours, when the numbness wears off, there's a very good chance I'm going to have a nervous breakdown. But for now, I just feel…nothing. Not nothing. I'm relieved. I'm relieved that Kohn is dead and so is his crew, but part of me worries the Russian will just find new lackeys."

August kissed his nose. "The Russian is on borrowed time. Archer's already on his way to take care of him."

"That's good," Lucas said, sounding like it was no better or worse than before.

"Do you want to go home?" August asked.

"Whose home?" Lucas asked.

August frowned. "Our home. Like you said, I like to keep my most treasured things close to me."

Lucas sucked in a surprised breath but recovered quickly.

"Has it occurred to you that we've only known each other a week? A week, August. Seven days."

"Ugh, yeah. I don't like when you say my name either. It sounds like I'm in trouble."

"See?" Lucas asked.

"We're getting distracted. What does time have to do with how you feel about me?"

"I shouldn't love you after seven days," Lucas said.

"Shouldn't or don't?" August asked, holding his breath as Lucas seemed to struggle with the answer.

"Shouldn't. I shouldn't love you, but I think I do. I know I do. I love you but I shouldn't," Lucas said, miserable.

August shook his head. "You're so hung up on time. It took me seven seconds to figure out you're it for me. If the passage of time is so important to you, I'll wait. Even if it takes you seven weeks or seven months or seven years, but don't let time be the only reason to keep us from doing what we both want. We don't have to explain ourselves to anybody."

He could see Lucas's resistance crumbling. "You know the rumor mill at work is already churning overtime."

"Then let's give them something to talk about," August countered. "Move in with me. I want to wake up next to you every morning and go to bed with you every night."

Lucas smirked. "You say that now. But you haven't seen me watching *Star Trek* in my underwear with Cheetos dust on my fingers."

A slow smile spread across August's face. "You paint a vivid picture, *umnishka*. But I'm willing to risk it."

Lucas pressed a long chaste kiss to August's lips. "Then

take me home. I want a shower. Oh, and that cheesecake you bought. It really was one of the best things I ever put in my mouth. Can we get that cheesecake on the way home? Please?"

"We should probably grab dinner, too."

"No. I demand a shower, sex, and cheesecake, the order of which is to be determined when we get home."

"Say it again."

"Shower. Sex. Cheesecake?" Lucas asked.

"No, home," August prompted.

Lucas smiled softly. "You are the world's most sentimental psychopath. Now, take me home."

EPILOGUE
AUGUST

August sat reclined in his office chair, Vivaldi playing in his ears. He'd canceled lunch with Lucas for a mentor meeting with a new student in the department. He normally wouldn't do that, but Bianca had asked for a favor since it was apparently her student.

There was a tentative knock on the door. August removed his earbuds. "Come in."

August's brows went up when Lucas stuck his head in and said, "Professor Mulvaney?" as if he had no idea who August was. Was Lucas having some kind of dissociative episode? And when did he start wearing glasses? Not that August objected to the thick black frames. They were sexy as hell on him.

August frowned but decided to play along. "Yes?"

Lucas raked his gaze over August in a way that made his cock take notice. "Hi, I'm Luke. Bianca sent me to talk to you?"

August glanced down at his calendar and realized the

name of the student was, in fact, abbreviated as Luke B. A hint of a smile formed before he schooled his features into one of casual disinterest. "What can I do for you, Luke?"

Lucas slipped in, closing the door and leaning against it, his fingers slipping behind him to twist the lock into place. He was certainly not dressed like himself. Lucas favored dark wash denim and cardigans for work. Luke, it seemed, preferred well worn jeans and a form fitting t-shirt the same shade of green as his eyes.

Lucas pushed his fingers through his blond hair and bit his bottom lip as he moved into August's space. "I don't know if Bianca told you anything about me, but I'm in a bit of a…predicament."

A slow smirk crept across August's face. "Do tell."

Lucas pushed the glasses up the bridge of his nose. "See, there was a mix up at the registrar's office and I was supposed to take your class but they never added me. If I don't have this credit, I can't graduate."

August gave him a pained expression. "I'm sympathetic to your cause. But I'm afraid classes are well underway and there's a wait list for my class."

Lucas dropped down to his knees before August, parting his legs with purpose. "That's the thing…Professor. I don't actually want to take the class. I was just thinking—hoping, really—that maybe you could *say* I took the class, and, in exchange, I could do something for you."

August shifted in his seat, hips sliding forward. "What exactly is it you have that I might need, Mr…?"

"Blackwell," Lucas offered, looking up at him behind

those dark frames, his palms running over August's thighs before he let his fingers trace the bulge behind his zipper. "Surely, you could think of something to do with me?"

August sighed, running his thumb over Lucas's full bottom lip. "If you want to receive full credit for a class like mine, I expect excellence. I need you to wow me. Do you think you can wow me, Mr. Blackwell?"

"I'd love to try, Professor." Lucas's nimble fingers made short work of August's belt and pants, freeing his now throbbing erection. His eyes got wide with mock innocence as he jerked him. "Oh, you're so big, Professor."

August snorted, but it quickly became a groan when Lucas's mouth closed over him, swallowing him down, only to drag his mouth almost completely back up. "Christ."

Lucas began to bob his head, giving August the sloppiest and most enthusiastic blowjob of his life. August had no idea what was happening, but he had to say, Lucas had committed to his part and he approved. His eyes rolled back as Lucas worked him over, taking him to the back of his throat until the muscles contracted around him.

Lucas pulled off, licking up one side of August's dick and down the other before slapping it against his tongue, his glasses fogging. "Mm, you taste so good. Am I doing a good job?"

August leaned forward, removing the glasses before closing his hand around Lucas's throat. "Very good, but I said you had to wow me."

The smile that spread across Lucas's face was borderline alarming. "I thought you might say that, Professor." He

stood, turning to face August's desk, dropping his jeans and lifting his shirt. "Can you help me with these?"

August leaned forward, unable to stop himself from biting at Lucas's side before hooking his thumbs in the waistband of Lucas's black boxer briefs, pulling them down to mid thigh. Lucas leaned forward, arching his back and pushing his hips into August's face.

That was when August caught sight of the hot pink plug nestled between his cheeks. Had he been wearing that when they left for coffee this morning? Had he lectured all morning knowing he was going to bend over for August later? He couldn't stop himself from squeezing Lucas's lush ass, spreading him apart to look, running his finger around his rim.

"Are you wowed, Professor?" Lucas asked, looking back over his shoulder, a smirk spreading over his face.

August didn't answer, just pushed the plug in deeper, his cock leaking as Lucas moaned long and low. "Bend over for me. That's it. All the way."

Lucas let out a shaky breath but did as August asked. He hooked his finger in the ring at the base of the plug, tugging it experimentally, almost as turned on watching Lucas's reaction as he was at the notion of burying himself inside him. After the tiniest bit of resistance, the plug slipped free, but August didn't remove it. He placed his hand on Lucas's lower back, fucking the plug in and out of him, watching as he tried to fuck himself on it.

"August…"

August's hand cracked over his ass, earning a shocked,

hazy look from Lucas. If he wanted to play, they'd play. "What did you call me?"

"Sorry, Professor," Lucas managed, voice no longer teasing but raw. He flicked his tongue out to wet his lower lip.

August wanted to explore the handprint blooming on Lucas's flawless backside. So, he did, running his lips across the heated flesh before he stood, letting the plug fall to the floor. He drove into Lucas in one easy motion, burying himself deep.

There was no time to muffle his shout and if August was being truthful, he didn't really want to. He pulled him upright, wrapping an arm around his chest, not even thrusting in and out of him but just rolling his hips, going deep the way Lucas liked.

"Touch yourself," August rasped against his ear. "I want to feel you come."

"Fuck me hard?" Lucas asked, wrapping his hand around his cock.

"Jesus."

August gripped his hips and gave him what he wanted, pounding into him, praying he could hold out long enough for Lucas to find his release. But it was impossible to slow his movements. The euphoric feeling rolling through him had him chasing his own pleasure, wanting Lucas to come along but helpless to stop working himself in and out of the tight heat of his core. He was so fucking close. "Come on, *umnishka*. I'm barely hanging on."

"Can I?"

August didn't need him to clarify what he was asking.

Could he drop his shields, could he ride August's orgasm? "Fuck yes. You never have to ask."

Lucas didn't have to ask, but August did have to slap a hand over his mouth because once he was in that headspace, Lucas lost all sense of reason. He was moaning, cursing, all but sobbing as August used him. When he finally went over the edge, Lucas came, too, his body spasming around August's cock, dragging out his orgasm until his brain went completely offline.

He fell back into his chair, pulling Lucas with him. They both sat there, sweating and panting, both of them looking like they'd run a marathon in the summer heat. "Well, that desk planner is ruined," August teased.

"I'll buy you another."

"What—" August tried again. "What was that for?"

Lucas's face fell in a look August was certain he'd practiced before he'd arrived. "You don't remember?"

"Remember what?" August asked, hooking an eyebrow up so Lucas knew he was onto him.

Lucas grinned. "It's our seven week anniversary."

"Our what?"

"You said you didn't care if it took seven weeks, seven months, or seven years. We made it seven weeks. Happy anniversary."

August snorted. "Please, tell me you didn't tell Bianca this was all part of your little plan? She'll be downright insufferable if she thinks she helped me get laid."

"I didn't tell her all the details. Just that I wanted to surprise you for lunch and that it was hard to do that when

we have lunch every day. Now that she's right across the hall from your office and not mine, she was much more inclined to oblige. She probably wanted to eavesdrop."

Now that they'd finally arranged the offices by department, Bianca was his new hallmate. When the blinds were open, she could stare straight into his office. August now kept his blinds closed.

Lucas waved a hand. "You know her. She likes to be included. Besides, she thinks if we're BFFs then she'll get all the hot gossip about us first."

"There's hot gossip about us?" August asked.

Lucas scoffed. "Didn't you know? There's a whole very sordid tale about us. Even the students know."

August raised a brow. "And what's that?"

"That I, the crazy, slutty—but super hot—mental patient, seduced you, the sweet, oblivious—but also super hot—billionaire into moving in with me after just seven days. And ever since then, I've been keeping you sated with my kinky, sexual exploits while I slowly syphon all your riches into an offshore bank account so I can leave you for the pool boy."

August grinned. "Wow. All that and grading finals. You're quite the multitasker, *umnishka*."

"I know, right?" Lucas said.

"We don't have a pool boy," August remarked as an afterthought.

Lucas shrugged. "We don't have a pool. It seems silly to hire a pool boy." He seemed to reconsider. "It might be fun to watch him walk around in one of those little Speedos,

though. No?"

August pinched him hard. "You will not be watching anybody in a Speedo."

"Except you?" Lucas asked hopefully.

"I'm not wearing a Speedo."

"Please?" Lucas asked.

"Maybe for our seven year anniversary," August teased.

Lucas's face grew serious. "Do you think you'll still want me in seven years?"

"Don't ask stupid questions. I'll want you forever. The question is, will you still want to put up with me in seven years?"

Lucas laughed softly. "The psycho and the psychic. We're truly not fit for anybody but each other. We're stuck together."

August kissed his forehead. "That suits me just fine."

"Me too," Lucas said before adding, "But I'm serious. We're literally stuck together. Let's go home so we can clean up properly."

"I have afternoon classes. So do you," August reminded him.

"No, you don't. I had Cricket ask your TA to take your afternoon classes. I pawned mine off on Robert's TA. We're free for the rest of the day."

August had hired Cricket as his secretary after his old assistant had retired. She mostly answered phones and ran errands but she was a quick learner, efficient, and got to take classes at the university for free. Plus, she didn't mind taking on any non-school, family related assignments. The

kind August could have never entrusted to his last assistant. It turned out having some people in the know actually worked out quite well.

"If anybody ever takes a blacklight to this office, we're both getting fired," Lucas teased, cleaning up at the sink before tossing the wet washcloth to August to do the same.

August pulled himself together, saying, "If they ever put a blacklight to my car, we're probably going to prison, so this is preferable."

"No, you're going to prison. I'll be running away with the pool boy and your millions," Lucas teased. "Oh, don't forget our butt plug, Professor."

August retrieved the toy and hastily stuffed it into his pocket. They were almost to the door when Lucas stopped him. "I love you."

"I know," August said.

Lucas's mouth fell open. "Did you just Han Solo me?"

"Would you prefer thank you?" August asked.

"You're so going to regret that when me and Orlando, the pool boy, run away together."

August pushed Lucas up against the door, wrapping a hand around his throat. "I know you're baiting me."

August hadn't known this side of Lucas existed. The side that teased and taunted and pushed August. The side that needed a little brute force for him to feel like August really meant it when he said they were forever. It soothed Lucas's frayed edges somehow. He wasn't a completely different person, but without the threat of death looming over him, he was…lighter somehow. Freer.

"Any man who touches you will find himself becoming acquainted with my father's woodchipper. Is that clear?"

"Crystal," Lucas murmured, leaning forward and licking his way into August's mouth. "Now, tell me you love me."

August didn't hesitate. "I love you."

Who was to say what love was to them? Maybe love to them was fighting and fucking and watching reruns of shows they didn't like just because the other person did. Maybe love was Lucas letting August have the last slice of cheesecake or August always making sure Lucas took his meds and saw his therapist. Nobody got to dictate what their love looked like. So, when Lucas needed the words, August gave them freely.

A smile split Lucas's face. "That's better. Now, tell me we're getting cheesecake."

"We're getting cheesecake," August said dutifully, opening the office door, letting Lucas lead the way out.

Lucas waved to Cricket, who sat at her desk, headphones firmly jammed in her ears. She waved back.

"Now, tell me you'll buy a Speedo."

August rolled his eyes. "I'm not buying a Speedo."

"You should totally buy a Speedo," Bianca called as they passed the door of her new office.

"See!" Lucas cried. "Please?"

"No!"

"But it's our anniversary."

August rolled his eyes. "How about we go home and you drop your shields and I'll psychically project me in a Speedo directly into your brain. You can even pick the color."

Lucas pretended to pout. "Ugh, fine."

August slipped his hand into Lucas's. It was better than fine. It was perfect. Lucas was perfect. Perfect for August. He was August's person. And August was his. Nothing else mattered but that.

DEAR READER,

Thank you so much for reading *Psycho,* Book 2 in my Necessary Evils series. I hope you loved reading this book as much as I loved writing it. Look for Atticus's book, *Moonstruck*, coming soon.

If you've read my books before, you have probably come to realize that I have an addiction to writing about the psyche and exactly how both nature and nurture often play a part in who a person becomes. I spent years working as an RN in a psychiatric hospital, most of those years I spent with children aged anywhere from five to eighteen. It took a big toll on me and my own mental health, which is why writing these characters has become my own form of therapy. While sociopathic bodyguards and megalomaniacal cult leaders are all works of fiction, my heroes and villains are all drawn from real people who I encountered in my time as a nurse.

The extreme violence towards women depicted in *Psycho*, while fictional, is sadly a reality for some. The statistics involving indigenous women and the rates at which they go missing is also unfortunately 100% true. If you want more information or feel called to help visit: www.mmiwusa. org. This is all a rather maudlin way of saying thank you for reading my books and loving my characters and allowing me to use these books as my own therapy sessions.

If you guys are really loving the books, please consider joining my Facebook reader group, **Onley's Oubliette**, and signing up for my newsletter on my website so you can stay up to date on freebies, release dates, teasers, and more. You can also always hit me up on my social media and find all my links here. You can find me literally everywhere, so say hi. I love talking to readers.

Finally, if you did love this book, (or even if you didn't. Eek!) it would be amazing if you could take a minute to review it. Reviews are like gold for authors.

Thank you again for reading.

ABOUT THE AUTHOR

ONLEY JAMES is the pen name of YA author, Martina McAtee, who lives in Central Florida with her children, her pitbull, her weiner dog, and an ever-growing collection of shady looking cats. She splits her time between writing YA LGBT paranormal romances and writing adult m/m romances.

When not at her desk, you can find her mainlining Starbucks refreshers, whining about how much she has to do, and avoiding the things she has to do by binge-watching unhealthy amounts of television in one sitting. She loves ghost stories, true crime documentaries, obsessively scrolling social media, and writing kinky, snarky books about men who fall in love with other men.

Find her online at:
WWW.ONLEYJAMES.COM

Lightning Source UK Ltd.
Milton Keynes UK
UKHW040639041021
391643UK00001B/84